THE
SAVAGE
HOUR

'An excellent, thoughtful book, written in a lyrical and intensely visual manner which no doubt owes something to Proctor's earlier career as a film-maker . . . It is a profound and deeply moving exploration of relationships . . . A superb novel that offers a fascinating picture of contemporary South Africa and a profound exploration of the human condition. I doubt that this ~~ar will bring along much to top it'

Margaret von Klemperer

Having made numerous political documentaries in her native South Africa, Elaine Proctor graduated from the National Film and Television School with her first feature film *On The Wire* (British Film Institute award for best first film). Her first book, *Rhumba*, was published in 2012. She lives in London.

THE
SAVAGE
HOUR

ELAINE PROCTOR

Quercus

First published in Great Britain in 2014 by Quercus
This paperback edition published 2015 by

Quercus Publishing Ltd
Carmelite House
50 Victoria Embankment
London EC4Y 0DZ

An Hachette UK company

A CIP catalogue record for this book is available
from the British Library

PB ISBN 978 1 78206 655 2
EBOOK ISBN 978 1 78206 654 5

This book is a work of fiction. Names, characters,
businesses, organizations, places and events are
either the product of the author's imagination
or used fictitiously. Any resemblance to
actual persons, living or dead, events or
locales is entirely coincidental.

10 9 8 7 6 5 4 3 2 1

Printed and bound in Great Britain by Clays Ltd, St Ives plc

Typeset by Ellipsis Digital Limited, Glasgow

For my brother David and my sister-in-law Linda who,
at great cost to themselves, have cared for our mother for more than
twenty years. Without the love they have bestowed on her every day,
when I was not there to do it, this could have been her story.
I am grateful to them that it was not.

And for Elisabeth Moeketsi, who raised us all.

For my children, Lucia and Jacob.

For David.

And, most of all, for my mother Lynda Proctor,
who will never be able to read this book but who made it
necessary for me to write it.

Die waarheid kwaak 'n karige geluid
The truth croaks a halting, meagre sound.

ELISABETH EYBERS

PART ONE

CHAPTER ONE

It is hot the day Ouma dies. A still heat. And quiet. The kind that comes at the end of a long drought.

A black-backed jackal on the hill behind the farmhouse searches for grubs under the sharp yellow grass. He hunts without the cover of darkness for reasons of scarcity and the demands of the starving cubs in the den just beyond the thicket of *wag-'n-bietjie bos* behind him. He stops, pricks his ears.

It isn't the routine lamentation that attends feeding time at the pig farm next door that alerts him to things amiss. Nor the feeble barking from one of the six panting dogs laid out like seals on the hot red sand.

It is the much quieter rattle coming from underneath the gracious, slowly fading acacia trees. The mysterious weight in the sound makes him whimper.

It comes again as a raw-boned farmhand whips a small herd of cattle into the scant shade beside the nearly empty dam. Klein Samuel, as he is known, forces a large Nguni bull into the deepest shadow with a percussive clicking of his tongue.

It comes again as a flicker of movement catches Klein Samuel's eye. He glances up to see a young girl dart across the red dust and into the shade. Cattle and girl mingle there, uneasy. Neither the farmhand nor the girl greets one another. It is a wasteful gesture on a day so hot. She regards the wheezing bull with vulpine curiosity until she has located him as the source of the sound, then swings herself up onto the wide, low branch of the wild fig tree.

Klein Samuel watches the girl stretch out on the ample branch, leopard-like, until only the edges of her are visible from below. He says her name in his head – *De-li-lah* – and wonders if the sixteen-year-old can hear the cowbell ring in it. *De-li-lah*.

Freckles and peeling skin compete for space on Delilah's nose as she lies in the pounding sun. Ouma has warned her that she will turn into a leather handbag if she roasts herself so, but the sun is the only thing that soothes her.

It is the *verlange* that keeps her cold in such heat, says her grand-mother. It is true that her insides are folded over with longing for her ma and pa and her brother Martinus. For her crumbling old home on the banks of the Pongola river.

The bull sucks breath into his lungs as if through a skin. The rasp echoes in the animal's cavernous chest.

It is the sound of defeat.

He sinks very slowly to his knees. Klein Samuel watches him list sideways and then lay his head on the dust – graceful as a maiden.

Klein Samuel christened the bull-calf Gundwane when he was born because the markings of his coat suggested a rat, long tailed and sharp nosed. He would have given him a more promising name if he'd known how big the animal would grow and how grand. Klein Samuel was a young man then, a migrant worker from poverty-stricken Zimbabwe with a wife and five hungry children left in Southern Matabeleland. Now he is middle-aged and his three surviving children, although grown, are still hungry.

He wishes it was his off-day so he could drink himself comatose and no longer hear the struggle of Gundwane's breath or imagine the sunken cheeks of his distant progeny.

Klein Samuel sits in the dust beside his charge and waves away the flies that swarm.

This is how it is the day Ouma dies.

Klein Samuel the farmhand works for Groot Samuel the farmer. Their names suggest that Klein Samuel should be small and the other large but they are both spectrally thin and as weathered as the roots of a tree. Long labour together under a desiccating sun has given them the demeanour of brothers, though one is white and the other black.

Groot Samuel's grand title comes from his family's ownership of the land but it is the land that has sucked the substance out of his once robust body. There are days when he is aware that the best of his insides, his *binnegoed*, lies on the road he built with red bricks to stop it washing away in the summer rainstorms or between the rocks of the perfectly hand-hewn *braaiplek* where he barbecues the meat for Sunday lunch.

He doesn't mind the presence of his lifeblood here so much because the *braaiplek* is at least beautiful.

Groot Samuel makes beauty where he can.

His hands and back remember where he found each rock for its floor and how he rolled or dragged each down the mountain to the house. It offended his wife, Ilse, that he took such care with the outside when their living-room roof leaked like a sieve when it rained.

He laid out the stones so the ripples on the rock, formed when the land was once a lake, flowed seamlessly together. The truth is that this prodigious labour eased the ache of what he still thinks of as his 'blue parts'. Those fine corners of his feeling world that have been bruised and pickled sour by cruelty. And he does it so his mother will find beauty, even here.

The two Samuels have laboured side by side on this smallholding for twenty years. If they talked they would be able to finish each other's sentences but they don't.

They do laugh though.

When Groot Samuel slipped in the irrigation ditch and hit his head on the spade sticking up out of the ground, Klein Samuel laughed like a hyena. Likewise, when Klein Samuel and his bicycle crashed into the tree at the bottom of the steep driveway, Groot Samuel laughed so hard the stitches in his head split open.

They do laugh.

This summer is the driest either can remember. The heat in the valley reaches its peak at midday. That is when Groot Samuel typically opens the pump at the dam to water the mutinous cattle. The scent of water snakes through the air. It is an acute smell, sweet, heavy. It is green.

Even Gundwane lifts his head off the red earth to suck it into his flaring nostrils. Klein Samuel seizes on the flutter of life that animates the animal. 'Get up, *jou luigat*!' Gundwane rises to his feet.

The bull and his skinny caretaker stumble to the dam. They slip and slide down through the reeds to the rising water.

As the liquid thunders onto the cracked mud, Groot Samuel watches both Klein Samuel and the bull drink. In the mud below them he sees the barbel flap shiny black against the red and wonders how such terrible creatures came to walk the earth.

Groot Samuel doesn't notice the straw hat caught in the reeds in the centre of the water. It is the hat his mother wears every day as she weeds the lawn with her legs stretched out in front of her like an African labourer. When the sun reaches its apogee the hat is broad enough to cast shade on both the old woman and the skinny yellow dog who lies beside her.

Her dog, Suffering. Her shadow.

Not even Delilah, who sits up on the branch and blinks away her torpor, sees the hat snagged in the yellow reeds. It is only when she half closes her eyes against the glare that she sees a shape tug itself away from the reeds and float up on the rising water.

Ouma's hat.

Delilah's alarm rises with it. The hat is so much part of her grandmother that on the odd occasion that Delilah has seen her without it, it is as if she has caught sight of the old lady with her bathrobe open. The hat and her grandmother go together like *pap* and gravy.

Did it blow off in the wind?

The thick stillness of the day answers her question.

Delilah slides her long body down the branch.

Groot Samuel turns away as her battered tomboy legs scramble down the trunk. He would prefer it if her kind weren't so potent when they emerged from one girl-state to another.

Delilah lands on the dust. She walks round the water's edge and peers into its depths. Then she stops. Everything in her body tells her to turn and walk away calmly so as not to disturb the natural run of things. So as not to have to say, 'I knew it.'

Delilah's ma says that the child sees tragedy wherever she looks. And she does. If Delilah had grown up anywhere else in the world, they might have thought her a savant, but in Pongola she is just a whiner, full of what her ma calls her '*piep en tjank*'.

She feels the ridges of the dried red mud under her bare feet as the force of providence draws her to the water's edge. She knows that she will, once more, see it before anyone else. She knows too that the shame of being the first to know it somehow makes it hers.

She steps into the mud up to her knees. Something pale and distant lies in the gloom below the watermark. She can hear her mother's voice, 'Ag, it's nothing Delilah.' How many times has she heard that phrase? Now she hopes it is right.

She stretches her arm towards the paleness below, aware that the way the water slows her hand removes its urgency. She wonders if it is cobweb made dense by the water? She touches the fine strands with her fingertips, then grabs at it, surprising herself. She lifts her hand out of the water. In her palm she sees a handful of silver hair.

She looks up to see Groot Samuel on the bank, Klein Samuel in the shallows with his bull. She sees the way the black fish twist around her feet.

She looks again at the fine silver threads emerging from the mud in her hand and only then does she scream.

All the next-door pigs at feeding time couldn't match the depth and terror in that sound. It makes everything else mute. The cicadas. The water. The cows.

The jackal on the hillside spins round to see what new horror has come his way, and then steps back, rattled.

CHAPTER TWO

Every last person living along the De Wildt side of the mountain would have howled with laughter if Jannie Claassens had confessed that he wanted to be a detective. They would have said all he wanted to be when he grew up was a *moffie*.

You had to be a man to be a detective. A real man. You had to go to police college. Be part bile, part grit. You had to *moer* people half to death if they crossed you and stay the distance until they confessed their wrongdoing. And above all, you had to marry a good woman, who would stand by you when the ensuing shit rained down upon your head.

Jannie defied them all. He graduated with distinction from the academy, put in his time as a policeman and was promoted to Detective Warrant Officer within five years and, soon thereafter, to Lieutenant.

He had something more sustaining than bile and grit to get him through. For Jannie, being a detective meant being a seeker after the truth. He was compelled to grow the muscles for that task very early in his life because nothing was what it seemed in the Claassens household.

His father was dutiful at church and always ready with a joke at the farmer's co-op. He behaved respectfully towards Jannie's mother on the rare evenings that they socialized with her extended family on their nearby smallholding. Then he battered her senseless behind closed doors.

Jannie forced himself to stay awake until his parents retired, to listen for his mother's stifled cries. If they came, he could do no more than creep under the bed and pray that it would be over soon.

In time, he learnt to see the storm of his father's rage building when it was still a long way off and he contrived to get his mother out of the house. They went to have a Coke in town or to Mr Patel's *spaza* shop for groceries. If it was at night, they hid in the garage until his father had ranted himself empty.

One mysterious day, Jannie's father's rage transferred itself from his mother to him. It happened in his teens, when the boy's fine, somewhat effeminate body, revealed itself as more adult than child.

He accepted becoming the decoy of his father's fury because at least it meant his ma was safe. What he hated was the giving of forgiveness afterwards. The way his father caressed his cheek and muttered, 'Sorry, my boy, sorry, *ag*, sorry,' and waited for his reply, '*Maak nie saak nie, Pa* . . . it doesn't matter . . .'

As soon as he was old enough he punched his father square in the face rather than say, again, what he didn't mean.

So his father beat him hard enough to break his ribs. The bone pierced the lining of his right lung.

Jannie still remembers how he arrived at the doorstep of Ouma's surgery gasping like a fish. She took one look at him and knew he needed more help than she could provide. She stopped the bleeding to keep him alive while they waited for the ambulance.

Then Ouma read to Jannie from the book of poetry that she kept on her desk.

Jannie listened, through his fear, to the strangeness of the words. They floated towards him, separate and potent, like slow notes on a piano. '*Waarheid.*' He raised himself up on his elbows to locate the sound. '*Kwaak.*' He saw the back of Ouma's pink ear move as she spoke. ''*n . . . karige . . . geluid . . .*'

He closed his eyes and the words rolled across the soft grey folds of his subsiding fear. *Die waarheid kwaak 'n karige geluid.* The seeker in Jannie knew that to be so. The truth didn't ever arrive fully formed. It came in skinny, inauspicious strips that laid themselves one on top of the other until they became denser than the air around them and therefore *were.*

Later, Ouma would claim that she hadn't read the fragment because she thought the poetry would have particular meaning for her patient. She just knew she had to find a way to slow the death-train clattering down the tracks towards him.

But that was not the whole story. Even *in extremis,* Jannie could hear that the words came out of her mouth slippery with her own feeling. Whether she knew it or not, she had shown him the door to her secret solace.

Once she saw that he would make it, Ouma telephoned Jannie's father and told him if he laid a finger on his son again it would be his last act on this earth.

Jannie was grateful for an end to the beatings but he felt even more indebted to Ouma for the poetry he believed had saved him.

Along with becoming the best detective for a hundred miles,

Jannie Claassens became the founder of the Elisabeth Eybers book club.

On the third Sunday of every month the mostly male members of the club arrived at his small suburban house. Jannie didn't see any of them outside the book club so it gave their gathering a special intensity. They came from far and wide to honour the great poet who, at her death, left twenty-one collections of work covering the whole span of her life from child to grandmother.

Some dressed in her image for these gatherings: glasses, pink lip-stick, and occasionally a nice necklace.

They ate cake, conversed politely and then read selected poems aloud. At these times Jannie was happier than he believed possible.

The way they saw it, Elisabeth Eybers was a seeker too. She hunted down the bloody truths of being a woman in mid century South Africa and then illuminated them in her restrained and digni-fied verse.

She illuminated Jannie and his friends too.

He has a special love for the poems of her middle period, like 'Meisie' with its call to live life to the full and thereby retain one's '*green-ness*' into old age, which is the chosen poem for today's meeting. Jannie is only halfway through reading it aloud when the phone rings. He considers ignoring it but he knows, even as he thinks it, that he does not have that freedom. Being a detective means that you answer the phone, even on rare days when you've managed to take refuge in a poem as delicate as this.

It is Jannie's mother, speaking on her cell phone, and he can't understand a word. '*Ma*, you can't talk on the phone and drive. *Moet asseblief nie. Jy weet hoe —*'

'*Bly stil*, Jannie,' his mother barks. 'I am just at the pig farm and what I hear . . . *ag nee* . . . is a terrible thing. They say it is the doctor.'

'*Ouma?*'

She shouts, 'They say Ouma is dead!'

Jannie's arms fall, boneless, to the sides of his body. All is silent but for the sustained hiss of breath leaving his lungs.

Chapter Three

Delilah stands in the dam looking down at the fulgent nest of silver hair emerging from the brown slick in her hand.

Groot Samuel stumbles down the bank towards her. Klein Samuel strides straight through the shallow water, stricken.

She knows neither of them can alter the terrible fact that she holds the hair from a human head in her muddy palm. No person on God's good earth can change that.

That is bad enough, but there is something else barrelling down the pike towards her and she is helpless, once more, to stop it.

Whose hair?

A wail comes out of her mouth. It travels along the branches of the acacia trees towards the corrugated-iron roofs of the pig farm next door.

The sow in the largest stall flops down onto her side at the sound of the human distress in the world beyond. She pays no attention to the hungry tussle of her suckling piglets. The strongest push and shove their scrawny runt brother away from the teat. The sow remains aloof to the runt's distress for no amount of nurture will alter the fact that the strongest will prevail and the weakest not. Just as it has always been.

The young woman, knee-deep in the sow's slop and excrement, stops her labour to listen to Delilah's cry. The sound seems to suck the brown out of her skin, leaving her indigo hued. This is Cheetah. She has a feral thinness about her. Wears a *doek* on her head and overalls four sizes too big.

Her father named her Cheetah because of the cat-like cheekbones her Khoisan ancestry gave to her face. She thought it was a good name because it meant she could run from trouble. She was wrong about that.

Cheetah shoves the runt piglet back into the fray with an unsentimental kick of her wellington boot. Then she steps over the wall of the pen and hurries along the long row of sheds. A voice calls out to her as she passes, 'Hey Cheetah . . . gimme a smoke . . . just a *stompie, asseblief tog.*'

But she pays no heed.

Cheetah reaches the dam in time to see the two Samuels make their first attempt to locate the body in the water. She doesn't call out to them or go to help, but waits, unseen, in the scrub beside the dam.

There is nothing stately about the removal of the corpse from its muddy tomb. The two men duck under and churn the murky water darker still. Bits of them, an elbow, ear, foot, break through the surface shark-fin-like as they slip on the algae and the fish debris littering the dam bottom. Sometimes they stand up out of the water gasping, clutching a leaf they thought was fabric or a handful of gelatinous frogspawn.

Delilah watches from the edge of the dam.

Cheetah would like to lead the girl away to spare her the horror of this emergence yet she does not move. It is not her place to give such nurture.

Delilah too wishes she could flee. *Go . . . go now!* she tells herself. But her body doesn't obey. The weight of what she has come to know as her fate once again roots her and so she does not move.

She watches as her capable uncle is reduced, in this element, to a fumbling, gasping fool. He shouts across at Klein Samuel, '*Tel saam . . . een, twee, drie.*' He could be counting out the start of a swimming race. They suck in a collective breath and vanish into the muck.

Time passes, too long for their screaming lungs, and then Groot Samuel rises out of the water with a body in his arms. He struggles to steady himself, sucks in a deep breath and bellows, broken hearted, like an ox, 'Gogo!'

The sturdy matriarch in the kitchen of the farmhouse on the hill lifts her head, iron in her hand, neatly folded pile of laundry on the table beside her. The sound of her name rolls across her broad, nut-brown face. Gogo. When Groot Samuel and his sister were near babies, Gogo had taught them how to say grandmother in her language – *nkgono*, but their childish tongues found the subtle demands of Sesotho difficult and had quickly found their way to the simpler Zulu version of the word.

'Gogo!'

She hears the alarm in it now but still she does not move.

She would prefer to stay where she is, in the peaceful dark. The cry comes again and this time she is defenceless against the sound of Groot Samuel's need. She turns off her iron and heads for the door.

'Gogo!' he calls once more as the old woman hurries across the grass.

Delilah watches Groot Samuel slip and slide his way up the bank of the dam, Klein Samuel at his side to keep the body from banging its head, or slipping from his arms. He lowers himself to his knees when he reaches the yet more slippery bank and begins to crawl up it.

Together, he and Klein Samuel lay the body on the dry dust at the edge of the dam. Then they turn away and suck in lungfuls of air. As they do so they both cough, a ripe, thick, cavernous sound. It is another thing they share – lungs as black as soot.

Delilah thinks about what might produce such a sound, because she is trying not to look at the body.

Surely that small crumpled shape is too slight to be the grand-mother who loved her and passed no judgement, not ever, not even on her *piep en tjank*.

Too slight *by miles* to be the woman who, when the tremor in her old hand made it impossible for her to suture a man with a knife wound that separated a large part of his lip from his mouth, made Delilah do it.

Of course the girl had refused at first but when Ouma insisted that her patient would lose his lip altogether if she didn't, she submitted.

'The anaesthetic stings when it goes in so be ready for him to move,' said Ouma gently as Delilah, scrubbed, gloved and masked, lifted the syringe.

As Delilah watched the flesh around the wound swell with anaes-thetic she could feel the man's eyes bore into her head. *God*, she thought, *forgive me*.

'Now remove the needle from the suture packet. I will show you how to knot it.'

And so she did. Delilah pushed the curved needle into his skin. She was surprised at the force required.

'*Kom nou, kind,*' said the old lady whenever she felt Delilah falter. 'You know worse than this.'

Her grandmother's belief in her made her capable. She worked, one stitch at a time, until there were seventeen neat sutures all in a row and Ouma declared it done.

Delilah took off her gloves and threw them in the bin. Then she turned to her grandmother and after holding her gaze for a moment she whispered in disbelief, '*Het ek so gemaak, Ouma?*' She touched her chest. 'Me?'

Her grandmother nodded. 'Delilah Susanne Magriet de la Rey.' And then she crowed like a rooster.

It didn't occur to Delilah to remind Ouma that in fact, strictly speaking, she was a Schoeman.

Delilah's Ouma would never lie as still and ruined as the form on the edge of the dam now does. The girl is sure of it.

But why then do Groot Samuel's shoulders shake with grief as he sits beside it on the dust?

And why has Gogo crouched beside the body to run her tender hand over the dead person's face?

A whimpering sound snakes its way out of the teenager's mouth, almost inaudible but more chilling than the louder cries that preceded it.

It brings Cheetah to her knees in the tangled scrub.

She watches Gogo sweep Delilah away from the dam, and up the driveway leading to the house. She sees the girl pull free and turn to look, once more, at her Ouma lying there.

Cheetah can tell that she looks to make sure that this terrible death, in all its mud and stink and horror, is not simply a figment of her cruel imagination.

CHAPTER FOUR

Jannie goes into the kitchen and puts the kettle on. Members of the book club drift away discreetly.

Had he had a lover amongst their number, he might have stayed behind to help Jannie through the ink of his seeping grief, but Jannie doesn't have lovers. The precarious balance of his life does not allow it.

He takes his mug of tea out into the garden and sits there, in his long blue skirt, sipping from it slowly. Today he doesn't care what his neighbours might think if they see him in a dress. The grass around him is dry as a stinking bone.

This time he doesn't move even when the phone rings. He hears only the steady pump of his blood and the swift in and out of his breath. He sits until Ouma's death has become fact inside him.

When he stands up and walks inside, his small, neat house feels like it belongs to someone else. Someone lonely and scared.

He changes his clothes and drives out to the sun-blasted granite hillside of the farm.

'She slipped,' Delilah tells Jannie as tears roll down her cheeks. She leads him to where Ouma's body lies on the dining-room table. It is a table meant for a large family. It assumes children and grandchildren will eat and fight around it for eternity.

Gogo puts a bowl of water into Delilah's hands. The girl looks down at its swirling contents.

'Hold it steady, child,' says Gogo.

'Yes, Gogo.' Delilah holds her breath and watches the sponge in the bowl slowly fatten with warm liquid. Her insides swell too, with grief.

Jannie wants to take the girl in his arms, to stay and give comfort to the community of souls gathered around the old lady, but he can feel Groot Samuel's familiar impatience and turns to take his leave.

'Don't go,' whispers Delilah. The child is washed white. She holds Jannie there with her need.

He hears Gogo say, as if trying to talk herself into knowing something unknowable, 'The mud sucked her down.'

Jannie leans towards her and says, '*Wat sê jy*, Gogo?'

'The mud, it made Ouma heavy from the inside.'

For all Jannie's contemplation in his garden, he is helpless in the face of this simple evocation of Ouma's actual blood and bones death. He can see it now: the slow sucking in of mud, stink and duck feathers. He can smell the fear. Feel the shutting down of Ouma's fine and fiery soul.

The misery of it.

And so, finally, he weeps.

Delilah puts down her bowl of water and takes Jannie's hand. The detective and the teenage girl stream with a sweet, uninhibited grief.

Groot Samuel looks away. Normally the most benign of men, he whispers, '*Bloody moffie*,' under his breath.

If you asked him why he said this, he would tell you it is because

Jannie is a snoop. Even as a teenager Jannie saw too much and asked too many questions for his liking. It has always been in Groot Samuel's nature to keep a lid on things.

Jannie looks up and sees the farmer watching him. Sure enough it is as if one eyeball has written on it *bloody* and the other *moffie*.

Jannie was still half a child when he first fell in love with Groot Samuel's fine, eighteen-year-old body and the lavish dark lashes that framed his eyes. It was Jannie who fretted most when Samuel was called up for his compulsory military service in 1990.

Jannie knew a thousand acts of cruelty and oppression had followed. It would drive you to do penance for the rest of your days. To build red brick roads and beautiful *braaiplekke* until your *binne-goed* lay smeared on the objects of your labour. And if that failed to still your self-hatred you could smoke your feelings all the way down into your stomach until your blackened lungs could no longer shrink and expand with your breath.

Jannie saw all that. If you asked him in a quiet and truthful moment, he might tell you that he loves Groot Samuel still, if that's what you call the resigned compassion we reserve for the stoical, wounded ones.

'You're wet,' says Jannie softly and Groot Samuel looks down to see the water drip off the ends of his trousers and onto the carpet under his feet.

'And you,' says Jannie to Delilah, who is shivering more from shock than cold. Neither seems able to move, or speak, until Gogo shoos them out. 'Go. Go get dry, both of you.'

The door bangs closed behind them. Jannie is full of sudden regret that he didn't put his arms around Groot Samuel as he passed. He would have liked to say, *I know how you loved her*. He can imagine saying those words right into Groot Samuel's ear as they hugged. It would have been the compassionate thing to do.

'*Eish*, Jannie,' says Gogo as she shakes her head, 'let us drink tea —' Jannie waits for the familiar words that complete the phrase — 'and then we can shut up.'

This saying has spanned the years of their friendship. It is short-hand for *Come sit with me, we can't do anything about the madness of the world but we won't let it crush us.*

Let's drink tea and shut up.

'Rooibos or English?' he asks, aware that her invitation is also a request for him to produce the calming brew.

She waves away his question and turns towards her labour.

He leaves quietly.

Gogo gently removes Ouma's old brown shoes with their mis-matched laces. She pulls off her sodden dress. She takes the sponge from Delilah's bowl and begins to wipe the trails of mud off Ouma's pale arm.

She remembers when Ouma's skin began to lose its elasticity and the muscle loosened from the bone. But she hadn't noticed this degree of emaciation. She had missed that. She doesn't know how.

For fifty years it has been the two of them, Gogo and Ouma. Of course they were not grandmothers at the beginning, nor friends. Gogo was hired to work in Ouma's kitchen and that is what she has done ever since.

In recent times, the day would begin with Gogo polishing the cracked red floor of the stoep while Ouma sat on the lawn below the house, legs stretched out in front of her, weeding. Suffering would be asleep in the sun by her side.

There was no other name for the skinny yellow bag of bones that showed up one day at Ouma's surgery with his tail between his legs and open sores on his back. *Suffering*.

Groot Samuel and Gogo were both secretly envious of the intense feeling that flowed between Ouma and her canine shadow.

The old lady hadn't taken to retirement easily. She stilled the churning that attended the loss of her role as healer-of-the-sick with hours of fractious weeding.

If she had forgotten her hat, Gogo would call across to her, 'Where's your hat, Ouma?'

The old woman would look up from her weeding. Her crinkled face burnt almost acorn dark, her blue eyes bright.

Gogo would click her tongue in disapproval and chide her, just as she herself did her granddaughter. 'The sun is making you into a leather handbag, Ouma.'

Sometimes Ouma didn't answer.

And sometimes she did, like when she hissed, 'Sshsht now . . .' Her arthritic fingers could have passed for tree roots as she yanked out the alien shoots. 'I'm thinking.'

Gogo slathered more red polish onto her cloth and polished. The polishing rag was silent but the wad of newspaper under each of her knees swish-ssh-sha-swished as she moved, 'Thinking what?'

'I'm thinking that those words are mine,' said Ouma.

'Which words?'

'The sun and the leather handbag story. Those are mine.'

'Tsta!'

This was not a new issue between them.

Like all people who live alongside one another for a long time, they pilfered each other's language without even knowing it. Gogo had the grace to accept the thievery when it was pointed out. Ouma did not. She dismissed Gogo with her hand in the air. 'It doesn't matter.'

'You can't own words, Ouma. Did you pay for them? Did you wrap them in newspaper like an avocado and hide them in the sack of *mielie* meal to ripen?'

'I have better ones even,' countered Ouma.

'*Haai*, like what?'

Ouma said nothing.

'Like what?' Gogo stopped polishing. If Ouma had a better way of saying something she wanted to hear it.

Ouma pulled at her weeds with greater intent but still withheld her answer.

Gogo snorted and struggled to her feet, the wads of newspaper still attached to her knees with elastic bands, and proclaimed, '*Eish* . . . you white people are full of nonsense.'

Ouma looked up at her. 'That so?'

The old black woman turned to walk away but stopped and added, 'Nonsense. Trouble and *NONSENSE*.'

There was a moment of silence.

Then Ouma crowed with laughter. Gogo felt her own laughter rising up to meet it. She tried to stem her mirth but her shoulders shook so that when she opened the door to the house Ouma could see that she was laughing too.

Gogo wonders that so ordinary a memory could sit so long in her mind while more recent ones chafed. Maybe it is the laugh, that growling, irreverent sound that softened the truths she and Ouma told one another.

She wants to hear that laugh again.

Gogo squeezes the sponge and water flushes the algae and mud from Ouma's wisp-thin hair. Her scalp underneath is blue and shiny as polished stone.

CHAPTER FIVE

Cheetah takes off her overalls and her *doek*. She fills a bucket of water and rinses the pig dirt off her face.

The quiet around her shack could easily swallow her with its emptiness if she let it. She is not immune to the longing people have when someone dies, to huddle together, gather, commune. She has seen it too much, that instinct and its cause.

She wanted to die herself when she first washed up at the pig farm. She was so thin you could see where the bones met at her elbow. The farmer said he wasn't running a bloody hospital but she worked harder than any healthy person that first day, so he let her stay.

When Klein Samuel first brought Cheetah to Ouma's clinic she accepted pain relief for her symptoms but told Ouma she could do nothing for her disease. At the end of each consultation Ouma would wrap her arms around the girl and whisper, 'Stay with me.'

Cheetah would rail faintly, 'Blerry fool old woman.' And she would turn to face the wall. 'Don't you know anything?'

But Ouma held on and said it again. She did this every time Klein Samuel managed to get Cheetah to come to the surgery. Then one day, finally, Cheetah began to cry. That was when Ouma knew she had won.

Cheetah was savvy about staying healthy once she decided to go on living. While Ouma fought with the reluctant Department of Health to get her hands on some anti-retrovirals, and then the pharmaceutical companies themselves, Cheetah swallowed twenty-two pills every day at the right time and in the right order to fight the opportunistic infections that blossomed in her body like Klein Samuel's green beans. It was not easy. She vomited when the dose was too high or when she hadn't eaten enough.

Oh, the grind of it.

'Shit, Ouma, what am I doing this for?' she asked.

'What do you mean?'

'What's worth saving about my *poes* of a life?'

It was not a question she asked in Ouma's bustling clinic but rather when the two lay, as they did sometimes, on the soft green grass under the leaky tap of the water tank. Long ago someone had planted a sprig of fragrant *buchu bos* there and it had sweetened the evening air with its scent ever since.

'You like to fall asleep in the sun, Cheetah?' asked Ouma then.

'On Sundays, sometimes,' she replied, wary.

'That's a reason for living.'

'That so?'

They were silent. Then Ouma asked, 'Make a nice butternut soup?'

'Soup is for white people.'

Ouma guffaws. 'You laugh sometimes and that's for everyone.'

'Ja, I laugh.'

'Dance to music?'

'I do that, yes.'

'Love someone?'

'He's more like a piece of wood.'

'He is good.'

'Wood.'

They smiled. Ouma looked at her and said, 'Eat some more, Cheetah.'

'I do. Two plates of *pap* last night . . .'

'Eat more, Cheetah! I can see your bones.'

'Okay,' she said, sheepish.

'You have a life to live.'

Cheetah glanced up at the old lady.

'I am old and mine is lived,' Ouma said quietly and she sat up to look at the orchard beyond.

Cheetah once asked Ouma what she would have done if she hadn't been snared by her vocation so young and she said without hesitation, 'A farmer. I would've grown *mielies*, tree ferns and red Barberton daisies.'

'Child, go and pick the . . .' said Ouma, and she hesitated a moment as she searched for the word. 'Go before the baboons get the ripe ones.'

'Pick what, Ouma?'

'The green thing.'

'What green thing?' Cheetah asked because she was still on her back and the sky did not contain any such hue.

'That!'

Cheetah sat up. Ouma pointed at a tree in the orchard.

'That's an avocado, Ouma,' said Cheetah and before she could stop herself she said, 'Everyone knows that.'

The silence that followed was sustained enough for them to become aware of the *swish-swish-swish* of the sprinklers watering the recently seeded earth beyond them.

'Not me,' whispered Ouma and her hollow cheeks flushed. 'Not me, any more.'

Cheetah waited. What do you say to someone who doesn't know that an avocado is an avocado? It was not the first lapse Cheetah had noticed, but this one made her want to shake the old lady and say, *Hey, don't forget yourself now, Ouma. You have people to save.*

She watched Ouma catch the silver strands of her fly-away hair and tuck them behind her ears, as if by organising her appearance she could also contain the turmoil of her mind and she heard her mutter, '. . . *getye ons nerfkaal stroop.*'

Ag, ja *well*, thought Cheetah to herself. She minded when Ouma recited *that blerrie poet*, for even though she understood the words, their meaning escaped her.

'*Afsigtelikheid kom reeds in sig*,' continued Ouma and if Cheetah had looked at her just then, she would have seen that it was indeed true for Ouma. Time *had* stripped off the skins of her competence, leaving her naked. And without language she did, truly, find herself hideous.

'You need to sleep more, Ouma,' said Cheetah.

'It is not sleep I need!' growled the old lady, and she struggled to her feet. It struck Cheetah that Ouma looked, briefly, like a dog chasing its tail as she found her balance.

'I'm nothing without my . . .' Ouma drummed her fingertips on her forehead. 'You see?' And she looked at Cheetah. The younger woman looked back at her, frightened now.

'Help me, Cheetah,' said Ouma.

The intensity of feeling in Ouma's words unnerved Cheetah further.

'Help you what?'

Ouma looked down at her feet and Cheetah could feel the air around the old woman grow still.

Then she saw what Ouma meant and couldn't say.

CHAPTER SIX

'She slipped,' says Gogo and then she runs her hand over her wide, iconic face.

The young investigating officer writes down the cause of death as '*aksident*' in his book. Then he and his two colleagues prepare to put Ouma's body in a body bag. The crisp metal-on-metal ring of the zip sounds alien here.

Gogo looks up at Jannie, bewildered. 'What are they doing, Jannie?'

'They must do an autopsy, Gogo,' Jannie says gently.

'What for?' There is a look of such incomprehension on her face that the uniformed men pause. They are all African; it is not their custom to pass the dead into the hands of strangers. Neither do they expect a white man to understand what it is to force the hand of an old woman protecting the dead. He doesn't know that they must honour her because if they don't the whole shaky-card-stack of their decency will fall. A cobweb of misunderstanding wraps itself around them all, swift and silent as a wraith.

In the silence that follows Jannie can smell something coming off Gogo's skin. It is the sweet, dense odour of fear. He doesn't think about its origins or wonder at its cause, he just knows it's there. He says quietly, 'It's routine for unexplained deaths, Gogo.'

The old woman looks down at her swollen hands while she considers Jannie's words. 'I know what you do . . . you people.' Bitterness rises up in her voice like yeast. 'I know what you do with the dead.'

Jannie glances at the investigating officer and, with great delicacy, the younger man leads his team out onto the stoep outside to wait.

Gogo takes a small pot of snuff out of her pocket. Jannie watches as she prises open the lid with her old fingers. He can see she is gathering her forces.

She sniffs the powder first into one nostril and then into the other. Then she closes her eyes to wait for the relief that follows. The sneeze unplugs her outrage. 'You steal body parts.'

She knows what they do, these white people. She knows. Because how? Because when her mother died Gogo reached into the coffin to take leave of her and her mother's body flopped forward like a cloth doll filled with sand. There were no bones. No ligaments. When she looked harder she saw her mother had been opened from top to bottom and stitched up again.

Her corneas were gone. And her shoes were full of a rolled up edition of the Sunday newspaper.

They'd sold her mother's feet.

Gogo looks at Jannie. 'That is why we black people stay with our dead until the end.'

Jannie looks at the old woman. He can see that he has become 'them', where only a few minutes ago he was 'us'. Still, he says quietly, 'It's the law, Gogo.'

She turns to face him and says softly, 'Then I will go with the body.'

'Jesus, you can't do that!' snaps Jannie in surprise.

'I can do it.'

And the old woman gets up and heads towards the door.

Jannie watches her leave, then he sits in the armchair in the corner of the room. He can hear the murmur of the policemen on the stoep as Gogo greets them in passing.

He sees the sodden clothing Gogo has removed from Ouma's body lying in a heap on the floor and notes, idly, that she was wearing a floral dress. It has been a long time since Jannie has seen her in anything but trousers and a shirt.

Ouma's arm has slipped off the table and hangs down into the dark space beneath. Her hand, fine-veined and long-fingered, is suspended there like a chandelier, the structure so clear, more like bits of stone than blood and bone.

The sun from the window beyond slants across the floor in a way with which Jannie is entirely intimate. He knows that it will hit the table in a matter of minutes and when it does the hand will be bathed in sunlight.

There it is. Luminous. The skin under the nails pink-hued, like the pads of a cat, so petal pale, as if it still lives. Jannie gets up out of his chair and catches the suspended hand in his. It is frigid to the touch. He reaches for her other hand without thinking and compares the two.

The subtle pink is not present under the nails of the left hand.

He is bowed over with the business of filtering what he has seen and smelt like a whale sucking plankton into its mouth and tasting the flavour of each particle. He wouldn't be able to put it into words, but the truth is that he is beginning to shift from grieving friend to *seeker*. It is an awkward metamorphosis; he sends shoots across the gap between one state and the other but none seems to take hold. It leaves him in no-man's land.

He crosses Ouma's hands over her chest. Stops. No, she would never want to appear so pious. He can hear her say, *Do not make me seem what I am not, Jannie Claassens*. So he stretches her arms out alongside her body and then, reluctantly, covers her with the sheet.

CHAPTER SEVEN

Inside her small brick two-roomed house Gogo washes her body using a bucket and a cloth. She rubs Vaseline on the bottoms of her cracked feet and on her hands.

The investigating officer and his policemen wait under the shade of the acacia tree in the middle of the lawn. One of them pulls the tender centre out of a luxuriant blade of grass and chews it slowly. The other lights a cigarette and watches Jannie hover in the dust outside the old woman's house.

Jannie wants fervently to accompany Gogo to the morgue. To lean over the shoulder of the pathologist as he works and whisper, *Look under the fingernails on the right hand*, but it goes against protocol to muscle in on someone else's investigation and he senses the man would take it badly. Jannie is known for playing by the rules.

Gogo dresses with care, as if for church. The room around her is pristine; her bed, raised off the floor on bricks, is draped with a series of white, starched, hand-embroidered cloths that speak to beauty and order.

Gogo binds her brightest and best scarf in an intricate turban around her head. Then she sails out of her small house like a stately ocean liner.

Jannie watches the police van labour up the steep driveway until it disappears over the brow of the hill.

If Jannie's diminutive mother sees the degree of her son's need as she opens the farmhouse door to him, she makes no sign of it.

'The bougainvillea by the gate is losing its leaves,' she says as she kisses Jannie on his forehead. He learnt long ago to lower his head for this purpose. It saves mother and son from having to touch anywhere but lip to head, sufficient to say you care but not enough to overwhelm.

Jannie was obscenely young when he understood the limits of his mother's power, yet today, just this once, he'd like her to hear him out and then keep standing in the rapids of his sorrow.

But she does not allow him that. Jannie feels, not for the first time, as if he has lived his life with sand under his skin.

The two of them sit in the small kitchen of the farmhouse. The room could be from another century with its old sink and free-standing gas stove in the corner lilting to one side on the uneven floor. The sparseness of it strikes Jannie anew. None of the succulent spices and flavours of the world's cuisine enriches the birdlike portions of meat and starch that are produced in this kitchen.

As Jannie watches his mother brew a pot of rooibos tea on the stovetop he wonders at her shrinking frame. When many of her community grew bulky in old age, his mother seemed to become yet more angular. In the days when his father beat her, her bruises told him what her words did not. She would never allow her son a bad word about her abuser. She cleaned, baked and sewed to create order out of the brutality that the fall of darkness unleashed in her house.

It is what she does now, in the small act of brewing tea and setting out the tray. She chooses an embroidered tea cloth. Conjured by her own fingers over many nights, it is her best work. She does it to comfort her son but also to honour Ouma's passing for herself.

Jannie's mother never found a way to say so, but she was infinitely grateful to Ouma for putting a stop to the beatings all those years ago, even if it meant her husband's rage turned inward and swept him to his own premature end. This indebtedness made it hard for her to resent the closeness that then grew between Ouma and Jannie, but she did miss her son.

The two women did not often meet, but whenever they did encounter one another, in the supermarket or filling up with petrol at the garage, Jannie's mother walked away from it knowing that Ouma and her vivacious life force would never have allowed anyone to beat her. Never. It made her feel that she was *not enough*.

Now that Ouma has gone, she hardly dares to hope that she might have more of him.

Jannie watches his mother take two shortbread biscuits out of the cake tin and put them on a small floral-patterned plate. Exactly two, just as it has always been; three would have been excessive, indulgent even.

She pours them each a cup of tea then sits at the table opposite him and pushes the small biscuit plate towards him with her arthritic fingers. 'Come, eat. You look thin.' She smiles up at him and takes a sip of tea.

'Ouma slipped,' says Jannie, and as he says those words he is aware that the whole story is not represented there.

'Ag, so sad,' says his mother and then she is silent. Her understanding of his loss sits in the way she waits, not even breathing, for him to speak again.

Jannie looks at his mother. The shape of her fine head, so still in this afternoon light, seems newly patient and tuned to his need. He notices the additions to the cobweb of lines around her eyes. Her jawline, so stern in his memory, now appears soft and perched on the edge of grief.

It does not occur to him that Ouma's death has altered the constellation of how mother and son *are* to one another but that is what it has done.

Jannie looks down at the tea tray. He sees his mother's care in the plate so frugally laden and the artistry in the tray cloth she has chosen. It is her way of making things better for him. She *does* know, after all, that this is a bad day.

She pats his hand and says, 'Come, eat a little.'

Jannie wonders, now, what it was that blinded him to the delicacy of her regard for him and his well-being. He smiles back at her and says, 'It's probably aphids.'

'Aphids?'

'On the bougainvillea. I'll look on my way out.'

'*Dankie.*'

He can see her shoulders relax at the idea that he will allow her love yet not overwhelm her with the story of his suffering.

'Thank you, my boy,' she says and takes another sip of tea.

Post-mortems in the Brits mortuary are usually conducted to the accompaniment of heavy metal music or township *mbaqanga*, depending on the mortician or in some cases the pathologist.

Gogo's insistent vigil over Ouma's body puts an end to that small pleasure.

The mortuary staff are familiar with devastated family members who come to identify their dead but the declamatory presence of this old African woman during the post-mortem is most unusual.

Less surprising is the six-foot-four-inch man who strides into the room with a tray of slides. Pieter Viljoen is always here, picking up samples, or performing an autopsy himself if it matters enough.

It is Gogo who is startled by his arrival. She watches him settle at the microscope in the far corner of the room and begin to work his way through a collection of slides. He is immediately so completely absorbed, so singularly unaware of her, and peaceful, that she remains glued to her chair. Like Gogo's father used to say, *he is without hardship*, as if that were the best one could hope for. Her tidings will deny him this hallowed state for a long time after. So she says nothing.

How many mornings has she seen Pieter slip from Ouma's house at the break of dawn and hurry barefoot and dishevelled up the driveway to the car parked in the bushes off the steep slope?

Gogo remembers, as if it were minutes ago, when she first stumbled across their love affair, if you could call it that. It was a hot summer night, the foreman at the pig farm had had an epileptic seizure and Gogo was despatched, across what she knew to be snake-infested bush, to call the doctor.

As she hurried up to the house she saw, through the bedroom window, Baas Pieter brushing the waterfall of Ouma's long, red-blonde hair.

The intimacy suggested in this silent communion ruffled Gogo's view of how things were. She assumed the single-woman nature of her and Ouma's shared lives would always be thus. *Eish!* Who was this interloper?

Gogo raised her hand to rap on the glass. She wanted to shout *What about the children?* but what she really meant to say was *What about how it has always been here?*

Of course she said neither. Long ago she learnt to moderate the thread between thought and lip but it didn't make her any more sanguine. In moments of such extremis she found it useful to band white people together in irredeemable sameness. God knows, she had seen banal cruelty from their kind aplenty, but was it also their province to behave like animals?

She stood and watched Baas Pieter plait Ouma's thick hair into a tail then lift her up into his arms.

Ouma's openness to being carried in this way took Gogo by surprise. Even through the window, she could see the trust Ouma put in the communion of their bodies, and the perfect care the man took of her. Gogo could not help but wonder if she herself did not sometimes long to be held by another in this way.

Pieter bows the tender pink of his almost-bald head over his work. Gogo sees the wire-thin tendons that connect his head to his shoulders, the wisps of grey hair that curl around his ears, unaware, yet, that Ouma lies lifeless at the far end of the vast room. It is too cruel.

Gogo gets up slowly. Memory snags her there once more, halfway up and poised in indecision.

Never in all her years of difficulty had Gogo heard Ouma weep; not at the death of her husband nor at the loss of her prior life, yet she did so that night.

It seemed to Gogo that she was more mewling small creature than human being. Pieter simply stopped and waited for her sorrow to pass like one would a rainstorm. He made no sound of comfort, just bore witness until she had cried it out.

Then Gogo watched him carry her to the bed. She could see that a more carnal communion would follow and she turned away. But as far as she was concerned, Pieter's tenderness and the surprise of Ouma's sadness had distinguished them from their barbarian race once more. It was for reasons of their mutual human need that Gogo preserved the privacy of this night for them both. The epileptic man from the pig farm was abandoned to his foaming seizure and Gogo tiptoed home in the dark.

Pieter does not look up as Gogo approaches his work station. She waits for him to notice her and when he does not she speaks quietly, '*Dumela*, Baas Pieter.'

He glances up at her then says automatically, '*Dumela*, Gogo. *Le kae?*' and returns to his work.

It is only then that he wonders at her presence there. He lifts his head again and he regards her grave face.

Neither speaks. Gogo wipes away the beads of sweat that have gathered on her forehead.

Pieter waits for her to reassure him that she is just passing through on some small errand and that all is well in the world, but she does not.

The devastation begins to gather in his eyes. He runs his hands through his hair and says, in Sesotho, 'I am sorry to find you here.'

'*Ehe*. I am sorry too.'

He puts his head in his hands and a whimper of what Gogo knows to be only the tip of his scorching, stoic grief escapes him.

Gogo looks away. '*Eish, my baas,*' she says in sympathy.

The drone of the pathologist working in the furthest cubicle fills the silence between them, '. . . *bruising around the ankle, liquid and mud deposits in lungs . . .*'

The suspension of time comes easily to Gogo; it has to do with the way she pays attention to things. If you asked her how long they remained there, she would not have been able to say.

She is aware, rather, of the crumbling and reassembling of Pieter Viljoen's feeling world.

'She did not marry me, Gogo,' he says quietly.

'No, Baas Pieter.'

Pieter looks away.

After that first night, Gogo came to understand that Ouma did not return Pieter's love in the way he wanted her to. She accepted his nurture and held him in high regard but she would not make a life with him.

Now Gogo sees that Pieter's dogged faith that one day Ouma would give him her heart, had taken him from youth to old age and the loss of this possibility, even more than Ouma's actual death, is what he now mourns. She sees all this.

The pathologist speaks on into the dictaphone, '. . . *findings consistent with death by drowning . . . no criminal act suspected.*'

Pieter walks slowly to the cubicle. As he nears it he turns his back on the body he sees lying there. He can't look at it; neither can he challenge the startled pathologist, nor the investigating officer at his side.

Later, Gogo wishes she had followed Pieter's lead and not looked too long at the abused corpse on the examination table but she feels its pull.

A long gash runs down the old lady's front from her neck to her hips; rough stitching puckers half of the skin together in a jagged line, the rest is open. Gogo growls in shock and alarm.

'Cover her,' says Pieter.

'Sir?' asks the pathologist.

'Cover her up!' barks Pieter. 'And when you've finished, send her home.'

'The magistrate needs to sign for the removal of remains,' says the pathologist.

'Not on a bloody Sunday,' Pieter snaps, 'so you will do it.' And he walks out of the room.

Gogo feels a stab of sorrow at his leaving. She turns to the pathologist and she hisses, 'Did you not hear the man? Cover her up.'

Chapter Eight

When Klein Samuel comes for her, Cheetah is sitting on her upturned bucket, scrubbed clean, wearing the dress she thinks of as her church dress but has had no cause to use for that purpose.

Klein Samuel, too, is dressed in his finest jacket, bought when he was a younger and fuller man. He approaches her deferentially, weighed down by his tidings, hat in hand. 'Ja, Cheetah,' he says, and then he clears his throat.

She looks at Klein Samuel but does not speak.

'*Die Ouma is dood*,' he says quietly.

Cheetah nods. She says nothing but her almond eyes tell him she already knows about Ouma's death. She glances at him and says, '*En nou?*' She smiles. 'Who will keep me alive now, Klein Samuel?'

He looks away.

'*Niemand nie*,' she whispers and it is clear she says it not as a question but as a statement. No one.

Klein Samuel lost his simple heart to Cheetah when she first washed up at the pig farm and it has been hers ever since. He wants to tell her that he will take care of her now that Ouma is gone but he is afraid she will laugh at him, so he vows it silently instead. It has been many years since his wife and children filled his heart like this.

Too many years apart. Too much hardship.

It wasn't easy to win Cheetah. In spite of her illness the workers at the pig farm were all eager bees to her flower. Klein Samuel was the most dogged in his wooing of her and merciless in exploiting his one great asset. Ouma. He made himself the bridge between the two until Cheetah believed her very survival to be bound up with loving him.

He had the wisdom to wait, also, for the delights of her body. It took almost a full year of his small attentions before she held out her hand to him one hot Sunday morning and led him into her room.

He had Ouma to thank for it. He feels a stab of fury at the old lady for abandoning him after such a long and fruitful association.

After all it was he who was waiting at the gate the day Ouma first arrived at the farm with a truck full of her worldly goods, a drunken husband, three sullen children, and Gogo. He waited as if he came with the land and expected to be passed like a slave from one family member to another. It was not how it was, but he hoped that by being there he could make it so.

The colour of Ouma's hair made him think of *rooigras*, a good grazing grass that turned red in verdant soil. She stood at the top of the driveway and looked, with dread, at the sight of her new home.

Back then, it was a thin, unkempt strip of bushveld, neither large enough to farm nor small enough to call a garden. Klein Samuel could see it shamed her.

Apart from taking food and water, Ouma didn't get out of bed for two months. The people in the valley said it was her husband's unruly thirst that lost them the big house in Pretoria. They said his family had thrown them this scrap of land by way of apology for their wayward son.

Klein Samuel made himself indispensable to Ouma. He worked in the garden. He dug plant beds, seeded spinach and *mielies* and dammed up the road to stop the red earth from washing away. And he waited.

He could not have known what a fireball of Boer ancestors occupied Ouma's mourning bed those many weeks. Raised to spawn a line of achievers, one of theirs now lay defeated there, her purpose forgotten. They nailed Ouma to the bed with the twist of their disappointment.

Then Petrus from the pig farm was knocked off his bicycle and Klein Samuel came to rouse the doctor.

He knocked respectfully on the front door and called out, '*Koh, koh.*'

But there was no answer. He pushed the door open, saying, '*Miesies?*'

Nothing.

It was his concern for the life being lost on the side of the hot tar road that drove him to break convention and open the door to Ouma's bedroom.

Ouma sat up, leaning on her elbow and holding the sheet to her chest. 'I'm not a doctor any more. Do I look like a doctor to you?' she had hissed at him.

He had no answer to that question so he waited, silently, eyes cast down, until Ouma cursed at him, sat up, swung her feet onto the floor and stood up.

She worked to stop the haemorrhaging until she was covered in blood up to her elbows. When the summer rainstorm hit them,

Klein Samuel held a beach umbrella over doctor and patient so Ouma could continue her efforts.

When Ouma saw, finally, that it was futile, she leant close to the dying man's ear and whispered something to him.

She brought his grieving wife and son to sit by his side right there on the road and hold his hand.

And they watched him slip away.

Klein Samuel recognised the driver who knocked Petrus down as a neighbouring farmer. As the cries of the dead man's widow filled the air the farmer shouted at her, '*Shaddup! Shaddup, meid!*'

Ouma raised her head to consider the farmer. He had called the widow *meid*. Maid. This woman, destined now with her children to live a life of extreme hardship.

'You must leave now,' Ouma said to him, quietly.

The man did not move.

'Get into your car and go.'

Still he didn't move.

Ouma reared up on her feet and roared at the famer. '*Loop!*' Her hair stuck to her forehead and bloody rain dripped off her fingertips.

He stared at her.

She roared again. 'Now!'

And, finally, he did.

Like Gogo always said, Ouma didn't choose sides that day. Nor any day after that.

That day she worked at saving this one life.

And then the one after that.

And so on.

Vir ewig en altyd, as Ouma liked to say.

She saved Cheetah's life too and so brought Klein Samuel untold riches.

He knows the black hole that consumes Cheetah now because he feels it too.

Cheetah tucks her thumb under her red bra strap and lifts it back onto her shoulder. It is a simple gesture but so full of sex that Klein Samuel has to look away.

In the way a hunter-cat catches sight of the far-away flutter of a bird wing, Cheetah knows she has awakened something in him. 'You got a cigarette?' she says.

He reaches for his packet and holds it out to her.

'Ta,' she says.

Klein Samuel digs for his matches. His battered black hands look unsuited to handling the fine sticks of wood and the soft paper drawer of the matchbox but his fingers move with surprising grace and refinement as he lights her up.

He watches the way Cheetah's brown lips suck in the smoke, and the heave of her chest as she expels the excess.

He whispers, 'It is time.'

Cheetah sighs. Then she gets up.

CHAPTER NINE

Gogo oversees the return of Ouma's body to the dining-room table in complete silence. She does not even acknowledge the investigating officer as he takes his leave with the respectful, '*Tsamaye hantle, mme,*' spoken in their shared language. She will not give him the grace of her forgiveness.

She dresses Ouma's body in trousers and a long-sleeved blouse to protect the family from the ravages of the post-mortem. Then she waits.

Groot Samuel is the first to arrive. He stands beside his mother's body and wonders whether he was born to suffer. There is no self-pity in his musing, just a factual question thrown out into the air.

After all, he had the bad luck to be born second out of three children – right in the middle and so forgotten. The bad luck to be in a marriage stubbornly short on happiness; even now his wife Ilse is with her family over the hill rather than by his side. The bad luck to be custodian of this blasted patch of earth, which defies him, every day, to make his living off it.

But even on the worst days Groot Samuel gives thanks that he has Gogo.

He watches her quiet competence as she rises from her chair to comb his mother's hair. It is an oddly tender sight, this coming together of Gogo's wide hands, the small comb, and the wisps of Ouma's nearly invisible, silver hair.

The song she sings under her breath as she works is the half-articulated African hymn Groot Samuel first heard as a child at Gogo's church under the willow tree on the pig farm.

In truth, it was Gogo who mothered him. Her nurture meant that he could preserve Ouma in his mind's eye as a salty, vast presence who knew what he needed even before he himself did. Who would never leave him. Never die.

It was not how Ouma was, but to remember her so blinded him to the intolerable truth that there was always someone who mattered more than he did; someone wheezing with tuberculosis or halfway through an impossible birth.

As children, Groot Samuel and his sister Aletta waited for their mother for hours on the red dust outside her consulting rooms. Before long, the young boy would come to wish that he was half-dead too so his mother would scoop him up and whisper, 'Stay with me,' the way he heard her say to the ones who were slipping away.

'Smoke, *baas*?' Klein Samuel the farmhand stands in the doorway to the living room with his hat in his hand to show respect for the dead. Cheetah hovers beyond, uncertain of her welcome. Delilah comes into the room from the kitchen, eyes swollen nearly shut from her grieving.

Groot Samuel takes out his cigarettes and joins Klein Samuel in the doorway. Groot Samuel sucks the smoke into his chest. His lungs receive it badly and heave him into a coughing spasm. Klein Samuel follows suit.

Cheetah steps into the room.

Delilah pulls socks onto Ouma's feet. She wonders how it is that old people's feet become so gnarled and twisted. It's as if all of their hardships and none of their grace are reflected there.

She looks up in time to catch Gogo's poisonous glance at Cheetah, who is now hovering in the shadows beyond where the body lies. Delilah doesn't like the storm brewing in that look. She smiles at Cheetah to ameliorate its bitterness.

Emboldened, Cheetah steps closer.

Gogo stops her with a bark, 'You!' She points at the door. '*Voetsak!*'

It is what she says to Suffering when he gets under her feet as she cleans. Cheetah hesitates.

'This is no time for you to be here,' Gogo spits, 'not someone like you.'

'Like who?' asks Cheetah.

Gogo will not give her more.

The two Samuels turn towards the fracas. Klein Samuel steps forward to intervene but his boss touches his arm and mutters, '*Wag maar*, you can only make it worse for her.'

Cheetah takes up Gogo's challenge, more out of habit than will. 'Someone sexy?' Cheetah pouts. 'Sexy like this?' She juts out her hip. The crudeness of the gesture reveals her ruin, as if a hard, bright light has fallen on the myth of her allure.

Gogo shakes her head. 'I said it long ago. I said it when I saw you coming down the driveway with your skin and bone. I said to Ouma, that one running from the gangs in Cape Town, she is bad luck.'

Cheetah looks at the old woman. Hurt intensifies the sound of the

Cape wind and sandblasted home in her retort. '*Gah!*' she spits. 'She loved me anyway.'

Gogo's face darkens.

'*Jy weet dit mos*. You know it.'

The two women look at one another. Cheetah takes a few steps back, afraid now of the dark in Gogo's eyes. But it's too late for retreat.

Gogo is upon her. She shoves Cheetah in her fine-as-a-bird chest. 'What do you know about . . . that . . . you *rubbish*!'

Cheetah is no match for her bulk.

Delilah calls out, 'Gogo!' But the old lady hears nothing.

'*Voetsak!* Out! *Isa!*' roars Gogo as she drives Cheetah out of the house and onto the red dust beyond it. She waits for her to turn and walk away. Then she puts her hands on her hips and spits into the dust.

You would've thought the sun had somehow moved closer to the earth so intense is the heat on the back of Cheetah's head as she takes the path to her room. It has mass to it, and density. Klein Samuel catches up with her and they continue in silence as far as the fence to the pig farm. The barbed wire catches her dress as she stumbles over it but she pays it no heed. Klein Samuel can tell by her half-blind forward motion that she is crying. He follows her over the fence but she turns back and hisses, 'Leave me!'

The small room feels smaller still as Cheetah clatters around in it in wounded fury.

'Help me, Cheetah,' Ouma had said again as they sat on the soft green grass.

'How?'

Ouma looked at her and Cheetah saw that what she meant was, *Help me die.*

Cheetah had never understood what *klapwoorde* were before – words that hit. And it was as if someone had hit her on the head with those three one-syllabled blows.

The sun caught the yellow pollen from the nearby *soetdoring* and held it in the air around the old lady's head, a cosmos of plump, open seed; some scurrying thing in the flowerbed sent the dogs yapping across the green grass; birds flew; crickets rubbed their hind legs together as if to say, *me, me, I am here.* The teeming sent Cheetah back down onto her back. She lay very still.

Did Ouma not remember that she had people to save?

'Fugoff, Ouma! You think I'm stupid?' Cheetah said as soon as she was able. 'You think I want more dying? You think I don't know what you are asking?'

Ouma had looked at her with tired eyes and said, 'I ask you *because* you know it.'

'Then *sies* on you, Ouma,' and she turned away.

Ouma put her hands over her face.

Cheetah would say it again right now if Ouma were standing in front of her. *Sies on you, Ouma, for taking me back.*

She takes off her church dress and hangs it on the single hanger on the back of her door. On her concave stomach, in big letters, are tattooed the words *Cassiems Forever*, without the apostrophe.

It is so much part of her that she doesn't notice it any more; it's like a freckle, or an irregular eyebrow. But today it is reflected in the cracked mirror beside the sink, and its backwards script startles her, *smeissaC reveroF.*

'You can be a high-up somebody, Ouma,' she said that day as the two women sat on the grass, 'but your death will be the same as anyone else's.'

It was like that with Cassiem. Even though he was, briefly, the brutal master of his corner of Lavender Hill, he was helpless when his end came.

He died buying a watermelon from Chrissie at the roadside stall on the corner of Prince George Drive and Military Road. He was handing over his twenty rand when a boy with a big hat, half hidden behind a corrugated-iron shed, pulled out a gun and fired a single shot. The boy knew he could advance his own story if he felled the big bull, so he did.

Cheetah looked down at Cassiem as he lay on the dirt road with sewage trickling by in the ditch beyond. His bowels released their putrid contents, his toes pointed straight up in the air and he died.

Cheetah waited but there was no bullet for her. She would've have liked one. It could've saved her a lot of struggle. She sat on the road next to the watermelons and cried.

'I was his, forever. See. Until his turn came,' Cheetah said to Ouma, 'and then he died just the same as everyone else.'

The old lady reached for her hand.

Cheetah wanted to say that Cassiem's death wasn't even the worst of it. The *everydayness* of seeing the fallen ones beside the dustbins at the back of the Pick 'n' Pay, was worse. First one young body then another and so it went on. But she didn't say it because just then Ouma whispered, 'Forgive me, child.'

Cheetah heard the regret in Ouma's voice. The two women were silent for a moment and then Cheetah said, 'I need you to be there at my end, Ouma.'

Ouma clasped Cheetah's hand and the young woman could see that she had remembered her calling. Then Cheetah said quietly, 'To show me the way to a better world.'

Delilah does up the cherry-red button on the right cuff of Ouma's blouse, then the one on the left. She empties the bowl of water out of the window and watches the liquid sink into the sand.

Delilah no longer expects constancy from the scattering of adults in her life, but she would never have foreseen Gogo's cruelty to Cheetah.

She reaches for the small plastic bag on the table that contains Ouma's sparse jewellery, removed at the time of the post-mortem and sent home with the body.

She considers the wedding ring nesting in its transparent folds and wonders if she should put it back onto Ouma's finger, then decides against it. She never once heard Ouma speak of her dead husband.

But she takes out Ouma's watch and begins to strap it to the old lady's slim wrist. She stops and considers it for a moment.

'Ouma was wearing her watch,' she says, and she looks up.

Gogo now stands in the doorway looking out. The old woman is so still that Delilah wonders if shame or grief have taken off with her insides and left her skin standing there. It is the kind of day for such thoughts.

Delilah turns to Groot Samuel.

He lights another cigarette.

She says it again. 'Do you see, Oom Samuel? It's a watch-day.'

Neither Gogo nor Groot Samuel seems to hear her. Or, if they do, neither is capable of a response. Delilah does not know what to do next.

Surely they must all know that there are watch-days and no-watch-days in Ouma's life? There are the sunny, early morning walks on the edge of the dam to look for birds, with her watch strapped onto her wrist to keep it all moving forward, and then there are the others.

Those begin long before dawn and are attended by an anxiety and disorientation so profound that the first morning Delilah saw her grandmother in such disarray she covered her face with her pillow and pretended she wasn't there.

On those mornings, Ouma stumbled to the door in the half-light, bathrobe open to reveal her concave chest with its diagonal scar from the removal of her breasts. She opened the door, gasping to get out, with a different shoe on each foot.

Delilah can imagine her grandmother slipping on such a morning.

But not on a watch morning. It comes to Delilah as an absolute fact.

Ouma didn't slip.

Delilah looks up at Gogo. She would like to, but she can't begin to describe the scorching passage that phrase makes through her body. There is no part of her or her world left untouched.

She did not slip.

PART TWO

PART TWO

CHAPTER TEN

Jannie's boss is not a patient man. He says patience is for pansies. If Mokheti Mokoena were a plant he would be a *kameeldoring*, a camel thorn tree, prickly, irascible and as enduring as the dust storms that bedevilled his desert childhood.

He had a lot to contend with as a boy. And he still does. As a capable black professional, this post-apartheid world should be giving him his moment in the sun, but it's not turning out that way.

It seems, some days, that he is powerless to stop the runaway train of burgeoning crime and corruption in his police district. He also has an extended family that spends every penny he makes. Their need keeps him in Soshanguve Township when all he wants is a quiet patch of green in the suburbs of Brits.

The house next door to Jannie's would do nicely, apart from the monthly gathering of the Elisabeth Eybers book club. He has heard about these great events and knows they would test him. He's a traditional African man and although he is fond of his poetry-loving detective, he doesn't want to see him in a dress.

It used to be that Mokheti insisted on spending Sundays with his wife and three children. He would potter in his early morning garden and then they would attend church together. More than a few beers would follow through the afternoon and teatime would find him noisily asleep on the sofa with the soccer blaring.

No more. His house has emptied out as his children have grown. He would never admit this but his last born, Bontle, is his favourite. She dazzled him with her wit and zealous determination from the time she took her first steps. Over the years he would look at her and wonder if she was not a changeling. Perhaps switched at birth with the offspring of parents with a more auspicious genetic imprint. After she finished school Bontle did her BTech in policing. Four years later, Mokheti saw her graduate with an Honours degree in criminology from Wits University. Now she is a working member of the Organized Crime Unit of the South African Police Service. It makes him very proud.

Bontle's departure from the family home left only the dry pips of Mokheti's marriage behind and a scattering of hungry-mouthed hangers on. Nowadays he prefers to spend Sundays in his office. He counts on it being more peaceful there on the day of rest but that is not always the case.

Today, mayhem at the local shebeen has filled the charge office to bursting with drunk and loquacious souls. Then there is Pieter, head pathologist, who has phoned Mokheti not once but twice to complain about Jannie's attempts to learn the results of Ouma's postmortem. 'Ag nee, *man*, what the blazes is he sticking his nose into this story for? The investigating officer has already asked the magistrate to close the docket.'

In Mokheti's overpacked and underpaid life, the accidental death of a seventy-six-year-old white woman on a farm in De Wildt shouldn't worry him. Except, and this is both his blessing and his curse, Mokheti thinks about these things. He cares. He has a lot of time for Jannie because he cares too.

In other circumstances their shared concern might have resulted in a long and careful investigation into the old lady's death, but not this time. In the Darwinian world of Brits area law enforcement Mokheti needs Pieter and his team of pathologists more than they need him. Most of the murder cases on his docket depend on their careful professionalism and, without a faultless chain of evidence from them to the forensic analysts and then back to him, he has no chance of convicting anyone. He can't have Jannie uproot that *mielie* field, even if Ouma was his best friend.

Mokheti stands in Jannie's doorway and snaps, 'Ja, Detective?'

Jannie stands up to show respect for his superior. 'Colonel?' he says.

'What are you doing here on your day off?' asks Mokheti.

Jannie couldn't answer the question if he tried. The truth is that, like a homing pigeon, he left tea with his mother and found himself here. He holds up his book to deflect further questions.

'Ja, reading,' says Mokheti. 'Reading what?'

'Poems.'

Ah, so it is serious, his grief. Even Mokheti knows that if Elisabeth Eybers makes an appearance, real pain is present too. He wishes, momentarily, that he didn't have to bring up Pieter's phone calls.

It has become something of a ritual for Mokheti and Jannie to share the dying moments of most days in congenial summary of the day's key events. These conversations are occasionally of a philosophical bent. Neither man has much time to ponder why crime in their country is attended by so much gratuitous violence. Mokheti leaves that to God to sort out and Jannie retreats to the solace of poetry when it troubles him. But every now and again, even though it doesn't get them anywhere, they muse on how far back the shadow of depravity goes. It is not the whole story, but both have come to believe, in their very different ways, that a cruel past makes a cruel present. And that lack of prospects for the poor keeps it that way.

Jannie closes his book and says, 'And I'm thinking.'

'About?'

Jannie gets up and goes to the window, a grated rectangle of glass too high up on the wall to frame the outside with any grace. It does reveal the sky and the gathering of cloud that marks the passage of the day from morning to afternoon.

Mokheti takes his chance while Jannie's back is turned. 'They're not too happy with you over at pathology, Detective.'

Jannie watches the cloud thicken but he says nothing.

Mokheti sighs. He sits down on Jannie's recently evacuated chair and picks out the words he finds scrawled across the paper on the desk. He is like a chicken pecking for corn: '. . . physician to farming community in De Wildt for thirty years. Survived by children Aletta, Samuel, Frans and two grandchildren.'

On the bottom of the page is scribbled in Jannie's hand, *AND ME.*

Mokheti glances at Jannie. The detective can feel his gaze but he does not meet it.

Mokheti reads the last line of the obituary aloud, 'She Saved Our Souls.'

He puts it back on the desk and says quietly, 'You write that?'

Jannie nods.

'Only Jesus can save us, my boy,' says Mokheti. He sounds tired.

Jannie doesn't turn to face his boss or respond to his comment but he can hear the feeling simmering there. You don't mess with Mokheti and his faith.

'The investigating officer has recommended this docket be closed,' says Mokheti.

Jannie runs his fingers through his hair. He can hear Mokheti breathing behind him. He has always wondered about the loud in and out of his boss's breath. Today it enrages him.

'She was an old lady and she fell,' says Mokheti.

'That so?' says Jannie.

'Leave it alone, Detective. And that's an order,' says Mokheti, and then he puts up his hand to silence the objection he sees coming full throttle towards him. 'If only to stop yourself being accused of failing the sixteen black corpses lying in the morgue with knife wounds in their chests in favour of an old white lady who died an accidental death. Don't do that to me or my police station, Lieutenant Claassens, *wa bona*?'

He says it with feeling and force, and then he gets up and walks out of the office.

As he makes his way down the long linoleum green of the passage, Mokheti wonders if he was too hard on Jannie. He can see that the young man's heart is broken and that he can't see straight for the chaos it has unleashed.

Mokheti longs, just then, for the certainties of his apartheid era youth with its good guys and bad, with its higher cause of emancipation that bound his countrymen and women together. He stops in at the kitchenette and drinks a glass of water. It doesn't help his thirst.

CHAPTER ELEVEN

Delilah watches the rain clouds come over the ridge as they do every afternoon during the hot season and then snag there on the thermals of burning air and darken.

It has been this way for months. The daily build up to rain. Then nothing.

The smallholding farmers and their labourers don't dare look up at the clouds in case the power that rules such things feels their longing and blows the cloud away in a perverse show of superiority.

They judge the likelihood of rain through their skin.

Today the sky is dark enough for an eclipse. Ink-black dark. The air gets wetter.

The pressure behind Klein Samuel's ear increases to an ache as he sits in the dust outside his shack hoping Cheetah will come to him. He longs to spread his succour over the bruise left by Gogo's lashing at Ouma's house but Cheetah is likely buried under her red blanket, belligerently alone in her grief.

If this feeling had a sound it would be a blade cutting through metal. He finds it so enervating that he does not even rise to his feet when he sees Delilah walk by pushing his battered red bicycle.

The bicycle is much too big for Delilah. The arch her body must make to clear the high middle bar as she pedals makes her sway dangerously into the busy road at the bottom of the hill.

She pedals furiously as a truck full of tomatoes clatters by. If someone asked her where she was going and with such intent, she would not have known what to answer, but the truth of it is that she has to do something about Ouma.

In the first few days after her arrival at the farm Delilah had tested every corner and crevice of her grandmother's patience.

'Take me home!' she screamed on the first morning. 'I want to go home right now.'

'Of course you do,' said Ouma, 'but come and see the dam; we have a canoe.'

That's when Delilah shouted, 'Stupid! That's a stupid idea.'

Delilah pedals past a huge mound of watermelons for sale on the side of the road. The young black teenager who mans the stall is sleeping on a striped red and yellow beach towel beside his produce.

The glimpse Delilah gets of the gentle heave of his slumber makes her suddenly aware of the burning passage of the breath into her chest. The metal chain of the bicycle rubs the skin on the bones of her ankles raw. The sun burns her shoulders pink.

Delilah's expulsion from her only known universe, her river, her home, her family, might have been easier to bear if a flood had left her orphaned. Being powerless to stop the bakery's dwindling earnings made her want to pull her hair out but the fact that her brother

Martinus stayed on while she was sent away made it worse. 'They would like it better if I was dead, not so, Ouma?'

Delilah waited for the old lady to scold her for her unforgiveable thought but she did not. Truth was, her grandmother was not appalled by any of the hideous things Delilah thought or felt and so she unburdened all her terrors, imagined and actual, into the old lady's imperturbable lap.

Sullen, silent days followed where Delilah paced up and down the driveway then sat on the concrete to wait for God-knows-who to rescue her from this exile. It felt to Delilah that she had fallen off the edge of the world.

Ouma let her be. She went about her business making sick people well, though the truth was that word of Ouma's lapses had travelled and only the desperate still showed up at her surgery. But Delilah didn't know that. All she saw was her grandmother's somewhat miraculous capacity to save souls. So, creeping sideways, she attached herself to Ouma and let her brave heart beat for them both.

Time came when she and her grandmother would paddle out to the forest of reeds in the centre of the full dam every evening. They would lie in the bottom of the canoe to watch the frenzied coming and going of the masked weaver birds to the nests hanging above them like lanterns. And of course she became acquainted with Elisabeth Eybers.

A township spreads across the plain beyond, vestigial from the days of apartheid but expanding still because of the grinding hardships that still face its people.

Delilah pedals past a struggling herb farm at the bend in the road. A half-built dream house next door, now abandoned.

It is a transitional, unsettled world.

The girl and her bike crest the hill. The town sits in the mountain-shadow below. The buildings are grim, as if the apartheid era architects who raised them feared that beauty and grace would somehow corrupt their nation-building purpose and send them packing.

Jannie doesn't say a word when he comes out of the police station to see Delilah waiting for him on the steps.

'She didn't slip,' says the young girl, breathless, before Jannie has had a chance to greet her.

'What?'

'Ouma.'

Delilah's words cause Jannie to stop in his tracks. His impulse is to run into Mokheti's office and insist that he stop the docket reaching the magistrate. Even as he thinks it, he knows his idea has no chance, based as it is on the word of this sixteen-year-old Cassandra.

Jannie looks at Delilah's burning face. He would like to cup her cheeks in his hands to cool them, but he doesn't dare.

A group of uniformed policemen sit on the steps behind Jannie, smoking. He feels their gaze in the back of his neck. His homosexuality is common knowledge. They might even have heard talk about his book club. Jannie sometimes wonders what clandestine pleasures the gay men among them allow themselves. He would like to know but cannot ask.

'She didn't slip,' Delilah says again.

Jannie picks up Klein Samuel's bicycle and slides it onto the back of his red *bakkie*.

The young girl waits for him to say something but he just holds the truck door open for her. He recognises in her the task of being truth teller to those who choose not to see. He would like to explain to her that his hands are tied, whether he sees or not.

As Delilah does up her seatbelt she says, 'It was a watch-day.'

'A what?'

'She was wearing her watch.'

'And?'

'She wouldn't slip on a watch-day.'

Jannie runs his hands over his face. 'I'll take you home.'

He walks round to the driver's side and opens the door.

They do not talk in the truck, not even when they reach open road and all they hear is the drone of the engine and the wind. Delilah's hands lie like fish in her lap.

Jannie glances at her. He sees the imprint of Ouma in the young girl's face. He scratches under the seat and pulls out a bottle of water. He hands it to Delilah silently.

She refuses it.

He insists.

She takes it. As she drinks, parched, snot and tears flow into the liquid and onto her lap.

He takes a deep breath and says, 'I'm sad too.'

Delilah tries to stem her impatience but it breaks loose and she roars, '*Sy het nie gegly nie!*' She says it in Afrikaans because she is angry. *She did not slip.*

He doesn't dare look at her.

She turns away from him.

He drives off the black road onto the concrete driveway and pulls up at the gate to the farm.

Jannie watches the child's skinny body stride away up the

driveway. The bike is almost as tall as she is. Her shoulders and arms are seared red by the sun.

It is only then that he considers what extreme effort it must have taken for her to cycle all the way into town.

When she gets to the gate she turns back to face him. He waves.

She makes no gesture in return. Just looks at him. Her stillness rattles him. He shoves the car into gear.

Delilah watches him pull out onto the black road and head back towards town.

Then she turns and pushes open the gate. As she passes through it she feels the black cloud open its mouth and suck her in.

She does not fight it.

CHAPTER TWELVE

The small town seethes in its sleep. The scavenger jackal, come in from the hills for food, tips over a dustbin and sorts through the rubbish with his nose. His scent rouses the dogs of the town to noisy wakefulness.

Jannie sits up in bed. He can't breathe in the stifling interior. Delilah's burning cheeks are with him there in the dark. He puts on his cotton dressing gown and opens the door to the garden. His burglar alarm goes off. It screeches through the suburban night until he types in the code number with clumsy fingers.

He steps onto his stoep, then onto the small patch of grass beyond it.

It starts to rain. Just like that. First one drop, and then another.

He is dimly aware that he should celebrate the breaking of the drought.

But it is too late for that.

The rain hits the hills above the farmhouse not long after the town.

Delilah hears the rumble of thunder as it rolls back the ozone and ushers in the forces that lie beyond.

She opens the window and looks at the succulent drops – too luscious, too wet, as they fall onto her outstretched palm.

Gogo is too broad for the narrow bench on which she sits in vigil over Ouma's body. Her back aches.

She has always hated this bench. It is for those tight-lipped Dutch Reformed relatives of Ouma's who show up from time to time to disapprove of how they live. The ones who eat their way through a groaning table of food without a smile. They are the people who build furniture like this. They are the ones who made the ugly town at the bottom of the hill.

Gogo shifts to a more comfortable position.

The rain is already drumming hard on his metal roof by the time it calls Groot Samuel back from his slumber. All the years of his life he has slept like this, closed his eyes and plummeted like a stone falling to the bottom of a well.

He hurries to the window and puts out his head to feel the drops wet his face; he needs this proof. Ilse, his wife, lies in the dark and watches him. 'Is it not on the way to somewhere else?' she says.

Groot Samuel glances up at the ink-purple sky. 'There's no wind from the west.'

'Might last then.'

'Maybe.'

Ilse sits up against the pillow and she puts her hand on the space where her husband's body slept. If he turns round now, he will surely see her invitation and come to her. She would like that.

Lightning flashes across the hill and makes the night day for a moment. In that flash, Groot Samuel catches a glimpse of his dogs, all five of them, scattering over the hills behind the house like a pack of wolves.

'Did you let the dogs out?'

'Ag now, Samuel,' says Ilse, and snatches her hand back. 'I've been telling you about that broken gate for half a year.'

She undoes the elastic band that ties up her long black hair, streaked here and there with fine strands of grey, and wishes she could erase the irritation and disappointment in her voice.

Ilse is known by people in the valley as 'the wife'. He is Groot Samuel and she '*die vrou*'. She knows it is because she doesn't measure up and she wonders how it came to be that way.

When she first met Groot Samuel at the doctor's surgery where she works as a nurse, he made her laugh. She had long resigned herself to life as a single woman but his subtle attentions gradually encircled her until she and he were bound. She saw the kindness in his eyes and believed he offered her a life of gentle communion. Indeed, the first few times she visited him on the farm, they walked the pathways he had built through the grasslands hand in hand, stopping now and then to observe the wonders of the wild fig he had planted, or the small wooden bridge he had built over the rocky riverbed.

What she didn't factor in was Ouma. The old lady's slow decline and the discreet closeness between mother and son tested Ilse every day. She wasn't proud of how she responded.

She barely dares to hope, as she sits on the bed, but Ouma's death could mark a new beginning for them. She longs for more from him than this duty – deep, stoical duty – dependable and deadly.

Groot Samuel can hear the dogs baying as they fly across the shiny granite hillside. The lightning cracks again and he sees a pack of baboons on the rocks ahead of them, waiting. In all his years Groot Samuel has never seen a troop so active in the night hours but there they stand, dogs and baboons facing off in the heavy rain. Their blood is up on this electric night.

Groot Samuel hurries, straight-backed, out of the house, across the garden and through the gate.

Ilse rests her head back on the pillows.

He scales the flat granite rocks behind the house as fast as he is able, but he is barefoot and is slowed now and then by patches of sharp yellow grass.

He hears a cry. It comes from the mountain and is dulled by the rain. Sounds like a baby crying. He knows it is not a sound his dogs would make. He has an ear for distress.

The sharp grass breaks through the skin of his feet but it doesn't matter. He breathes heavily, his blackened lungs in revolt. The cry comes again.

Groot Samuel sees the baying dogs, all hunched and hungry in a group, growling at something in their midst. Snapping.

He talks the dogs down, '*Kom, kom, kom nou*. Hey, boy, hey.' They look up at him, uncertain.

He walks into the centre of the pack and looks down into the grass.

There, on its back with eyes as big as pools and a gash in its side, lies a small baby baboon.

Groot Samuel kneels down.

He pulls off his raincoat. The pyjama top underneath is at least partially dry and still warm from his body. He wraps it around the small body and then draws it into his chest. It is too wounded to protest.

He feels it shiver.

A bubble of feeling erupts at the bottom of Groot Samuel's spine and he is felled by how often he has longed to hold his own young this way.

God knows he and his wife would have both been grateful for that. They met too late perhaps.

He holds the baby ape and savours the secret joy it gives him.

The rain soaks into the parched ground. Klein Samuel stands in the doorway of his shack. He listens to the rain with the ears of a bat. He hears the small rivulets cut a course through the red dust outside his house.

A light goes on in the small shack beyond the fence. Klein Samuel moves towards it. He ducks under the barbed wire and as he does so a trickle of water washes over his feet. He knocks on the door.

A voice answers, 'Ja – what?'

'It's me.'

The door opens to reveal Cheetah wrapped in her red blanket.

'The roof leaking yet?' asks Klein Samuel.

She steps aside to show him the blue bucket catching drips on her bed and the frying pan on the floor.

He can see she's been crying. He puts his hand on the door frame and says, 'Can I just sit inside with you?' The rain runs streams down his cheeks. 'I swear. Just sit.'

She opens the door.

'Samuel. Just leave it,' says Ilse gently when Groot Samuel stumbles in with the baby still clutched to his chest. She stands in the kitchen in her dressing gown, dishevelled with worry for him. She shares his grief at being childless and can see some of that feeling in the way he holds the baby baboon. But she's a farm girl and she knows the wild world rarely responds to human ministration. She would like to comfort him but he doesn't allow it.

He believes it is his salvation not to hear the peaks and troughs of her unhappiness.

He takes the milk from the fridge and a baking syringe from the cooking drawer.

'Where's your shirt?' she asks.

He does not answer.

His naked torso is so imperfect — concave where it should be round and round where it should be flat — that Ilse wonders for a moment how she could love someone so ordinary?

Her stomach lurches as he turns to go. She would like to beg him to stay with her, but she doesn't trust herself not to cry so she sits on the ebony chair in the corner and closes her eyes instead.

Klein Samuel hears the rivulets join up and spread out on the firm redbrick surface of the road racing to the dam.

'Enough now,' he says under his breath.

But the rain keeps coming.

Cheetah taps him on the shoulder and he turns with a start to face her. She holds open the red blanket of her bed. He crawls under it gratefully.

The small shape of the baby baboon lies on Groot Samuel's lap still wrapped in his pyjama top. She does not respond to the milk he dribbles into her mouth. Does not stretch out her toes in pleasure at the taste or even open her eyes.

He blows hot breath onto her face and her feet. She does not respond. She is rigid, cold, light as air.

It was too much work to keep that small heart beating.

A pit opens in Groot Samuel's grieving, middle-aged chest.

He wades through mud and water to the base of the broad oriental spread of the acacia tree. As he digs, a heaving, growling sound catches in his nose and spit fills his mouth.

If you ever asked Groot Samuel what it cost him to see Ouma on her watch-less days, he would have walked away from the question, straight backed and silent. He would have fixed a fence, or dug a hole for a new peach tree.

His mother's disorientation simply didn't fit with his view of her. He could not allow that disease was its cause and so he gave it an intentionality it didn't possess. He would rage, sometimes to the verge of cruelty, at her lapses.

'It's *your* house, Ma!' he would shout as she wondered, on a bad day, whose house she was visiting for dinner. And when she asked again just a few minutes later as he knew she would, he would rail, 'Just sit down and be quiet!'

For Groot Samuel these evenings were made nigh unbearable by his mother's confusion and his wife's loneliness.

As Ouma's incontinence grew more persistent he would turn his back on her when she needed cleaning up, even when Gogo was not available. He could not bear her soiled, birdlike nakedness. When Ilse, out of compassion for her husband, stepped in to help, Ouma would beseech him silently not to let her daughter-in-law wash her down.

'She's helping me, Ma,' was all he would say, and he would walk away from the house so he didn't have to hear Ouma shout, deep-voiced, '*Jy is die duiwel se kind!*' as Ilse pulled off her clothes, gagging at the smell. *You are the child of the devil*. But it was Ouma who sounded like the devil. And it was he, her son, who walked away from her.

Once he woke in the dead-pitch of night to find his mother standing next to his bed.

His heart thumped hammer-hard in his chest. 'Everything okay, Ma?' he asked.

She wore a different shoe on each foot, her robe hung loose over her bony shoulders and her eyes were ink-dark and wide with fear. 'The people who own this place are coming . . .' she said as he followed her out onto the stoep.

'What?

'. . . to pack us into a truck and send us away.'

'This is our farm, Ma.'

She wagged her finger as if to say, *No, young man, you are mistaken*. Groot Samuel saw the depth of her disorientation and the whole of his insides flipped over to face the other side of his body.

She looked at him and he could see an idea flush colour into her cheeks and, God knows, *mission*, into her eyes.

'We must go out there,' she said, and she waved her hand into the blackness, 'and find the most *vul-ner-a-ble* person –' she said the word like each syllable lived separately and was only revelatory when brought together – 'and we must tell them . . .'

He didn't want to hear any more, but her eyes held him there.

'. . . that they are not alone.'

Then she sat down on the small outdoor sofa, slowly, exhausted.

He sat beside her. The two of them looked out at the night. If he could've he would have held her close and whispered, 'Stay with me . . .'

Instead, he reached for her hand and so pinned what was left of her to the earth.

She leant back against the back of the sofa and whispered, 'I must leave you, child.' She said it with such tenderness, such gentle regret and such concern for him that he could hear that it came from her sentient self.

A blood-filled rush of grief and alarm got him to his feet.

He walked out onto the wide red dust in front of the house. When he looked back at her, caught there in the cold glow of the stoep light, she appeared transparent, as if part of her had already departed.

The noise of the rain and the darkness of the night protects the privacy of Groot Samuel's grief as he buries the baby baboon. He weeps, great chunks of loss.

His arms reach out for the soft mounds of wet earth around the grave and he fills the small pit, armful by armful, until the baboon is buried, along with the farmer's rare show of feeling, and his shame.

PART THREE

CHAPTER THIRTEEN

Anriette le Roux's violet eyes have always been her saving grace. Almost everything else about her is ordinary but, like Ouma said, her eyes are as startling as Elizabeth Taylor's kohl-rimmed orbs in Ouma's favourite film, *Cleopatra*.

Anriette and her family have been part of this valley for generations. There are some who say she inherited her grandmother Biddie's melancholia. Her children know that she bursts into tears if the milk tart comes out of the oven with a dip in the middle. They know that if they share her disappointment even for a moment, she covers them with fierce, sharp kisses until they smile.

Senuweeagtig, as her boss at the forensic science lab says, highstrung, but definitely the good side of unstable. She was born to work forensics. Her attention to detail creates order out of chaos. It doesn't always lead to convictions and when that happens she fumes and wishes she had been born in Sweden where there are fewer killings and each one can get its due.

She's a year away from retirement and she is weary from the slaughter that fills her every day. Anriette and her husband have bought a small cabin in the hills outside Cape Town and she dreams of retiring there with good music and even better wine.

She plans to erase all the terrible things she knows, one day at a time. If she gets there, that is. She knows the data and she can see that in the scheme of things, no one can escape the random nature of the violence besmirching her land forever. One day it will be her turn.

It's not easy being Anriette.

She's one of the few women who has ever been invited to join the Elisabeth Eybers book club. She would have done so, were it not for her prior passion: the study of raptors, which she approaches with the same degree of obsessive attention as she does everything else. It takes her to far-flung parts of the country whenever there has been a new sighting and her job allows the travel. The black sparrowhawk is her favourite.

Jannie is waiting for her in her driveway as she opens her front door with a travel cup of rooibos tea in her hand and a half-eaten carrot in the other. She knows why he's there.

'I can't help you, Jannie,' she says as she unlocks her ancient blue Volkswagen Golf.

Jannie leans back against his red truck. He looks tired.

Anriette throws her handbag onto the seat. The truth is she views the young man as hers and she can feel his frailty. It gives her pause.

'I just want to ask one thing,' he says.

'Ag *nee*, Jannie.'

'Did you see the results of the post-mortem?'

'Why would I have? The docket has been closed by the magistrate already, Jannie. There's no investigation,' she says and she turns away.

'There was something under Ouma's nails,' Jannie says quickly, 'on the right hand.'

Anriette stops. The hair on the back of her neck bristles. Jannie knows she can't resist a mystery, nor tolerate unfinished business.

'Stop!' she hisses. 'I loved her too, Jannie, but I can't even put my toe into that water.'

She loses her carrot as she gets into the car. Jannie picks it up off the driveway and waits while Anriette rolls down her car window to retrieve it from him. As she does so she says, 'I need my pension to get to the mountains, Jannie.'

He nods his head. 'I know.'

'And tell your ma to feed you some stew. You look sick.'

She guns her engine if such a thing were possible in such a car. To her mind, anyone stupid enough to drive a new car in this poverty-stricken place deserves to be hijacked.

With her violet eyes she sees Jannie turn away from her, but not before he has looked at her in *that way*. The way he's had since he was a boy, of seeing and hearing nothing else when following the trail of an unanswered question. Like he's caught the tail of a hissing serpent and must hold on for fear of being bitten teeth-sinking deep if he lets go. That's the look she sees as she heads out of the car park.

The open highway sweeps Groot Samuel and Delilah through the morning mist that follows rain in these parts.

Delilah sits in the passenger seat, hair still wet from her morning bath. She sings along with the melancholy ballad on the radio. It steadies her.

Her mother used to say that even a good voice could drive you mad if you hear it every waking hour. So she banished singing at the table, and in the car.

Groot Samuel doesn't mind if Delilah sings in the car. It makes the world outside the window seem kinder.

When the broad, six-lane highway first went in, Groot Samuel wondered whom they built it for.

Then the shopping malls went up and he saw them as follies. What fool would spend their ever-dwindling rands in their vast, echoing halls?

He was wrong. They thrived. More were built.

And Groot Samuel could see that the people would come. And that, one day, there would be no more room for farmers like him.

He turns up the volume on the radio so that Delilah must sing louder to match it. When she does so, he smiles at her and increases his speed.

She smiles back.

In the whole time she's been on the farm, Groot Samuel hasn't conversed directly with Delilah more than a few times. She's never been offended by it but now she wonders if he welcomes her presence there.

She has watched him sit on the stoep every night, hunched over his glowing cigarette. Alone. She's never known a person more deeply solitary than her uncle. It wakes her *piep en tjank* from its slumber to occupy the tender spot just behind her Adam's apple.

Could it be that a physical place, and one peopled by *her* family, could be the source of this suffering? As if it bubbles out of the earth and comes to rest on whoever finds themselves there.

The idea steals the song out of her mouth.

*

Groot Samuel buys himself coffee in a paper cup from the vendor at the airport. As an afterthought he gets Delilah a fruit juice and they sit on plastic chairs in the arrivals hall to drink and wait.

The press of people flowing past Groot Samuel reminds him that he does not like human beings very much. His happiest Christmas was before he was married, when Ouma was still close to Aletta and was with her for the holidays. Gogo went to see her family in the the Free State and Klein Samuel to a shebeen to drink himself closer to death. For ten blissful days Groot Samuel worked hard and spoke not at all. He has rarely been so at peace.

He hears the hiss of air in the straw as Delilah finishes her orange juice beside him. She crunches the box into a flat oblong and then breaks the silence with, 'Do you think he meant Ouma to die?'

'Who?'

'The one who pushed her?'

Groot Samuel doesn't reply but he pauses long enough to wipe the sweat off his forehead.

'Do you?' Delilah asks again.

He looks pointedly away from her and says gravely, 'I think it is better to think before you speak.'

And he turns back to his coffee. Her question bubbles in his body along with one of his own. It is a question he can now never ask but that doesn't stop him wanting to shout it into his mother's face, so close that he can feel her ensuing shame settle like fog on his cheeks.

Ouma knew that Groot Samuel's central purpose lay in taking care of her, better and more devotedly than she had managed to do for him. How then could she have asked him to help her leave this world? Because they both knew that that is what she was saying, even if indirectly. *I must leave you, child*, she had said, with the expectation that he would make it happen as he always did.

If she had said, *The ants are back, Samuel*, he would've put down the poison and flushed away the small black bodies with the hose when the deed was done. But Ouma's final request went too deeply against his sense of guardianship over her final days and so, then and there, he forbade her to speak of it again.

Groot Samuel kicks out his feet and pushes his full weight against the back of the airport chair to stop himself from cursing at its memory.

Beauty Sephamla, whose job it is to clean up and make tea for the detectives three times a day, collars Mokheti on this raucously busy morning and complains that Jannie, the sad white *moffie*, is taking over her kitchen. She's never seen him this bad. He has yet to drink the first cup before he is at the tea station making the next. It offends her sense of order and thrift.

Mokheti probably wouldn't say it aloud but the news of Jannie's continued unease adds a new burden to his day. He depends on his young Boer detective more than he would like. Just this morning, Antjie Basson, head of finance, pulled him aside to say that not one, but two of his detectives had shown up for work driving new cars.

'A Mercedes CL500! How did he do it, boss?' she had asked, feigning ignorance.

Of course Mokheti sees the slow seep of graft trickling its way into every crevice of his institution. He knows that more is coming, fruit of the poisoned tree of new power.

He knows that the car thief slips the keys of his stolen car into the pocket of the young detective in return for his silence. That the government official, with a trail of graft of his own, stuffs an envelope and slides it across the desk to the investigating officer.

Of all Mokheti's detectives, Jannie is the most immune to temptation. The cynical would say it is because, as the sole heir to his family's modest land, he doesn't need the money. Whatever the reason, Mokheti depends on him being in the trenches, not distracted by a quest of his own.

'You okay, Detective?' he asks Jannie as they pass one another in the passage.

Jannie's head flicks up in surprise. He stops and the two men hover awkwardly in the middle of the strip of green linoleum.

'So?' says Mokheti.

'Gogo says they stole her mother's feet when they performed her post-mortem,' says Jannie, and the moment the words are out of his mouth he sees what a non sequitur this must be for his boss and he mumbles, 'Sorry, I can't get it out of my mind.'

Mokheti looks at him and says, 'Gogo?'

'She says it happens all the time. Ligaments, corneas, bones stolen from our morgues. Especially from the unclaimed bodies. Did you know that?'

'Who is Gogo?' asks Mokheti.

'Just Gogo.'

'She your grandmother, Jannie?'

'No, she's my friend.'

Mokheti waits for a moment. He can't help but have a jaundiced view of close relationships across the races. He would never say it out loud but he believes they can never be truly intimate. That they call one another names connoting familial connection, *mama, sisi, gogo*, makes it even more of a shared fiction. Sometimes he can laugh at it but today it enrages him. He turns to walk away.

Jannie watches him go a few metres and then calls out, 'Colonel!'

Mokheti turns back in time to see a wave of black despair rise up in Jannie's eyes.

'I'm trying to see who would stand to gain from Ouma's death,' says the detective quietly, 'but I can't. It was for nothing . . .' and he blinks '. . . *nê?*'

Mokheti is silent for a moment; not even his breath marks its usual resonant passage in and out. *Nê*. A mere pip of a sound, yet meaning *This is the real truth, not so?*

Mokheti sees the battle his detective is fighting. 'You asking me if there is such a thing as evil in this world, Jannie?'

Jannie looks at him and nods, barely.

Mokheti sucks in an involuntary breath, forced by his empty lungs to do so, and he says, 'What do you think I'm doing here, Detective?' and his gaze is full of matching darkness.

'*Dankie*,' says Jannie softly and he watches as his boss walks away.

CHAPTER FOURTEEN

Delilah weaves amongst the throng in the arrivals hall and plays out in her mind then and there all the truths about Ouma's death that she'd like to tell her mother.

She can already hear her response: *Ag stop that now, Delilah. Stop that piep en tjank.*

When she spots her mother emerging through the glass doors into the arrivals area, she looks like a stranger.

She is older. Not old, not like Ouma was old, but emptied out. When she hugs her, she feels light, small. Her blonde hair sticks to the back of her neck in a way Delilah does not recognize. Her clothes hang loose on her fine bones. Delilah wonders where her flesh has gone.

She was once so dense.

She watches her mother open her arms to Groot Samuel. The childhood stories she told Delilah always included her brother. She never said 'me' or 'him' when she spoke, she always said 'us'. She and Groot Samuel made a wholly uniform *us*.

Now Delilah can see both are unsure as they reach across the intervening years for sight of the shape and glow of their youthful faces. The disappointment of *who they are now* is cluttered with the verbal niceties of the adult world. 'So nice to see you, *boet*.' 'How was the flight?' 'Have you had rain?'

'Thula Baba' pops unbidden into the young girl's mind and she doesn't know what to do with it. Everyone knows that unless you are stark raving mad you can't start singing 'Thula Baba' at a crowded airport but she wishes she could because it would help them find their way.

'Thula Baba'. When Aletta and Groot Samuel were babies, Gogo would tuck one child into the blanket tied to her back, hold the other in her arms and rock them both to sleep as she sang.

> *Thula thul thula, baba*
> *Thula, sana . . .*

In her turn Aletta sang it to Delilah and her brother Martinus. It is an old Zulu lullaby, sung by a mother to her child as she rocks it to sleep. When Aletta felt the song losing its power for her children she took the liberty of adding a bit of story here and there, in English, to make it more engaging.

Ouma sang it to Delilah on her first night on the farm, when the only thing the child could see after she closed her eyes was her parents walking away from her into a field of sugarcane on the banks of the Pongola river.

Delilah picks up her mother's suitcase and waits for her to emerge from her uncle's silent embrace.

There came a time when Delilah and Martinus didn't want to hear lullabies at all so their mother pulled out the cello that stood in the corner of the spare bedroom and played it instead. She played until she was oblivious to all but the music. At times like this Delilah could see the woman her mother might have been. She felt it rather than understood it. She heard it in the music.

Waste.

That was the word that Ouma used most often when she spoke about her daughter and she said it with a bite.

Delilah wondered how someone could waste herself? Did they have to give out their talents to undeserving others? Or did they have to leave bits of themselves in the sun to rot?

Ouma had not raised her children to hanker after material enrichment. In her early childhood Delilah heard her ma describe baking bread as a dignified occupation. Making a good staple food for the poor with fresh ingredients did seem a lofty idea and worthy of Ouma's respect.

But the challenge of fulfilling that mission when the forces of change swept all but their most deprived clientele out of the centre of town proved too much for them. Delilah stopped hearing her ma talk about the higher purpose of her occupation a long time ago.

The day came when her mother stopped playing the cello too. So Delilah picked it up. It was instinctive, as if her ma had thrown the instrument over the floodwaters of the Pongola river and Delilah was the only one standing there to catch it. It just happened.

At first the child tried to teach herself. She did it long and loud enough so her mother sent her to Tannie Trix for lessons after school even though she could ill afford it.

As her mother steps away from Groot Samuel, it strikes Delilah that she does not look like someone who can play the cello any more. Was this what Ouma meant?

'Hello, Ma,' says Delilah.

Her mother turns to look at her and says quietly, '*Skattie.*'

No one else uses that endearment with her. They look at one another, shy.

'You are taller,' her mother says.

Delilah shrugs. 'Where's Martinus?'

Her mother shakes her head and says, 'He's working at Klipwal.'

Delilah looks at her, uncomprehending.

'The gold mine. They wouldn't give him leave because he's doing the training.'

Delilah looks away from her mother and says, 'And Pa?'

'Working also.'

Sour regret at her father's and brother's absence from this important family event holds her there a moment. She has not yet learnt to manage the gap between her longing for things and how they really are.

This time, thank God, her mother senses her disappointment and has the good sense to wrap her arms around her.

The smell of their bodies saves them from the trickery of their minds. There she is, her whole and present mother. Both are liberated by it. As they weep quietly into one another's shoulders her mother says under her breath, 'Oh thank God for you,' and again, 'Thank God.'

Cheetah has always said that pigs are clever. Klein Samuel laughs when she says it but she knows that there isn't much they can't sense. She has a special feeling for the sow in the second pen. She is the oldest and most bountiful. Cheetah sometimes comes to sit with her in her pen, just to be there. She named her Tannie Hendricks after her neighbour on Gracie Street who fed her Cup-a-Soup as a kid when she was hungry.

This morning Tannie Hendricks's snout crinkles back like a concertina and she sucks in the air around the girl. She doesn't seem to like the disquiet she smells on Cheetah's skin. Cheetah doesn't like it either.

She can see the road leading down the hill to Ouma's farm from Tannie Hendricks's pen and that's how come she sees Jannie park his car in the thick bush just above the dam. She watches him get out, careful not to slam the car door and, in the light-footed way that comes from a wiry body and a purposeful mind, he slips into the surrounding bush and is gone.

'There goes trouble, Tannie,' murmurs Cheetah to the pig and she flicks a fly off the sow's big, hairy ear with the tip of her finger.

Jannie emerges from the thick scrub on the side of the dam. As he walks he scans the long grass around him for a sign. A message left in distress? A broken twig or a smear of blood on rock.

He moves swiftly on to the far side of the dam wall, mindful that he is momentarily visible from the house. He kneels down to examine the indistinct indentation in the earth, which might once have been a footprint but is now washed clean of any useful detail.

In the bush beyond him he hears Gundwane lower his head and low, long and parched. The cattle lumber into the clearing around the dam. Jannie knows that Klein Samuel, the most diligent of herders, will not be far behind. He tucks himself into the brush to avoid him.

One breakaway heifer stomps around the muddy edge of the water, oblivious to the barbel burrowing desperately into the mud to escape her hooves. Some of the fish do not move quickly enough and soon their soft, black detritus floats on the surface of the muddy water.

Jannie watches from the bush as the rest of the cattle churn the dust and crush the grass around the edge of the water. He wishes he could drive them off before they obscure the small signs that he hopes might be hidden there. '*Gah! Go. Out!*' But of course he can do nothing but wait.

So confined, the dry dust and cattle smells of his childhood rise up. Stored more in his body than his mind, they fill him with shreds of vestigial shame.

After his father died, Jannie took to riding his bike over to the farm after school every day and so took up the space of Ouma's absent son.

Frans, her firstborn, attended boarding school and only came home for the holidays. Whenever he did so, his friends from the district converged on the farm. Tough barefoot boys, all decent enough alone, Jannie knew, but together they were trouble.

They caught Jannie under the wild fig where he hid to watch Groot Samuel swim in the dam. The boy was helpless to conceal the firecracker of his desire.

They hung him from the tree, feet first.

Fokken moffie.

Shame stopped him from calling out for help. By the time Ouma found him his feet were swollen corpse blue. She cut the rope that bound him, shoved a clipboard into his hand and put him to work. She knew the only way to restore him was to give him the chance to think about someone else.

With great diligence he noted the names, addresses and basic medical histories of the ailing souls waiting outside her surgery door.

Black people – *daardie mense*, those people – unknown to him until now. Jannie's father had refused to employ black labourers. He chose, instead, itinerant whites who drifted by in the hope of easy money. They stayed only briefly before stealing what they could and moving on.

Jannie bent his head and listened dutifully to the lives he had missed. He remembers the first one best for its ordinariness and the grace with which it was told.

Palesa Moshoeshoe, so named because the flowers on the *mokwane* tree were plentiful the year she was born, contracted tuberculosis at the age of five. It was never treated.

She married when she was just eighteen and soon thereafter her husband left to seek work in Pretoria. She bore him a child and then waited for three whole Christmases for him to return to her. She despaired and went to the city to look for him. The woman in whose arms she found him called herself his true wife.

Palesa got a job and tried hard to nurture the toddler playing in the dust beside her but the black spot in her lungs bent her double in the mornings, more so every day. Ouma feared that this new manifestation of the disease was associated with HIV and suggested testing but Palesa refused politely. '*Ehe*, I cough with blood,' she said simply and lowered her eyes as if that were all that was to be said or done.

Jannie wanted to give her the coins in his pocket as well as his bicycle but Ouma stopped him. Later she would say, 'And what will you give the next person when your bicycle is gone? If they are well, each can earn their own money.'

What Jannie heard that day revealed lives of such startling new-ness to him that it wasn't long before he sought out Klein Samuel for his story too. Klein Samuel was sitting, Jannie remembers keenly, just as he is now, on the edge of the dam watching the cattle drink.

'Ja, Baas Jannie,' Klein Samuel had said as Jannie sat beside him. Jannie could tell he was somewhat surprised to see him there; life did not bring them together much.

'Ja, Klein Samuel,' Jannie said in reply.

Neither of them spoke for a moment. Klein Samuel rolled himself a cigarette. Lit it and took a long, slow puff.

'Ouma tells me that you are the only one who can get the vegetable garden to grow on these rocks.'

'She said that?' said the farmhand, and his eyes crinkled with pleasure.

'And that it all died when you went away.'

'I had a big fire in my head that time.'

'In your head?' said Jannie. And so Klein Samuel told Jannie about his brush with the powers that be at Weskoppies Psychiatric Hospital.

He would've preferred Ouma to have ministered to him as she always had, but she said he needed more than she could give and sent him off to Outpatients at Pretoria West. He wondered why the nurse bothered with his height, weight and blood pressure when it was his head that hurt but he didn't say anything because in his experience these learned ladies could be cross over nothing. With each step of the examination Klein Samuel grew progressively less responsive. Even the sound of the nurse's voice caused him to wince in pain whenever she asked him a question.

The nurse looked at him askance, scribbled on a slip of paper, handed it to him and told him to wait on the pavement for the small white bus that would take him where he needed to go. This was how Klein Samuel found himself in the acute care unit at Weskoppies.

'I told them, *wa bona*, I said,' and he holds up his hands to indicate a force field around his head, 'it is like a whole choir is singing inside my head.'

He may have had a choir singing in his head but he wasn't blind to the looks the nurses exchanged; he knew they meant trouble for him.

He made a run for the door. When the security guard tried to stop him, he lashed out. The man needed stitches when he was done with him.

Klein Samuel clapped his hands together. The ringing sound of his laughter softened his account of the brutality of being put in a straitjacket and pumped full of anti-psychotic drugs. It was only a month later, when he had slipped into unconsciousness, that they did the lumbar puncture that revealed acute hepatitis.

He held two fingers within inches of Jannie's young face and said, 'This close, Baas Jannie . . . I was this close to joining my mother in heaven.' Klein Samuel laughed at Jannie's horror and ruffled his closely cropped hair. 'Soft, like new grass,' he murmured and lowered his own head for Jannie to touch his hair.

Jannie hesitated.

Klein Samuel prodded him gently.

So Jannie put the palm of his hand on Klein Samuel's springy head and laughed in surprise at its texture.

Cheetah does not notice the ants as they pour out of the underground nest and over her bare feet. They are always more active after the rain but today she doesn't stop to wonder, as she has before, if many of their kind were lost in the flood. She is too busy watching for the re-emergence of Jannie from the bushes.

Sure enough, as Klein Samuel coaxes the cattle onto the road homeward, the detective steps out of his hiding place and follows the washed-out dips and peaks of indistinct human spoor down the bank of the dam.

They seem to tell him nothing. Then he notices a piece of corrugated-iron that lies halfway up the bank. As Jannie lifts it Cheetah can see that he has found something that matters. She watches the detective take out his phone and dial a number.

Someone answers Jannie's call and Cheetah hears him say, indistinct and jumbled, 'Anriette . . . listen . . . no . . . please . . . footprints . . . make moulds. Yes. Footprints. Good ones.' Then Cheetah hears his shrill voice say, 'Hello,' and again, 'Anriette?'

Then she sees Jannie look at his phone as if it has slapped him.

Cheetah shadows Jannie on her side of the fence as he runs up the hill to his truck then back again. She watches as he kneels beside the footprints and tears open the plastic bag of fine, white powder.

Just then the bell rings at the pig farm and Cheetah must turn reluctantly towards the pens for feeding time.

When Anriette opens the door to Jannie her first instinct is to take him by the scruff of his neck and walk him straight back to his car. His presence there means nothing but trouble. It is only her abiding fondness for him that stops her from acting on it.

She can't help but be moved by the tilt of his head and the grace of his long slender fingers as they hold out his offering. She often wonders how it is that his father's abuse caused no coarsening of his face or spirit.

'You want tea, Jannie?' she asks.

He shakes his head. 'I've had too much today already.'

He holds out the plastic bag, and after a moment's hesitation she takes it and says, 'Is this the footprint nonsense that you are giving me?'

'Ja, Tannie.'

It doesn't go unnoticed by her that Jannie calls her auntie for the first time in years, but it doesn't help his cause.

'Well, I don't do that kind of forensics, Detective.'

'I know.'

'I do biology.'

He nods his head.

'Blood, semen, skin. It's like asking a brain surgeon to remove a gall-bladder.'

'Ja, Tannie,' he says. He waits a moment to see if she'll hand the packet to him but she does not.

'Thank you,' he says, and turns to walk back to his car.

Anriette watches him go and wonders, once again, why it is that his essential aloneness catches so in her throat.

She manages to resist opening the packet for ten minutes after he has gone. She would like to talk herself into throwing the whole lot into the bin, but instead she tears it open and goes into her small home office to dig out her magnifying glass. It takes her but a minute to see that Jannie's moulds are useless.

She gives him the bad news over the phone. 'There's no detail. Even I can see that.'

He asks if she can help him make the moulds again.

'I don't know *how*, Detective,' she says. 'I'm going to make borscht and go to bed.' And then she says, 'It's beetroot soup. Don't you know anything?'

She throws the moulds into the bin beside the door and silently prays that this will be the end of it. The truth is that had there been anything worth investigating in those moulds she would not have been able to refuse him.

CHAPTER FIFTEEN

Not even the shadow cast by Ouma's passing can dampen the rare bubble of excitement that swells in Groot Samuel's chest as he turns onto the dirt road leading to the farm. His sister, the first and most important witness to his early efforts as a craftsman and farmer, is about to see his *braaiplek*. He trusts that its beauty will tell her the story of how he has spent the intervening years because he can't begin to put it into words.

People used to think he and his sister were twins. *Patoot* was the word they made up for Frans because he could be cruel. *Gaarvits* was shorthand for when their father was fall-down drunk. *Blokskap* was for Run! Run! Run! There is trouble coming.

They had their language. They had the veld. And they had each other.

Every second Sunday they had Tannie Truida too, their embittered auntie, who filled their minds with stories of Boer women suffering in the British concentration camps. In the veld later, with clumps of smoking grass and ants as their army, they quelled the bastard English and freed their imprisoned kinfolk.

They came home sunburnt, with battered knees and scraped

elbows. They were always hungry but it was not their mother they went to for nourishment. It was Gogo.

It pleased her to watch them stuff their mouths with her home-made fish cakes, her tinned tuna pie, and her dry rusks. Even after their mother had sent her to cookery school Gogo remained a peasant cook, perfectly tuned to their starving childish palates.

Beyond all of that, the two children shared, silently and unself-consciously, their mother's neglect. Both sat, shadow-like, at the door of the surgery while people came and went. Both were somehow comforted by the presence of the other.

Groot Samuel is mindful of the presence of the hooded cobra in the nearby groundcover as he parks the truck under the shade of the wild gardenia. He has seen the snake there many times but this spot provides the best vista for the *braaiplek* and he wants it to be the first thing his sister sees when she steps out of the car.

He feigns nonchalance as the dogs bark and jump up on Aletta and Delilah as they tumble out of the truck. Out of the corner of his eye he sees Aletta make her way through the yapping canines and stop in front of the stone structure to silently admire it. She runs her hand over the ancient pattern in the rock then turns to glance at him. She can see the art in it. Groot Samuel grins, just a sliver of light in his face, and then he turns away to lift her suitcase out of the back of the truck.

Ilse hovers at the front door of the house with a fresh-picked bunch of veld flowers in her hand, a gift for the new arrival. Shyness is in her nature and it is complicated today by the difficult-to-manage fact that she and Aletta are sisters in marriage yet complete strangers. It keeps her hidden just a moment too long. When she pulls open the door she sees the trio already making their way across the lawn to Ouma's house.

Ilse can see Gogo waiting on the stoep to meet them with her prior claim to Aletta's attention, so she slips back into the house and pulls the door closed behind her.

Gogo does not call out a greeting as they approach, but the gravity in her face says more than words can about her feeling for the woman who walks across the grass towards her.

She can see the life that has settled on Aletta's face and made her lined and pink where she was once pale as sugar.

She takes her into her arms. Aletta allows herself to be absorbed. They rock in a barely discernible motion. A low keening comes out of the younger woman's mouth. And an answering murmur from Gogo follows. Delilah and Groot Samuel are forgotten in the bright sun of their reunion.

Groot Samuel turns and walks away. Delilah follows wordlessly. They look like a parent duck and duckling as they make their way to the orchard.

Delilah sits on the pile of earth and watches Groot Samuel work. He pays her no heed, lost as he is in the blessed oblivion of the spade entering the red earth and then leaving it, loaded heavy.

'My brother is a good digger,' says the girl after a time.

He doesn't answer. Nor does he pay any attention to the reddening sun that signals the coming of evening.

'He wanted to be a doctor, or a philosopher,' Delilah says. She hopes he doesn't ask her more because to this day she's not sure what a philosopher does, apart from *think* about things, which was what

Martinus was born to do. She cocks her head and asks, 'Did you ever meet him?'

He shakes his head.

'Not even see a photo?'

Groot Samuel mumbles, 'Maybe once.'

'Did you think he was good-looking?'

Groot Samuel stops digging and looks at his niece. 'I don't remember.'

Delilah turns away.

Suddenly Groot Samuel is concerned that he has hurt her feelings. He is like this, one minute he is a thousand miles away, the next he is in so deep he can hear the other person's heartbeat.

He says, 'Do *you* think he's good-looking?'

Delilah turns to face him and she says with feeling, 'There's no one even close in the whole of Pongola. But he's clever too and that's more important for a boy. My dad says so.'

'Well, it must be true then.'

Delilah looks at him. 'I wish I was pretty.'

Groot Samuel coughs and the stew of phlegm in his chest heaves. He digs again. 'Who says you aren't?'

'Aren't what?'

'Pretty.'

She laughs and shakes her head. 'The mirror says it, Oom.'

He sees Delilah stuff her toes into the mound of red earth growing ever higher beside his hole.

She says, 'Ma says Tinus is working on the mines.'

'I didn't know that,' he says quietly.

Delilah shakes her head. 'He was going to be a philosopher.'

It strikes Groot Samuel that his niece might want to dig a little.

That she may be in need of the comfort of work. He hands her the spade and they swap places wordlessly as if by prior agreement.

The small muscles in Delilah's arm bunch and harden as she works. Then, without any warning, she rests her head on the handle of the spade and weeps. The thought forms itself then that her parents sent her away not to punish her but to save her from Martinus's fate. In families like hers, the duty falls to the firstborn to help provide for those who follow.

Delilah pays no particular heed to the tears that run silently down the handle and stem of the implement. They are like the slime trails that snails leave in their wake. Integral to how they are.

Groot Samuel is shaken by how much he wants to put his hand on his niece's head. He moves closer but Delilah looks up before he finds the courage.

She wipes her arm over her face and leaves a thick smudge of red mud in its wake. 'He didn't even finish high school.'

Groot Samuel would like to gather the child's skinny body into his arms.

'I was hoping he would come so I could see him again,' she says.

He would like to kiss the top of her head and then let her go.

'But you don't always get what you want,' she looks up at him and whispers, 'hey?'

All he can do is help her out of the ditch, take the spade, and walk away from her, stiff backed and silent.

Delilah watches him go. She doesn't wonder at his retreat; she simply accepts that he's had enough of her sad story.

She walks silently through the descending dusk to the window of Ouma's dark dining room and peeks in. She sees her mother and Gogo beside Ouma's body. The silence is so dense with grief that Delilah would have to stand in front of her mother burning in flames for her to pay her any heed.

Delilah sits on the front steps to wait.

When Aletta emerges she is so emptied out that she creeps straight into bed.

Delilah takes her mother's hand as she lies under the covers.

'Sorry, *skattie*,' says her ma.

Delilah nods her head. 'It's okay.'

'I will be fine tomorrow.'

'Good,' says Delilah.

'Then we can catch up.'

'Yes.'

Delilah tells herself that she will tell her ma about Ouma in the morning. Truth is, the urgency of that mission is fading in the face of her more piquant desire to be held by her mother without fuss or consequence – to have nothing of import to say.

She waits for her to fall asleep and then she opens the cupboard at the far end of the room.

The cello is propped up behind the long dressing gown. A spider scurries thick-black-legged across the floor when Delilah lifts the instrument out of the dark.

She plucks a string and lays her ear against the wood to listen, then gathers it up into her arms as if it were a living thing and leaves the room.

Night approaches. It's a headlong fall from bright to dark. The birds shriek and scurry to get to bed before the night hunters emerge.

Gogo returns to the dining room to sit beside Ouma's body. The old woman longs to go to sleep in her own bed. She wants to climb up onto its height and feel the reassuring weight of the thick blankets on her body.

But for the second night running she spreads a blanket on the hard wooden boer-bench and pulls a quilt over her. All the years of living skin to skin with this family does not help her understand why one of Ouma's own progeny is not here keeping her safe in death.

If Ouma were alive, Gogo would complain loudly, as they took their goodnight cup of rooibos together, about the children's lack of decency. *Straight talk breaks no friendship* is what Gogo's own mother used to say. Ouma would listen with her head bowed until Gogo had talked out her ire and then she would say, 'Rotten children, all of them.'

Gogo would wait a moment and then say, 'Not rotten, Ouma. Just not thinking right.' And her compassion for Groot Samuel and Aletta would fill the place in her heart her own son occupied when he was still breathing.

The first time Gogo saw the garden of the grand house in Pretoria she said '*Modimo*' under her breath. She said it because she could see the hand of God in its verdant beauty. She searched under the flowering shrubs for the spinach plants or *mielies* she was certain would be there, but she found no food amongst the beauty.

She called Ouma *miesies* then, as was the way of things. Every Thursday she polished the dense black wood of the leaden bench on which she now lies. When she reneged, it cracked and twisted as if to admonish her.

Gogo often rested on the bench to be close to the sleeping children as she waited for Ouma and her husband to return from an evening out with their friends. It didn't offend Gogo's body to sleep on it then. She was a farm girl with few expectations.

It was from the bench that Gogo witnessed the end of Ouma's marriage. She can still remember how her stomach lurched at the sound of the front door opening. Seven recent robberies in the neighbourhood had her expecting the worst but it was Ouma who came into the house. Alone.

Gogo waited for *meneer* to follow but he didn't come. *Meneer*. Gogo never had any other name for Ouma's husband. It didn't sound polite when she said it in English but in Afrikaans *meneer* was a form of respect.

Ouma went to bed.

Gogo heard *Meneer* calling from the garden some time later. She got up to open the front door and she saw him lying on the steps leading up to the house. He tried to sit up and failed. He turned to look at Gogo.

She could see he was frightened so she leant down to help him to his feet but she heard Ouma shout from her bedroom, 'Leave him.' And again, 'Leave him there.'

Gogo stood looking down at the drunken man.

'*Susanne! Kom!*' Meneer had shouted to his wife.

Silence greeted his show of bravado. He opened his mouth to shout again and Gogo found herself putting her fingers to her lips to silence him, 'Sshsh.'

He gestured for her to come close and so the young black woman kneeled beside the prone man.

He whispered, '*Ek is nie genoeg nie.*' Tears of self-pity dribbled into his mouth. 'I am not enough for her.'

'*Kom nou, meneer,*' Gogo said, and helped him to his feet. He slipped, boneless, back down onto the floor. Gogo crouched down and lifted his thin form into her strong farm-girl arms.

She carried him to the bench in the entrance hall like she would a child.

She laid him down on it and covered him with the blanket. Then she shuffled through the kitchen to her small room at the back of the house and closed the door.

Gogo turns over on the hard wooden bench and sighs. The density and scale of her body is transformed from those days.

When Ouma once commented on her expanding girth Gogo snapped, 'It is everybody's suffering sitting here on my hips.'

That silenced the old woman.

Ouma wasn't the only one who saw hardship.

A long melancholy note snakes its way through the hot night. Gogo finds it soothing when Delilah plays; it reminds her of Aletta's childhood when the girl would sit under the acacia tree and practise her scales for hours. Gogo could sing easily, and from her earliest years, but she is mystified by the skill it takes to make music in this way.

She hears Delilah pull her bow across the strings again, the sound building in soulful confidence.

Aletta's voice calls out, slurred with recent sleep, 'Not now, Delilah!'

Gogo wonders if she should intervene, the child so clearly needs the comfort offered by the music, yet her mother's voice is so weary. Their conflicting needs freeze Gogo in indecision.

'Shshsht now,' says Aletta again with a long, sibilant insistence. Then there is silence.

PART FOUR

CHAPTER SIXTEEN

The people come rolling down the driveway in their cars and down the mountain paths on their feet. They ride their bicycles. They come by battered communal taxi.

The large green bus that this morning has gathered mourners from Soshanguve township, the plot-lands surrounding it and the perversely named semi-suburb of Wonderpark, turns into the dirt driveway; it's ancient suspension whines at the weight of the people within. The driver stops at the top of the steep hill for fear of plummeting down the gravel track that leads into the valley. It is not only Klein Samuel and his bicycle that know the hazards of this slope.

The passengers pour out of the bus and walk down the road, older mourners in black, while the younger wear more colourful attire.

Local people to the north come along paths that snake over the back of the mountain.

Gogo stands beside the grave, dug now in the hillside overlooking the dam and the two houses beyond it. She watches the mourners walk slowly towards her from every direction. She nods at Baas Pieter, enclosed by a skin of private, illicit pain and dressed in conservative black, hat in his hand.

There are many more black people here than white. Most have been Ouma's patients for years and have come to pay their respects to the old lady who saw them through many of life's hardships.

As Delilah and her mother take their place beside Gogo, Aletta says, 'Where is he?'

Gogo shakes her head.

Groot Samuel waits on the crest of the hill, looking out over the arriving crowd. He is looking for someone. His sense of familial duty insists that he should be here, doing that.

Gogo and Aletta know he will take it badly if their brother Frans doesn't show. He glances back at them. Aletta shakes her head in sympathy. It has always been so between them.

He was the dutiful one who stayed while she and Frans fled, with only fitful visits back home over the following decades. She knows the weight he has carried and what it has cost him.

Now she sees the sag of his shoulders as he gives up on his brother and turns back into the crowd.

It is Frans's absence that moves Groot Samuel to pluck Jannie from the crowd and ask him to be a pallbearer. Jannie almost weeps with gratitude. He tells himself it doesn't mean he is forgiven for all his missteps, yet surely it is an acknowledgement of his place in Ouma's life? He admonishes himself silently for needing it.

The coffin is heavy in spite of Ouma's small frame. It takes Groot Samuel, Klein Samuel, Jannie, and two workers from the pig farm to get it out of the house.

A lone voice rings out to accompany the passage of the coffin up the hill. It's a sound of such sharp purity that all eyes seek out its source. None who see that it is Klein Samuel can quite believe it.

The most startled of all is Cheetah, for whom the very African-ness of this lament comes as something of a surprise. Her Cape origins are, by their nature, more urban and mixed up than the undiluted sounds she hears coming from her paramour. And as an outsider to most of life's proprieties she is sensitive to the dark, unspoken xenophobia she feels towards him from the other mourners.

Still, the ravaged farmhand lifts his head and fills the valley with his Ndebele lament. It marks him as a foreigner indeed; he too is aware that not everyone is comfortable with its prominence in this leave taking.

It is only when his song has drawn to its singular end and been replaced by a Sotho hymn led by the priest, that the other mourners join in its fervent chorus.

This is music that belongs to them all, to the grass, the red sand and the local ancestral shades that look on from times past.

The pallbearers lay the coffin in the grave by lowering it down on ropes. It is hot and the sweat pours off their faces as they strain to ease the heavy wooden box down, hand over hand.

The priest leads them in prayer. He delivers the homily in a mixture of English and Sotho. He himself was a patient of Ouma's and he knows her to have been an unbeliever in spite of the scattering of Dutch Reformed *dominees* that populated both sides of her heritage. He sees his function here to be a source of comfort to the believers amongst those left behind.

It is Delilah who alerts her mother to the car coming down the driveway.

Aletta says under her breath, 'Ja, well then. He has come.'

The man who emerges from the battered Mercedes is tall and fair, his long frame dressed with a nonchalance that verges on the disrespectful.

Gogo names him without enthusiasm. 'Frans.'

Delilah watches Groot Samuel walk across to greet his brother. Even her childish eyes can see that her work-loving, hole-digging uncle is *ordinary* in comparison. Yet he holds his ground as he takes in his more charismatic brother with his sharp blue eyes and says quietly, 'Hello, Frans.'

Frans turns away from his gaze.

Delilah watches Frans lift her mother off her feet with his embrace. She turns to Gogo and whispers, 'Is he pretending, Gogo?'

The old woman takes a deep breath, '*Haai wena* . . . you see too much, Delilah.'

Gogo always said the two boys were like Cain and Abel. Like opposite ends of a long, thin road. If Samuel wanted to play Boer War games, Frans wanted to play Dracula. If he allowed himself to be talked into the Boer War, it was on the grounds that he had to be the general first. When it was Samuel's turn, Frans would find a way to change the game.

Frans's rivalry with his younger brother was tolerable most of the time but as they grew older it was stoked by jealousy into something darker. Aletta and Samuel's easy intimacy drove Frans into a corner.

The swing that the brother and sister built together in the old eucalyptus tree was a precarious affair. Small slats of wood nailed to the trunk made steps that led to a larger plank. It was on this wobbly perch that they stood to slip the stick and rope swing between their legs and jump off into nothingness.

There was a precipitous fall before the rope grew taut and sent the children sailing smoothly through the air.

Samuel and Aletta swung themselves sick before they even thought of offering Frans a turn. It wasn't a conscious cruelty. There was just no room for him in their universe.

Frans would creep out to swing in the dark so they wouldn't see how much he longed for it. But swinging alone felt like slipping on ice, shocking and sour with disappointment.

One night, almost as an afterthought, Frans loosened the knot on the swing. Then he went to bed.

Samuel fell slowly at first. As if he didn't entirely believe it was happening and could therefore make it stop. He gained momentum as he plummeted earthward until it felt to him as if he had gathered the force of a meteor.

Gogo had never heard a noise, before or since, more fearful than the snapping of Samuel's bones as he met the hard red earth.

Delilah sees that Frans keeps his eyes down as he walks towards the grave. She can tell he does that in order not to have to see where he is, that his swagger barely disguises his unease.

She looks away quickly so as not to see any more. Never again does she want to know what others do not. But, of course, it is not long before she seeks him out again. She is chronically curious about the missing members of her family. She measures each against the empty space the bare idea of them once occupied in her.

Now Frans is closer and she can observe the flare of his nostrils as he takes in the unfamiliar smell of the bodies around him and their easy grief.

He scans the crowd. His face seems to be saying it can't possibly be *his* mother they have come to take their leave of, all these black people. Yet they claim her with a calm and confident ease.

Delilah wonders what he did to bring the tinge of yellow to the skin around his mouth and the vivid lines around his eyes. She suspects it was too much of something, like her friend in primary school, Belinda van Rooyen, whose mother drank herself stupid. Belinda's mother had that same look.

She can tell Frans does not expect to mourn his mother long but when he sees the small coffin lying in its deep earth home, something darker than simple leave-taking rushes at him from the shadows. It is a shocking surprise to him that his grief has such a kick to it.

For a moment, Delilah sees his face collapse into the folds and crevasses of real feeling, but then he rights himself and calm returns to his features.

Groot Samuel is the first to fill his hand with earth and throw it into the grave. It hits the wooden casket louder than hail on a tin roof. Aletta is next, then Frans, Delilah, Gogo and Jannie.

Handful by handful, the mourners fill the grave with earth. The air becomes dense with red dust cast high on the wind by many, many hands.

Jannie watches the red cloud grow. The sun behind doubles the density of the haze and endows this leave-taking with a powerful otherworldliness.

He sees Pieter slip away up the driveway without seeking leave and wonders at his hunched shoulders, bent with grief. He watches Groot Samuel herd the family together into a sort of receiving line.

He sees Cheetah and Klein Samuel shuffle awkwardly towards it, unsure of this practice.

Ilse offers her hand to Cheetah when her turn comes. Jannie sees horror settle on Ilse's face as Cheetah refuses it. Instead, the farm girl puts her fingers to either side of her head to make ears, like a . . . like a what? And she pants. Like a dog! She pants like a dog.

Suffering!

Cheetah is being Ouma's canine shadow. Her friend. Her constant.

Jannie almost stumbles in this moment of revelation.

Where is Suffering?

The question sends the blood rushing to the vein in his temple.

Gone. The dog is gone.

And so the last meagre strip of fact lays itself down on all the others that have come before and is, finally, denser than the air around it. He moves from suspicion to certainty with the help of Cheetah's gesture.

Jannie searches out Delilah to share this revelation but sees she is engulfed by mourners who reach for her, as Ouma's youngest, to commiserate and weep. He can see the rising cherry-red patches on her cheekbones that reveal her growing discomfort. Why is it that in the giving of their insistent comfort, the mourners take more than they leave?

Jannie is pulled away from Delilah's plight by the demands of his discovery and he must follow where it leads. He knows that had Suffering been there on that fateful morning, as he always was, he would have barked until someone came to Ouma's rescue. He would have woken them from their slumber, he would have bared his teeth and howled until they answered his call.

Jannie knows then that somebody made sure he was not. He knows it in his body. Absolutely.

Ouma did not slip.

CHAPTER SEVENTEEN

Delilah stumbles into the house and pulls the front door closed behind her. Relief at being alone rings in her ears. She can feel how close she came to snarling at the well-meaning funeral guests who burdened her with their grief. Without thinking she reaches for the cello propped up against the chair. She wipes it clean with the back of her hand.

She sits on the wooden chair.

And begins to play.

Single notes at first, with gaps in between, then her fingers find the first note of 'Thula Baba'. She plays crudely, discovering the sounds as she goes. She gets it wrong as often as right so the music has an unstable, mercurial, quality to it.

Outside, amongst the milling crowd, Groot Samuel's head snaps up to listen. Likewise Aletta's. And Frans's head too.

If someone asked Delilah whether she wanted to raise her grand-mother up on the very day of her burial, she would have looked at them as if they were mad but it is what she does. In spite of its primitive execution, she plays as if someone is drowning and her music can pull them from the water.

She plays for the life of the woman whose absence makes her world a much more hazardous place.

It does not escape Delilah how different the quality of this music is to the practised Bach she played for Ouma on her final visit to their home in Pongola two years earlier.

Her grandmother had arrived without warning and so Delilah's mother was, as always, baking bread.

Ouma saw her, covered, corpse-like, in a fine dusting of flour, and she made her visible to Delilah too. The girl saw that every day from dawn to black night her mother baked cheap bread to stock the shelves of their small bakery. Whenever she turned from her work, there stood Delilah and her brother Martinus, wanting what was left. No room for music in that life. Delilah made sure of that, just by being. Not only for her mother but now for Martinus and his musings too.

Before that January visit, they hadn't seen their Ouma in years. Delilah's father, Tertius, regarded the relationship between his wife and her mother as one of life's mysteries. How two people with so much feeling for one another could live so long on the fruit of their misunderstandings seemed to him cruel. Delilah knew that when he had suggested that they talk and make up, her mother had turned on him and hissed, 'Shaddup. You don't know anything!'

But as far as Delilah was concerned, Ouma brought only sunshine into their shadowed house. Even their neighbours the Nanjis seemed to love her. She gave them prickly pears from the farm and Gogo's apricot jam and the Nanjis invited her over to sit on their gold sofa.

In their view, Ouma was a better class of person than her progeny and they wondered what had happened to make it so.

Mrs Nanji pinned Ouma down for the better part of an afternoon with an inventory of her aches and pains. Any other time Ouma would have jumped to her feet and said, 'Ag nee, go for a walk, Mrs Nanji, the sun is shining outside.' But Ouma made herself listen because she knew Martinus loved Aarti, the Nanji girl. Ouma and her grandson had a lot to say to one another about what Ouma called *love, life and other misadventures*. It was clear that she considered Tinus and his ambition something the ancestors would be proud of.

On the evening of the second day, as they all sat on the stoep after supper, Delilah laid her head on her grandmother's shoulder and said, 'Tell me a story, Ouma.'

Ouma thought for a moment, then asked, 'Have you ever heard about the word thief, child?'

Delilah shook her head. Ouma continued, 'He visits me all the time. He hides my watch too, so I don't know what time it is.'

'Then he's the time thief as well,' said Delilah.

Ouma kissed her head spontaneously, as if she belonged to her.

'Go on, Ouma,' said Delilah, emboldened.

'Ag shut up, *sissie*, give her a chance,' snapped her brother, resentful of their closeness.

'*Moenie so praat nie*, Tinus,' admonished his father.

'Shaddup yourself,' murmured Delilah to her brother.

'Quiet, both of you,' hissed her mother.

Delilah remembers how softly Ouma's voice drew them out of their squabble and into Cheetah's story.

'Cheetah?' the child had asked.

'So named by her father because she looked just like a wild cat. With eyes like bullets and of course those tear trails down her cheeks,' Ouma murmured to Delilah confidentially. 'She has those because she has lived a hard life.'

'She has tear trails?' whispered Delilah and she imagined that if she herself had marks from every time she cried there would be no clear skin left on her face.

Ouma nodded. 'Just here,' and she pointed to her cheeks.

'When she first came to my surgery, Cheetah was very sick. In those days we were still learning how to treat the disease she had and I had to fight and beg and sometimes even steal to get my hands on the drugs she needed. She had to take twenty-two pills every day for six months.'

'I could never do that,' said Delilah, who could barely swallow an aspirin even when her head was splitting from her *piep en tjank*.

Ouma's gaze was steady. 'She knew that if she didn't she would die.'

Delilah was silenced, and she moved closer still to her grandmother. Aletta glanced at her husband and both adults shifted in their chairs, wary.

'Go on, Ouma, go on,' said Delilah, and this time nobody admonished her.

'As Cheetah's doctor, it was my job to make sure there were always enough pills for her treatment,' Ouma paused and closed her eyes, 'but one day the *muti* thief . . .'

Delilah claps her hands. 'There is a *muti* thief also?'

'Ag shaddup, Delilah!' barked Martinus, so caught up in the story he could not abide any distraction.

'There *is*,' said Ouma, 'and when Cheetah came for her *muti* I opened the drawer and it was empty. No trays of antibiotics, no bottles, all gone. I still remember how Cheetah looked at me and asked, "What has happened here, Ouma?"'

'The *muti* thief!' screeched Delilah.

'Of course,' said Ouma, 'but, when I opened my mouth to tell her that, I knew the word thief had been there too.'

'Oh no,' whispered Delilah.

'D'you know what Cheetah did?' Ouma looked at Delilah and she brought her head close. 'She swore. Like a sailor. And she threw a glass against the wall.'

Delilah looked up. 'I would've just cried.'

Ouma sighed. 'She did that too.'

The old woman continued, tired, 'And so did I because I knew that her sickness would blossom in the place left by the *muti* thief until I could replace her medicine, and then she would have to fight double hard to get better all over again.'

'Poor Cheetah.'

'Ja, poor Cheetah,' said Ouma quietly.

Aletta looked at her mother and she whispered, 'And poor Ouma.'

Her mother looked up at her and her eyes said, *Please, oh please understand what this means to me.*

Aletta looked away from her mother's gaze and reached for a rusk on the tea tray; she didn't bite it though, just held it in her hands.

'Play for me, Aletta,' said Ouma, gently.

Aletta shook her head. 'I don't play. Any more.'

'Don't play?'

Aletta shook her head again. 'Not for years.'

Ouma looked at her and Delilah could see her grandmother's eyes well with sorrow.

So Delilah slipped off the sofa and returned with the cello in her hand. She couldn't tell you why she chose the Cantatas, they just were there when she pulled her bow across the strings, and they broke the pall of silence that had descended over them. The music freed Martinus to slip away for his assignation with Aarti and released her father from witnessing, again, the jagged to and fro between his wife and her mother.

Ouma listened to Delilah play so acutely and with such silent stillness that Delilah feared she had fallen asleep.

'Ouma?' she asked softly when she had finished.

Ouma lifted her head and Delilah could see the feeling on her face. 'Thank you, my child,' she said.

If Ouma had said goodnight and gone to bed, then and there, maybe the healing would have continued. Maybe the family would have gone up to the farm for the Easter weekend to see Ouma and Gogo and Groot Samuel.

But Ouma was running out of time.

She looked at her only daughter and she said quietly, 'Help me, Aletta.'

And the way she said it made Delilah's *piep en tjank* clamour.

Ouma took her mother's hands and said, 'This is a very hard thing to ask but I do so to spare us both.'

Aletta pulled her hands away and hissed, 'What do you want, Ma?'

Ouma glanced at Delilah and said, 'Maybe you should go to bed, child?'

'No!' said Aletta. 'I have no secrets from her.'

Ouma looked uncertain but then leant forward and whispered in Aletta's ear.

Whatever she said caused her mother to pull away as if she'd struck her.

Ouma called out to her daughter as she retreated, 'Please. If not for me, do it for your brother. He is the least able to cope with what is coming.'

If Cheetah had been watching she would have recognised the force of the *klapwoorde* on Aletta's face, but all Delilah knew was that Ouma's mysterious words were like a meteor crashing through their fine-as-cobweb reconciliation.

Her mother was silent for a long time and then she got up and said to Ouma, 'Please leave in the morning.'

Delilah cried into the bones of her Ouma's chest when she said her goodbyes.

And Ouma?

She packed her small suitcase into the back of Groot Samuel's ancient truck. When she got to the main road she wondered whether home was to the right or to the left.

Delilah drops her head down lower to play. Her forehead almost touches the strings but it brings no musicality to the endeavour.

Koh, koh. A knock on the front door threatens to derail her from this stumbling memory. Delilah curls her head closer to the cello and swings her bow across the chords with added intensity. Now, finally, it is coherent music and it flows across the top of Jannie's head and down his back as he waits at the door.

He remembers, too, Delilah's sunburnt face, streaming with tears as she shouted, '*Sy het nie gegly nie!*' She didn't slip.

Inside the house, Delilah pulls her bow across the strings one last time. Her arms fall to her sides and all is silent.

CHAPTER EIGHTEEN

The workers from the pig farm have gathered to eat at the far end of the lawn.

Cheetah and Klein Samuel sit slightly apart, an alliance of oddballs.

It does not escape either one, as Jannie approaches them across the lawn, that Jannie is an oddball too.

The detective crouches down beside them. He turns to face Cheetah and puts his hands on either side of his head just as he saw her doing to Ilse.

She looks away.

Jannie asks, 'What's this, Cheetah?'

She mumbles, 'A *moffie* with horns on his head.'

Klein Samuel laughs.

Jannie nods. 'A stupid *moffie*. I didn't even notice Suffering was gone.'

Cheetah shrugs.

Jannie looks at her. 'What happened to him?'

Cheetah shrugs again. 'Maybe a jackal?'

'I don't think so.'

She says nothing.

'We need to find out,' Jannie says.

'No policeman I know ever did any good,' she replies, straight as a bullet.

Jannie looks down at his hands and asks, 'Why Ilse?'

Klein Samuel is listening now, alert in an entirely different way.

'I need to know why you chose Ilse?' says Jannie quietly.

Cheetah looks up at him, there is a moment when she almost speaks, but then she decides not to and looks away.

Jannie leans in close to Cheetah's face and hisses, 'Why her?'

It is Klein Samuel who steps in to answer Jannie's question. 'You go ask Miesies Ilse why Suffering he not bark the day Ouma died.'

The farmhand's gaze is steady. Cheetah leans fractionally closer to him as if to say *I defer to you*.

'You go ask her,' Klein Samuel says again. His dark eyes say more than his words. They brim with regret, as if he wishes he didn't have to speak badly of Groot Samuel's wife. *You go ask her*.

Delilah leans the cello against the wall in the corner of the room and walks to the front door. She doesn't open it. She would rather stay here in the solitary half-light of the living room than brave the company of people. She can hear them call to one another and laugh.

She moves over to the window and sees Gogo and her mother at the food table. Groot Samuel is at the *braai*, his face red from the heat of the coals. She looks around for Frans but does not find him.

Delilah half closes her eyes and the funeral guests become a pattern, she imagines, of sand wafted this way and that by one another's movements. It makes for a constant, swirling reconfiguration, like the dense flocks of green pigeons swooping out of the sky to feed off the wild fig at the bottom of her street.

A disturbance at the centre of the pattern causes Delilah to snap her eyes fully open. Jannie, head down, runs with intent across the lawn and up the stairs to Groot Samuel's front door.

Delilah watches him disappear into the house then drags a chair under the window and sits down to wait for him to re-emerge.

It is dark inside the farmhouse, the hum of the mourners' voices outside dulled by its thick walls.

Jannie calls out, 'Hello?'

He knocks on the door. He has not been in this house for many years and it feels like a foreign land. There is no reply.

He steps into the shadows and a chill accompanies him. He sees the jacket that Ilse wore at the graveside slung over the back of a chair.

It is the living room of a nature lover, scattered with dry grass arrangements, stones, and shells. He can hear the dogs barking at the gate. The fact of Suffering's absence hits him again.

He hears the faintest rustle of sheets. Someone is there. He moves towards the sound. At the bedroom door he stops and glances in.

Ilse is on the bed. Open eyed, dead still. She looks at him and blinks. Makes not even the slightest attempt to respond to his presence in her bedroom.

'Ilse?'

She turns her head towards him, fractionally, and whispers, 'Listen to them.'

'Who?'

'All the people.'

And he listens.

She closes her eyes.

'Where is Suffering, Ilse?' he asks.

She sucks in a breath of air and whispers, 'Suffering?'

'Ouma's Suffering.'

Silence falls so he can hear the breath in the back of his throat.

'Yap. Yap. He yaps all the time, that dog. Even in the morning before there is any light in the sky he yaps.'

Jannie's heartbeat quickens. 'Where is he now?'

Ilse says nothing.

He tries again. 'Do you know where he is?'

'He never ran with the big dogs; he just sat in the old lady's shadow.'

'He was her friend.'

'Ja well . . .' and Ilse turns away from him.

'Ja well what?'

'We all lose things we love.'

'Did we lose Suffering?'

She says nothing.

Jannie sighs. He sits in the chair beside the bed and puts his head in his hands. From here he can see Ilse's bare feet on the bed, sinewy and tough, from a life lived barefoot. It would have been better for her if she had occupied a world less complicated than this place, somewhere where skin and sand communed to grow things and that was that.

It wasn't long after Ilse moved into Groot Samuel's house, with her long black hair and her hope for a happy life, that she and Ouma had their first fight.

As was their habit, Gogo, Ouma and Jannie were drinking tea together on a Sunday morning when a gunshot echoed against the orange rock of the hillside behind the house.

They rose as one and ran.

Ilse was standing in the dusty courtyard outside the surgery with a small handgun in her hand.

A young black man stood at the other end, terrified. He had a wounded arm, wrapped in cloth to stop the bleeding. A pack of dogs, their teeth bared, bayed around his feet.

Ouma shouted above all the noise, '*Bly stil, julle!*' and the dogs immediately sat, submissive, in the dust. Then Ouma turned on Ilse and barked, 'What is that?' She pointed at the gun in Ilse's hand.

To this day, Jannie wonders why neither he nor Gogo found it in them to soften the edge of Ouma's judgement that morning?

Ilse's voice had trembled as she said, 'I thought . . . he didn't stop when I shouted.'

'And why would you shout?' Ouma asked.

Ilse turned to Jannie and Gogo as if to say *You know why – just look at where we live.*

And it was true; fear was their common bedfellow. Jannie worried that he would be the victim of reprisals from the criminals he had put behind bars. Gogo feared that her age would make her an easy target for flick-knife wielding pickpockets every time she took a taxi to the shops.

A day did not pass without news of a local brutality to confirm that view. The collective trauma ran deep enough to bring Ilse to this moment, gun in hand. Yet neither Jannie nor Gogo said a word in her defence. So Ilse looked at Ouma and whispered, '*Sorry.*'

In a way, Ouma had been lucky, Jannie thought as he waited

beside Ilse's bed. The cataclysmic loss of her prior life in Pretoria had goaded her into making community with the people in this valley. Even though she was not a believer, he knew Ouma regularly thanked God for the riches that rupture had brought her.

'This is Tobias Mhlangu,' she said to Ilse then, 'I have known him since he was a baby. He works at the tree fern nursery. It looks to me like they were putting up some new fences and he cut his arm.'

She looked at her patient for confirmation and he nodded, '*Yebo*, Ouma. The razor wire.'

The young man was trembling with fear and desperate for help to stem the blood pouring out of his arm.

And Ouma saw to it that the wound was cleaned and stitched and bandaged. As she worked, Jannie, Gogo and Ilse waited awkwardly in the dust outside the surgery. Something unfinished about the earlier conversation held them there.

When Ouma emerged with Tobias, Ilse stepped forward to offer her apology but the old woman stood in her way and would not move. Jannie could see that Ouma now considered Ilse a threat to the delicate co-existence she, Gogo and Groot Samuel had built in their thirty-year relationship with this patch of earth and the souls who peopled it. She would not allow the new arrival to undo what had taken so long to build.

Jannie saw that he and Gogo were part of the fabric of her certainty and so were mute.

From then on, living on the farm for Ilse was like sliding into the thin, airless bolthole between heaven and hell.

Jannie did not envy her the annihilating force of Ouma's disapproval.

*

'Tell me what you did with Suffering?' Jannie asks Ilse as she lies on the bed.

She does not answer him.

He says very quietly, 'I will shame you in front of all those people sitting on the grass outside, Ilse.'

Her body goes still. He can tell she is listening. He feels his outrage at her cruelty rising. It makes him sweat to hold it in check and gives him the *krag* to say: 'And take you to the police station in handcuffs, if I have to.'

He watches Ilse slowly uncurl herself from her foetal position until she is sitting upright against the pillows. She covers her eyes with her hands.

'I couldn't stand the barking.'

'Did you kill him?'

'I took him to the shelter.'

'The one at Hartebeespoort?'

She nods.

'So they could kill him?'

She closes her eyes.

'Did you tell Ouma?'

There is a moment of silence then a cold sucking in of breath and Ilse says, 'She would've known when she woke up.'

In a moment of clarity Jannie sees Ouma walking along the edge of the dam calling for her dog. He hears her voice, 'Suffering? Here, my boy. *Kom, my liefie.*' He can see her concern when the dog does not answer. 'Suffering! Come, *bokkie*, come.'

Jannie groans under his breath.

Ilse looks at him for the first time. 'She made me feel bad.'

'So you took her dog.'

'I wanted to make her cry. Like I had cried.'

'When did you do this?'

There is silence. Then she continues, 'When it was still dark. I tied him up at the gate.'

'On the day she died?'

She puts her hands over her eyes. 'Yes.'

Jannie stands up.

'She took my husband.'

Jannie shakes his head. 'She was his mother.'

Ilse's eyes shine with bitter hurt. 'But she left no room for me.'

Jannie can hear someone amongst the mourners laugh, an otherworldly sound in a moment so bleak.

Ilse looks at him and in a sudden change of mood she says, 'You must hurry now, Jannie.'

He hears the urgency in her voice.

'I don't know how long they keep the dogs for before they . . .'

Jannie is on his feet. 'Before they?'

'You must hurry.'

CHAPTER NINETEEN

Jannie stumbles out of the house, propelled by Ilse's warning and poorly remembered talk of the daily 'euthanasing' of dogs at the overcrowded shelter. Was it the evening, for reasons of smell, or was it dawn? That he can't recall fills him with panic.

He runs past mourners still communing in small groups on the lawn. Past Aletta and Gogo clearing up the food table.

'Jannie!' a voice calls out and he turns to see Delilah emerge from Ouma's house. He does not respond. She runs after him. 'Wait!'

'Can't!' he shouts.

'Just wait!' She closes in on him. He guns the engine. She pulls open the passenger side door and clambers in. 'Where are you going?'

'The shelter at Hartebeespoort.'

'What?'

'For Suffering.'

'Suffering?'

Then it hits her: where is Suffering? 'Oh God, Suffering!' she screams. 'Drive. Drive!'

The red truck roars up the steep hill to the gate.

*

Delilah does not ask how this all came to be and Jannie doesn't tell. She just seizes hold of the side of the door and holds on for dear life.

It wasn't long ago that Delilah had walked past Ouma's bedroom door and seen her lying on the bed. Suffering was stretched out long and thin beside her, his head resting in the cup of her shoulder.

In the normal course of things Delilah would have stopped and maybe even crawled onto the bed with them but something about the way Ouma's arm had fallen across her face told her she needed privacy. It was only when she was halfway down the passage that she heard her grandmother say, 'The green thing with the pip inside. What's that called?' There is heavy silence and then she says, 'The baboons like it.' A rustle that sounds like a dog's tail hitting the covers. *Thump, thump.* 'Gogo wraps them in newspaper and puts it them in the *mielie* meal to ripen.'

Thump, thump, thump.

'You don't care, do you, Suffering?' *Thump, thump.* 'That I am stupid.'

There was silence and then, 'A person without words. As stupid as a piece of wood, without stories even, without Elisabeth and her poems.' Then she hears Ouma begin to cry, hard, dry gasps.

Delilah hurried to her door and, once again, what she saw made her stop.

Suffering was licking away the salty tears that flowed down Ouma's cheeks, dutifully and without sentiment. Delilah could see her grandmother had no need of human solace.

Rows of low cages fill the back yard of the shelter. Jannie and Delilah split up; he heads up one aisle and she another.

'Suffering!' calls Delilah.

Their two voices make a chorus in the uneasy quiet. 'Suffering! Come, boy. Suffering!' And the word is true of all the creatures whining for their attention in their cages, as if aware of what is to come.

Delilah has seen people show up at Ouma's surgery with injured dogs lying across the back seat of their cars. The old lady never turned them away. The nearest vet was over an hour away. Mostly they came with puffadder bites or biliary.

She lingered over their care. And if, rarely, she suspected the owner was responsible for the injury she offered to buy the dog there and then. That is why the dog population at the farm had been known to swell to over ten at one or other time.

Delilah can still hear her say, '*Bokkie*, remember the way we treat our animals is a true measure of our *peopleness*.' She said it like she was speaking Afrikaans, *ons medemenslikheid*, our humanity.

They do not find Suffering in any of the cages. Jannie knows where the animal crematorium is because he has had to deliver dead animals there from time to time.

The incinerator roars and clatters indiscreetly when it is running at its peak. And every week the number of animals to be cremated rises.

The double doors leading into the crematorium are open. Delilah heads towards them.

'You don't want to go in there, Delilah,' shouts Jannie.

'I'm going,' she says.

Through the open door she can see what looks to her like a giant ant but what she knows to be a man in an overall with a protective visor over his eyes. He throws something heavy into the incinerator like he would a bag of sugar or *mielie* meal.

Delilah stops in her tracks. *What's he doing?* The question sits in her head but she doesn't dare answer it.

Jannie passes her and steps into the gloom. It takes a moment for his eyes to adjust. Then he sees Suffering curled up in the corner of a cage, just he and one other small white dog. Jannie knows they do it without injections when the volunteer vet has failed to get to the shelter before the truck that collects the dogs. Sometimes Jannie wishes he didn't know the things he knows.

The attendant shovels fuel into the furnace. The roar of the flames and his visor make him deaf.

Jannie tries the gate and finds it open.

Suffering doesn't move when Jannie crawls into the cage and holds out his hand for him to smell.

As he kneels, so prone, Jannie is floored by the dull heartbreak in Suffering's gaze. He sees Ouma as she often was, leaning down in her chair to touch her forehead to that of her canine companion. They would rest there for some minutes and then Ouma would sigh.

The dog's nostrils twitch at Jannie's familiar smell. His tail wags tentatively and then falls still. He growls once as Jannie picks him up and then he allows him to carry him out of the cage.

The sight of Delilah standing in the doorway startles both man and dog.

'Let's go,' Jannie snaps.

She shakes her head.

'Come, let's go.'

Ons medemenslikheid. The phrase sits between Delilah and flight. She says, 'Tell him to turn it off.'

Jannie looks at the attendant who senses their movement and turns to see them. He lifts his visor and says, '*Baas?*'

Jannie indicates Suffering in his arms and says, 'My dog.'

The attendant shrugs, one less to contend with.

'Tell him to turn it off,' says Delilah again.

'He's got a job to do, Delilah,' Jannie says.

'What kind of job is that? Hey?'

Jannie takes her shoulder. She pulls away. 'What kind of fucked-up job is that?'

She and the attendant look at one another. The uncharacteristic crudeness of her language sits poorly on her youthful face.

The black man holds her gaze. In it, she sees his resignation. He cannot alter the course of this day's work. He depends on it.

Her face crumples.

The attendant turns to nurse the flames once more. While his back is turned, Delilah darts into the cage, grabs the small white dog out of it, and runs.

Ilse moves from window to window of her darkened house. Dogs lie around the room, on sofas, chairs and the floor. They sigh in their sleep, grateful for the cool interior. The ridgeback watches her passage around the room. He tries to fit her peregrination into his canine frame of reference, and fails. It unnerves him.

She maintains her vigil through the afternoon. Pacing, thin-skinned, from portal to portal, as if anticipating the rising of the waves outside her window.

She sees the funeral guests finish their lunch and slowly trickle homeward. She can tell, by the lightness of their faces, that they've satisfied their need to bear witness to Ouma's passing.

But Ilse is not interested in the humans.

It is the uncertain return of Suffering that she is waiting for.

CHAPTER TWENTY

The rays of the descending sun blast the top of Klein Samuel's head as he crouches on his heels outside Cheetah's small corrugated-iron room. '*Eish*,' he says under his breath and then again, '*Eish, eish, eish.*'

Cheetah sits on a stool in the doorway. She throws a handful of loose leaf tea into a small pot bubbling on the kerosene stove, '*Eish* what?'

Klein Samuel lifts his head but his eyes remain closed. He shakes his head and says in his native Ndebele, 'They have forgotten me.'

'Say what?'

'The *amadhlozi*. The ancestors.'

She can see there is trouble coming. 'I miss Ouma too, you know,' she says.

He still doesn't look at her.

'When you speak that Shona of yours it sounds like oil bubbling in your mouth,' she mutters.

Klein Samuel's eyes flash. 'Ndebele.' He gets to his feet and walks away towards his shack. 'Not Shona. N-d-e-b-e-l-e.'

'Okay then, Mdebele.'

He swings around. 'Not Mdebele, *N, N, N,* Ndebele.' He thumps his chest and turns away.

Cheetah watches him walk and she calls out, 'Does the Ndebele *outjie* want some tea?'

'*Ga!*' he says and carries on walking.

She sees him disappear into his shack and come out with an unlabelled bottle of clear alcohol. He sits on the upside-down bucket in the dust outside his room. He unscrews the bottle top.

It's all very slow at the beginning. She sees him lift the bottle to his lips. He drinks deeply then screws the cap back on. He is nothing if not methodical. It is as if good manners will make the drinking less of a giving in.

Cheetah turns off the stove and puts the lid on the pot. She knows it won't be long now before Klein Samuel's body lies comatose on the sand. Dead. Drunk.

Dead to her.

Cheetah wanders out of her shack and across the dry veld to the path that runs along the base of the steep hill. A small troop of baboons sways knuckle-first over the rocks into the darkening orchard to knock an avocado or two from the trees but she doesn't see them.

Klein Samuel puts the bottle to his lips and tilts his head back. The dregs burn the back of his throat and then are gone. He puts the empty bottle on the muddy earth beside where he sits and he waits.

The trembling in his hands has long ago subsided; now he waits for the alcohol to numb his loss. He sighs. He will need more.

He gets to his feet and walks slowly, careful to compensate for the dulled communion between his eyes and brain. He walks along the path to the garage and slips a key off the hook and then climbs into Groot Samuel's white truck.

Klein Samuel never did get his driver's licence but Groot Samuel doesn't seem to know that, or care enough to ask. Every week he entrusts Klein Samuel to drive the loaded truck to the dump to offload their refuse.

Klein Samuel releases the handbrake and after just a brief push it rolls silently down the hill. It is only when it reaches the gulley below the house that he starts the engine.

Frans, sitting with the others on the stoep of Ouma's house, is the only one who sees Klein Samuel and the white truck slowly climb the hill and then disappear from view. He has a talent for noticing the furtive.

Cheetah takes the path to the back gate that leads onto Groot Samuel's land and then to Ouma's surgery.

This is where she came when she needed Ouma's counsel in the daylight hours. Ouma let her sit in her consulting rooms even if she was busy, just so she could be near.

And sometimes, on the evenings when Ouma was alone, the two of them would drink tea together after the old lady had finished her dinner. It gave them comfort. Cheetah was wise to Baas Pieter's occasional visits and kept away when she saw his truck parked in the bushes.

Nights on the farm always seemed solid-black to Cheetah, no matter what the moon did. In Lavender Hill, where she came from, it was never dark like this. Powerful streetlights towered above the several-storey blocks of flats that made up the bulk of the housing. No bird-spiders or snakes could live in amongst all those feet.

Cheetah didn't grow up afraid of creatures that come out at night apart, of course, from the men and boys in the gangs that sprang up on the sandy flats like bitter weed.

But the farm night seethed with living things. The *nagapies* in the trees with their eyes round as pools. The pearl-spotted owl hunting moths in the light from the open door of her shack, so small that you would expect only a chirp from its diminutive mouth, but the sound it made was immense.

Lucky, Cheetah thought, to have such a gift.

It was only when she saw the snake that hid in the acacia tree swallow the owl's eggs that she changed her view. It ate them one by one, until its length was marked with intermittent bulges like a string of beads.

Bad things happen to all of God's creatures.

Cheetah didn't mind braving the night creatures to see Ouma. Only once did the old lady break their rule and ask a question about the bad old days. She put the kettle on for tea and she asked, 'Where's your ma, Cheetah?'

If anyone else had wanted to know, Cheetah would have told them to *fugoff* and stick their rat-nose into someone else's story, but it was Ouma who asked and they had an arrangement.

Cheetah shook her head, 'Long dead.'

She didn't know why but on their nights of gentle communion the language she and Ouma used was English, even though Afrikaans was both of their mother tongues. Maybe Cheetah felt English communicated her better self.

'I can't remember her.'

'I wonder if my girl remembers me,' said Ouma quietly.

'Who?'

'Aletta. My daughter.'

The arthritic bulges on Ouma's finger joints slowed her down as she clattered cups together with unmatching saucers. 'I haven't spoken to her in a year but every time the phone rings I hope it's her. I can't stop myself.'

Cheetah felt a stab of jealousy for this missing child who had the power to cause Ouma such pain. Who occupied the sacred place of *daughter*.

'She's a bloody fool to turn her back on you,' mumbled the girl.

Ouma took Cheetah's hand. Briefly. And held it against her cheek. The papery surface of her fingers and the tremor in her hand travelled up Cheetah's arm and made her want to put her head in her hands.

Ouma sat at the table with her tea. 'Come, put your feet on the heater.' She picked up the shirt she was mending and took a needle out of her sewing basket.

Cheetah sat, pulled off her worn socks, put them and her feet on the metal heater and groaned with pleasure.

Ouma threaded the needle and then asked quietly, 'How did she die?'

'My ma?'

Ouma nodded.

'By the knife. My pa said she had it coming.'

Ouma waited for more, patient. The needle flew in and out. 'Your pa raised you?'

'For a bit.'

Cheetah picked at the bubbles on her jersey. Sipped her tea. 'Don't know where he went after that.' She bit her fingernail. Nothing there, bitten to the quick, tattered. She tucked her hand into her sleeve.

Ouma didn't look up or speak. She knew this moment, this creaking open of the door. She knew not to look at Cheetah. She knew to sew, and wait for her to be ready to talk some more.

A rustle of movement calls Cheetah back and she scans the floor of the abandoned consulting rooms for its source.

A slithering?

She turns to look behind her. But there is nothing there. The scrape of scales against stone comes again. Was that a tail curling by in the shadow?

In a flash Cheetah sees what will become of this place. Roots will grow up through the floor. The roof will sag. *Nagapies* will nest in the ceiling, lizards in the walls, and in all the dark corners snakes will lay their eggs and multiply.

Cheetah turns and runs. She slams the door closed behind her and she runs so the pink rises into her cheeks and her heart thuds. She runs back along the path and through the gate to the pig farm.

CHAPTER TWENTY-ONE

Klein Samuel is not a good driver even when sober, but the brew already coursing through his veins and the bruise of Ouma's passing reduces his aptitude yet further.

Her death demands his reluctant attention. He can feel its certain progress through his feeling world and he pushes the wheezing truck to its limit to escape it but to his surprise it is the spiky shards left by Ouma's lapses when living that assail him first.

He saw them for what they were long before Groot Samuel did because he depended on Ouma to keep Cheetah in this world. From the day he opened the abandoned shed to find a store of sawn-off plastic milk containers full of light brown fluid he knew trouble was coming.

The smell of urine burnt the membranes in his nose. He wasn't entirely surprised; he'd seen the old lady pluck the empty bottles out of the rubbish bins behind the house. When Gogo had asked what she was doing she had said, 'Hush, Gogo, it is my business.'

He saw her spray the liquid over the arum lilies at the foot of her stoep when she thought no one was watching. She used a wide-armed movement, head lifted high, as if they contained holy water.

As a farmer Klein Samuel understood the value of this fertilizer but the furtive way in which Ouma stored and spread it spoke of things amiss in her. It was as if she could not bear to waste even the cast off liquid from her own body.

Soon after, she forgot Cheetah's *muti* two weeks in a row and then, to make matters worse, she denied it.

'Don't talk rubbish, Klein Samuel. I don't forget such things.'

Out of fury and fear Klein Samuel lost his head that day. He walked to the shed and emptied out all the urine bottles and threw them away.

You would have thought he'd stolen all her money the way Ouma shouted and swore at him. *Hayi!* An old lady should not speak in such a way.

Ouma claimed he had betrayed her. 'No, Ouma,' he had said, 'it is you who have forsaken us.' And she had, she had failed the greater mission of keeping Cheetah healthy. Did she not know she was their Noah's ark?

Klein Samuel pulls up outside the shebeen without a thought to the people and cars that now have to heave themselves through the bottleneck caused by Groot Samuel's white truck.

Mercy, the shebeen queen, and proprietor of this establishment, is a talkative woman, and voluptuous. She's trying to provide for two fatherless children and it gets harder every day in this *gemors* of a place.

She is fond of Klein Samuel in spite of his Zimbabwean origins. He is a good customer and polite.

She doesn't think the same of that girl of his, Cheetah, who accompanied him once. She took one look at her and she could see her used-up-ness. She knows what women like her have seen and done. You would think it might make Mercy kind but, in her view, kindness is not what girls like Cheetah need.

She is glad to see that today Klein Samuel is alone and smartly dressed. She pumps her toxic brew from a tin oil drum into an empty Coca-Cola bottle.

'We buried Ouma today, *sisi* Mercy,' says the farmhand and he looks down at his hands.

'Oh, I am sorry to hear that, Klein Samuel, really.'

Mercy knew Ouma too. She had turned up at the shebeen to find Klein Samuel after he had been there for two straight days.

The old lady had shown no fear in entering that place where sightings of white people were rare. Ouma put her hands on her hips when she saw Klein Samuel asleep on the bench in the corner of the room, a silver line of dribble hanging from his mouth.

'Look at you, Klein Samuel. Lying there like a fool while Cheetah wonders if you are still breathing and the spinach plants shrivel and die.'

Even in his drunkenness Klein Samuel knew that the plentiful rain over the past many days had taken care of the spinach plants but he didn't say anything.

Ouma was there because she needed him.

Klein Samuel could barely walk to the truck and she made him sit in the back on the way home because he stank.

The strange thing was that Klein Samuel was glad she had come. It meant he would not be forgotten there, even as he forgot himself. More than that, if such a feeling was possible in a relationship of such inequality, it confirmed Ouma's love for him.

It rattles him deeply now to know that she is no longer there to do that. Klein Samuel counts out payment from a thin sheaf of dirty notes and takes a long sip from the bottle. The commotion outside doesn't cause either Mercy or Klein Samuel much pause until they hear, '*Who is the mutha fucka who thinks he owns this road?*' spoken in Zulu.

Klein Samuel has the illegal immigrant's hardwired fear of all things official but there is a chasm between that and the terror he feels when confronted by the criminals who run these streets.

Klein Samuel hears in that one sentence the presence of such a person and his heart begins to pound. He looks for a way to escape out the back of the shack. But what then would happen to the truck?

Mercy says, 'You'd better run, my friend.'

As Klein Samuel emerges from the shebeen he tucks the bottle under his arm. A man in a red T-shirt stands between him and Groot Samuel's truck and he does it in such a way that suggests he owns this road.

Klein Samuel claps his hands together as a mark of his servility. 'Sorry, sorry. I will move. Sorry.'

The man cranes forward so his face is unduly close to Klein Samuel's and says in English, 'What did you say?'

'Sorry, my brother,' Klein Samuel says in Zulu.

'I'm not your brother,' the man replies in English.

Klein Samuel stops. Blinks. A cold rod of fear stiffens his back.

'You speaking my language, boy?' says the man, in English again.

'Yes, brother. No! I mean, sir . . . boss.'

'It is not yours to speak, you fucking rubbish.'

'Yes, boss, I know, boss.'

'And this is not your country to be in.'

'Yes, sir.'

If Klein Samuel had been less afraid he would've told him how much he'd planted and reaped in the man's country, how hard he had worked to make his labour bear fruit. But he takes one look at the man's face and knows that only silence can save him. So he hangs his head and is quiet.

He can see the man's feet. They remain rooted to the dirt road and make no move to let him pass. Fear rises like yeast in Klein Samuel's body. It fills his mouth and his eyes and, much too late, he turns and he runs. The wall of bodies now gathered around to watch the fracas impedes his progress and he falls.

The man in the red T-shirt is on him like a dead weight. Klein Samuel's slight form beneath the man's corpulence is bird-spider-like.

Somewhere in his sound mind, Klein Samuel knows that the best thing to do is to lie very still and allow his assailant to do his worst, but he is beyond that. He lashes out where he can and he kicks.

He sees blood on the man's mouth and smells his sour breath as he says, 'Let's go for a ride, *Zimbabawe*.'

CHAPTER TWENTY-TWO

Ilse is no longer watching for the return of Suffering but she can't seem to find the animation for anything else. She lies on her back on the sofa with her eyes closed and longs for the escape of sleep; for *who she is*, what she has become, is a dog killer.

As if that thought had just been shouted out in canine speak, all five dogs rise up and thunder out of the living room.

A sharp, high bark sounds outside, separate and distinct from the others. She stumbles to the window just in time to see Suffering emerge from Jannie's truck. Ilse's insides fill up with relief. *Oh, thank God.*

She watches the small yellow dog lower his nose to the ground and follow the scent trails of his home turf, tail upright. Then she steps away from her window and sinks slowly into a chair, released.

She hears her dogs yap and whine to greet their pack-mate and in her mind's eye she imagines them asking forgiveness on her behalf.

Then she walks slowly into her bedroom and takes a suitcase from the top shelf of the wardrobe. She puts it on the bed and unzips it. Its pristine dark green interior shows little wear and tear. She looks into its depths, then sits on the bed beside it and puts her hands in her lap.

Outside, Groot Samuel sees the small yellow dog bounding across the grass towards him. He crouches down to greet him then looks beyond, half expecting to see his mother come out of the bushes, back from her evening walk to the dam. But it is only Delilah.

Groot Samuel sits on the grass as the dog spins in a joyous circle around him. The grown man's shoulders begin to shake. He laughs. And laughs. He tries to stop himself, 'Sorry.'

Delilah sits down beside him. She can sense there is as much grief in the laughter as joy so she whispers, 'It's okay.'

It escapes from him like the air from a tyre and he fights to get the words out. 'I thought the jackals had got him.'

Suffering licks Groot Samuel's hand.

'We found him at the crematorium,' says Delilah quietly

'Why the crematorium?' asks Groot Samuel, his laughter fading.

Delilah shrugs. 'Just did.' She couldn't say, just then, why it is that she doesn't tell Groot Samuel. Perhaps she sees he's had enough grief for one day or maybe it is she herself who cannot bear to see him embrace one more sadness.

'He from there too?' says Groot Samuel, indicating the small dog in her arms.

Delilah nods. They sit in silence for a moment, then Delilah says, softly, 'I used to see bad things coming a long way off. I mean, not exactly, see . . . but . . .' She trails off. Her mother told her not to tell anyone about her *piep en tjank* because it made her sound crazy.

Groot Samuel watches the girl rest her head on her knees. After a while she says, 'Now I only see them when they are on top of me . . . and by then it's too late.'

He has no words of comfort for her, neither can he conjure them. Instead he lays his broad hand on her bent head. This first touch, this tenderness, happens so easily she barely notices it.

Gogo approaches across the grass and Suffering jumps up to greet her, tail wagging. '*Haai!* Watch those feet,' she admonishes the dog but her smile reveals her feeling for him. 'Where have you been hiding, *wena*?' Then she sees the small white dog tucked under Delilah's arm and she says, 'And who is this now?'

Delilah looks down at the skin and bones in her arms, and she says, 'You name her, Gogo.'

The old lady looks at the shivering pup and she says, 'We will call her *Important*.' She looks down at Delilah and grins. 'Important de la Rey.'

Gogo cocks her head at the dog. 'You, Important . . .!' The dog looks up. 'No dirty feet in the house. No dead birds. No snakes, dead or alive, *wa bona*.'

A scratching sound and they look up to see Suffering at the door to Ouma's house.

His anguish escalates as the door fails to open. He runs around the side of the house and emerges, moments later, with Ouma's hat in his mouth. It is a trick the dog used to perform when Ouma forgot her hat. She'd say, 'Suffering, *die hoed*.' He would run off and because she always left it in the same place on the bench in the kitchen he would be back with it in his mouth before she could spit.

Ouma always said it was Suffering's way of saying thank you for his rescue.

Today he doesn't know who to give it to.

It is as if he has just learnt what they all already know. A wailing sound comes out of him that gives voice to canine and human mourning alike.

It adds to Cheetah's growing worry as she sits on the upturned bucket outside her shack and eats a cold potato. The sun has fallen beneath the horizon, the *nagapies* are beginning to rouse themselves in the trees above and still there is no sign of Klein Samuel.

When the dog's mourning howl fades to silence, Cheetah turns on the radio. It normally lifts her spirits to hear music. She has a special passion for jazz, especially the hybrid sound of the Cape townships with its power to raise you up, away from here. But today it doesn't do that; today it just confirms her fall. She calls out, 'Fuck you, Samuel!' into thin air.

Cheetah had fully expected to find Klein Samuel comatose on the dust outside her house when she returned from her visit to Ouma's surgery that afternoon but only the empty bottle lay where he once did.

Even his sleeping form would have given her some comfort.

She sighs. One bottle is never enough on dark days like this one. Sometimes he stays away for two days at a time, comatose on the floor of the shebeen, his body swimming with the brake fluid Mercy uses in her brew. That's where he is now. She knows it. *Mr Dead Drunk and Far Away.*

Aloneness settles on Cheetah like a shroud. She turns off the radio and sighs.

In the silence that follows, Cheetah hears singing. A lone voice singing in what even she recognises as Zulu. It is the kind of song a herdsman would sing to his cattle as they grazed lazily on the slopes above the sea.

She gets up to follow the sound.

There, ahead of her, just off the path in the discrete bushes, a young man is bent over a small pink bucket, washing his clothes. A pair of jeans, a white shirt, and two pairs of socks have been carefully laid out on the nearby bushes to dry in the evening air.

It is the calm and heft of the song that holds her there.

She sees the muscles of his bare back bulge and stretch as he scrubs at a pair of blue work overalls. The bubbles of soap on the surface of the water sway with the movement of his hands. Water sloshes over the lip of the bucket and turns the surrounding earth to dark mud.

She has seen him before, this man; he arrived a few months ago and is already a foreman in the feeding sheds. She can see he is a person with a future.

He turns to see her standing there. He has noticed Cheetah too. The wide cheekbones and the sexy sway of her hips as she walks. Instead of blushing shy at her unexpected presence, he says, '*Dumela, sisi.*'

'Ja, hello,' she replies.

He rings out the overalls he is washing and dips them in a second bucket for rinsing. Then he spreads them out carefully over another bush. While he works he introduces himself. 'Me, I am Dumisane, from KwaZulu-Natal.'

'Cheetah,' she says, following his lead, 'from Cape Town,' as if naming her place of origin will somehow tell her story.

Cheetah knows she should take her leave but she doesn't seem to be able to.

Dumisane picks up a litre bottle of Coke from the dust at his feet and unscrews the top. He holds it out to her. 'Come.'

Any other time she would have shaken her head and walked away. But today, she knows he was sent by God to ease her loss.

She steps forward, just one step. He does the same. He passes her the bottle with both hands.

Chapter Twenty-three

The falling dusk makes it hard for Jannie to work as he kneels, for the second time, beside the spoor on the bank of the dam. This time Delilah sits beside him. 'Is it dry yet?' she asks.

'My friend said it would take longer if it was runny,' says Jannie. 'And then she said she didn't know why she was telling me how to do it when she didn't know herself.'

Delilah leans forward to prod the plaster with her fingertip. 'Feels hard.'

Jannie looks at his watch. 'Twenty more minutes.'

They sit in silence. Both are aware of the encroaching dark and the shrill noises of the night rising.

'Maybe you should go up to the house, Delilah,' says Jannie softly.

'Why?'

'What would you say if someone found you here?'

'What would you say?'

That silences him.

'Where's Groot Samuel?' asks Jannie after a minute.

'Feeding the cows. Klein Samuel's gone.'

'Ilse?'

Delilah shrugs.

'Gogo?'

'I told you, she's in the kitchen feeding Important.'

'Who's Important?'

'My dog.'

They are silent, then Delilah asks, 'D'you always ask so many questions when you're scared?'

'Ja, so they tell me,' says Jannie and smiles fleetingly. There is a rustle in the nearby scrub and they both look in the direction of the sound. Suffering emerges from the bush, nose to the ground, following the spoor of his absent owner.

'He's looking for her,' says Jannie.

'How long will he do that before he gives up?'

'Until the scent fades.'

Delilah turns to Jannie and says, 'You should take him home or he'll look all night.'

'He is not mine to take,' says Jannie. They watch the dog walk in circles, nose to the ground. The screech of the *nagapie* interrupts his mission. He looks up and sniffs the air for its associated scent.

'We'll find him, won't we, Jannie?'

'Find who?'

'The one who pushed her.'

He sighs. 'I don't know.'

Once again, the shrill night fills their silence.

'It's always your fault, hey?' whispers Delilah.

Jannie glances up at her.

'If bad things happen to one of *yours*, your people, your friends,' she continues.

She takes his silence as his assent. 'I should've seen how Ouma was that morning and followed her to the dam. You know?'

He shakes his head. 'Don't.'

She sighs.

As a young child, Delilah roamed the banks of the Pongola river that made up the western border of her town. The river was home to crocodiles and snakes. It fed and watered birds, cattle and the sugarcane growing on its banks. It also hid men with pangas in its reeds but the grown-ups didn't believe Delilah when she told them that.

The river burst its banks two or three times a year.

Delilah saw how the raging rapids rose up and swept cows, trees and people over the falls and into the hungry mud and rock below. She wondered when it would be her turn.

But it wasn't the river that swept her away from her family.

It was the failure of her parents to make a living, plain and simple, although they wouldn't say as much.

She carries on. 'It would've been better for the family if I'd got a job instead of playing the cello.'

'Now that is nonsense, Delilah.'

'And the stuff! I even wanted a gold sofa,' she says, 'like the Nanjis.'

'Who?'

'Our-neighbours-the-Nanjis.' She says it as if it were a single word of many syllables. 'Our houses are so close that if you spit over the road you can watch your spit dribble down their window.'

'You did that?' asks Jannie.

'Martinus did when he thought no one was watching but the

grandmother saw. She told him it confirmed the *savagery* of the Schoeman family.'

She says *savagery* with an Indian accent just like grandmother Nanji must have done. A guffaw escapes Jannie's mouth.

Delilah pauses; she wants to tell Jannie how she saw the raggedness of life in the Schoeman household. To her, everyone on the Nanjis' side seemed flush with food, love and purpose. Even their washing, lengths of vivid sari and kurta silks, beat the hell out of the faded Little Mermaid pyjamas and paper thin bed sheets drying on her family's washing line.

It made her worry about the future.

When she asked her parents if they could have a gold sofa like the Nanjis', her mother looked at her and said, 'And who are you – Nefertiti?'

Her mother turned bitter when she was worried about money. Delilah could see that they would never be able to give her such a thing.

So Delilah put all her pure, blind faith in Martinus, the doctor/philosopher. He was the only one of them who could give the family a shot at the kind of future that might include a thing of such beauty as a gold sofa.

Martinus wasn't haunted by floods and he didn't stumble upon men hiding in the reeds with bloodshot eyes and pangas in their hands.

No. Martinus raced barefoot through the thorny grass and catapulted himself off the branch into the river with jaw-dropping boldness. Even Aarti, his first love, was a prize. He was full of brains and ambition. For even Martinus's able wings have been clipped by the banal need for rands and cents.

Delilah looks at her hands and her dread slips off into the air, thin and high as a gong. She says, 'They say that Aarti is at university learning to be a lawyer.' She pulls her fingers through her hair until she encounters a bird's nest then gives up. 'Martinus is under the ground at Klipwal gold mine to earn our keep. And he's never going to get away.'

Jannie doesn't try to talk her out of her guilt because he can see it is simply part of her, like her red-blonde hair. He sits beside her close and quiet.

She wouldn't know how to describe what passes between the two of them as they sit in companionable silence, except to say that it is like sand, molecules of sand made up of *them*. If Ouma had been there she would have said it was grit, Jannie-grit and Delilah-grit. She knew its value better than most.

Delilah's sixteen-year-old mind wonders if this is what good friends do, share one another's stories, carry one another's loads?

Groot Samuel stops in the doorway of his house and wipes his muddy boots on the mat. No one has turned the lights on. Ilse is sitting at the dining-room table. The high-backed chair makes her posture unsparing.

He takes in the pile of half-eaten biscuits on the table in front of her and he knows she has gnawed the edge of each in one direction, then the other.

He wishes that it were not so, today of all days. But he walks over to her slowly and he touches her hand.

'Come,' he says.

Ilse looks up at him, chocolate biscuit paused in its passage to her mouth.

'Come,' he says again and he holds out his hand.

She doesn't take it but she does get to her feet. Groot Samuel walks into the bedroom. He sees the empty suitcase open on the bed and he zips it closed and puts it back in the cupboard. In the half-light he takes her pyjamas from under her pillow. As he hands them to her he says, 'It will be better in the morning.'

She does not put on the pyjamas but climbs under the sheets in her clothes. Groot Samuel sits on her side of the bed. 'Water?' he asks.

She shakes her head.

Groot Samuel gets up and walks round to his side of the bed. He lies down on the cover, fully clothed, leaves even his shoes on his feet. Ilse begins to cry very quietly. He closes his eyes.

'Time?' asks Delilah.

Jannie crouches over the footprint and carefully lifts out the plaster mould. He turns it over and looks at it.

'Did it work?' says Delilah.

'Can't see,' he says. 'Come.' And they gather up the tools and packets and climb up the bank of the dam to the path that runs along its rim.

The still, black water stretches out on one side of them as they walk, the fragrant bush on the other. Both are aware of the sharp perfume coming off the hot earth as it cools. As they near the far end of the dam a voice sounds out in the gathering gloom: 'There's a crested barbet with chicks in this tree.'

It stops them in their tracks. They peer into the gathering darkness and see Frans sitting on the bench under the acacia tree. What would be an entirely plausible location on a sunny day feels somehow sinister in this gloomy coming of night.

Jannie wonders how long he has been there and what he has over-heard. 'Your ma put up that nest. She'd be glad,' he says.

'Is my car still parked up at the top gate?' asks Frans.

Jannie nods. 'Last time I looked.'

'Not scratched?'

'I didn't see any damage.'

'Somebody could easily . . . you know . . . with us jammed together like that.'

'I suppose,' says Jannie, and he wonders why Frans cares about the well-being of his battered Mercedes at a time like this. Jannie doesn't *know* the face turned now towards him, not really. Frans went to boarding school after his father died so was not an active part of life on the farm in the early years of Jannie's friendship with Ouma.

But Jannie does remember the laughter of him and his cronies as they hung him head first from the acacia tree. *Blerrie moffie.*

He'd like to get away from Frans but he can't seem to find how to do that gracefully. It's as if the obliterating power the teenager once wielded still holds sway and Jannie can't move without his permission. It would have been better if Frans had asked them what they were doing there in the fall of night, or even what they carried in their hands, but he says nothing.

'You staying here tonight, Frans?' Jannie asks, finally.

'Not on your life.'

'No?'

'It closes around you like the mouth of a fucking whale, this place, and you never see the light again,' says Frans.

Jannie is stung by his crudeness; does he not realise Delilah lives in this so-called whale? Then he sees that Frans has said it directly to the girl, as a kind of warning. She blinks in startled silence.

Suffering whines at their feet and Frans turns to Jannie and says, 'Delilah's right. You should take the dog home with you. Be merciful, *jy weet*, at least to those in the valley trying to sleep tonight.'

Jannie considers Frans. So he did hear their conversation. Alarm seeds itself in his gut as he and Delilah take their leave.

Cheetah emerges from the bush as Jannie and Delilah arrive at Jannie's truck. Her slight shape is made slighter still by the dark.

'You not sleeping yet, Cheetah?' Jannie asks.

'He's gone again,' she says and they both know she's referring to Klein Samuel.

'Drinking?'

'Maybe.'

'Then he'll come tomorrow when he's sobered up.'

'Ja,' says Cheetah and she crouches down to scratch Suffering's ears. She speaks directly to the dog as if to an old friend, 'But you're back, *ouboet*, and that's something, not so?' She uses the phrase her pa would have chosen – *old brother*. It feels true to her.

'We found him at the shelter,' says Delilah.

'Lucky,' says Cheetah as she strokes the top of the dog's head.

'Ja,' says Jannie, 'lucky.' He throws his equipment in the truck.

Cheetah gets up and as she turns to go, Jannie can see in the way she moves that she has not got the comfort she came for and he calls out, 'He always comes back, *nê*, Cheetah?'

She doesn't turn or stop walking, simply lifts her hand to acknowledge his certainty.

Jannie watches her disappear into the bush and then opens the door to his truck.

Delilah asks again. 'Take Suffering, Jannie. I've got Important to worry about.'

'Important?' asks Jannie.

'Don't you go losing your mind now, Detective, *asseblief*.' She's always loved the rhythm of the word, *as-se-blief*, and that it means please without sounding like pleading.

'Shit, sorry. Ja, your dog,' he says.

Delilah watches the lights of his truck crest the hill. She's not alone in doing this. Cheetah watches Jannie leave from the clearing and then closes herself and her dread into her shack to wait out the night.

Cheetah's not one for mumbo jumbo. She would never claim that she somehow *knows* what she can't know. What she *would* say, if asked, is that a dark feeling has arrived in her, and that it takes up more space every hour that passes without Klein Samuel's safe return.

Delilah heads back to the house; she hesitates on the road, at the turn-off to the dam, then runs, light and silent, back to the edge of the water.

At first she can see nothing but then she makes out the shape of Frans standing by the water's edge.

She watches as he kicks off his shoes, then puts first one foot and then the other into the shallow edge of the dam. Delilah can tell by how slowly he moves that the mud is filling up the gaps between his toes. One more step, and then another. In this way he moves deeper.

With each step Delilah relives her discovery of Ouma in the water and she imagines, as he must be doing, the old lady's passage to her end. Did she tumble as she went? Did she cry, shout or tremble.

Was she afraid?

Frans stops when he is waist deep, as if he can feel the smudge of his mother's existence passing out of the world. It looks to Delilah like he has stopped just where Ouma finally lay.

A single burp of grief bursts out of Frans's mouth and he begins to weep.

Delilah turns and runs home in the dark.

In the cold early hours, the small yellow dog crawls onto Jannie's bed for warmth.

Jannie hesitates, then curls his drowsy body around Suffering's skin and bones. It occurs to him that he has never woken to a lover's warmth beside him. He has always stolen his intimacies. Sex as a young man was always furtive and desperate. Now it is easier for him to be celibate.

Why he should be thinking such thoughts he doesn't know but they make his insides ache. He savours the small, warm body next to his and waits for sleep to take him to a kinder world.

PART FIVE

CHAPTER TWENTY-FOUR

Monday morning at the Brits police station is a calm window in an otherwise busy week. All the carnage that washed up there on the weekend has passed on. The employed people in the surrounding townships are on their way to work and those who are not are sleeping it off.

Mokheti is often visibly present at times like these, like a cheerful maître d' bringing peace and order to troubled parts. Today he is nowhere to be seen. Jannie could do with his reassuring presence.

His first morning as a dog owner has not been easy. He took his leave of Suffering reluctantly and was yet to pull out of his driveway when he heard the dog begin to howl. He did what he often did when faced with challenges of a domestic nature, and phoned his mother. 'Ag but, Ma, I can't leave him crying like this.'

'Leave him, he'll stop as soon as you are out of sight,' she'd advised.

Jannie made himself wait a full ten minutes in his truck on the corner, listening to Suffering's escalating cries, before he stumbled back into the house and covered the dog with guilty kisses. It is a first for him, this care of a dependent creature, and he is startled by the protective feelings it conjures.

Now the dog is asleep on a scrap of blanket underneath Jannie's desk. A bowl of water and a folded up towel mark his corner of the world. It's as if it has always been there. Jannie kneels down on the floor to take in the sweet in and out of the dog's breath when he hears Anriette's voice.

'We've got something this time, Jannie.'

Jannie scrambles out from under the desk to see her in the doorway.

'Enough to persuade them to open a docket?' he asks.

'Maybe,' she says and smiles.

'Just . . .' he says and runs out of his office.

One of the anomalies about Jannie's place of work is that it was built without a single communal area for people to gather. And so no one does. In an effort to boost morale the department put a patch of green in the courtyard with a sign on the wall saying *The Gathering Place*. No one ever gathers there, no one even goes there alone, so when Jannie finds Mokheti sitting on the bench in a closed-off, bowed-over posture, he knows something is amiss.

Jannie crosses the green lawn. Mokheti looks up, still deep in thought. 'Ja, what, Detective?'

Jannie doesn't realise that Suffering has followed him and is standing beside him.

'Who the hell is this?' says Mokheti, looking at the dog.

'His name is Suffering,' says Jannie.

Mokheti glances at him. 'You serious?'

Jannie nods, and Mokheti laughs the great belly laugh for which he is well known.

Jannie waits for it to fade away before he asks, 'Is Colonel waiting for someone?'

Mokheti knows Jannie only uses his formal rank when he has something important to say.

'No.' Mokheti shakes his head. 'I'm here to cool off.'

'From what?'

'Ntombela and Bezuidenhout were meant to give evidence in the Mhlangu trial but they didn't turn up,' he says.

Jannie gives silent thanks that it wasn't something he did that is the source of Mokheti's irritation.

'Not yesterday, or today, and the bastards are not sick – they're just gone.' Mokheti shakes his head. 'Now the commissioner wants me to tell him why.'

The unsettling truth is that Mokheti wonders whether the cause of Ntombela's and Bezuidenhout's disappearance is perhaps more sinister than simple negligence. In this, he and Delilah are the same, the two Cassandras, tuned finely to catastrophe. Like her, his antennae for trouble have been dulled of late, overworked, tired, wanting not to know.

As the person in charge, he knows he will be held accountable for what his forces do, good and bad. He heaves himself to his feet. Suffering barks in alarm at his looming bulk.

Mokheti snaps. 'Where does this bloody dog belong?'

'With me, now.'

'You can't keep it.'

'Why not?'

'Because it needs place to run.'

Jannie looks at his boss and he says, 'He was Ouma's dog.'

'Ag ja then, there is not one simple thing in this world,' says Mokheti and he sits down again.

Jannie joins him on the bench and the two men say not a word.

Mokheti wishes sometimes that Jannie wasn't gay. Then it would be easier to have him home for a *braai* and a few beers. Years ago he visited more frequently and it was okay but come the end of lunch, Jannie would be washing dishes in the kitchen with the women while Mokheti got quietly and profoundly drunk alone in the sun outside.

'What have you got to tell me, Detective?' asks Mokheti finally.

Jannie looks up at him, yet can't seem to form an answer.

'What the hell is wrong with you, Jannie?'

'Ouma didn't slip, boss,' the detective says.

Mokheti lets out a long, thin stream of air and sighs, 'That so?'

'Ask the prosecutor to request the investigation of criminal charges, please?'

'No,' says Mokheti, and he wipes his face with a handkerchief. 'I said no.'

Jannie speaks quickly before the window closes forever. 'We found some tracks at the dam. If forensics can ID them, it may be grounds enough to open a criminal case.'

Mokheti snaps, 'And what else?

'Ouma's daughter-in-law took Suffering to the animal shelter there in Hartebeespoort the day the old lady died.'

Mokheti considers Jannie. 'So?'

'She may have been an accomplice, to get the dog out of the way.'

Mokheti is silent.

Jannie glances at him. Something about the twist of his mouth and turn of his head alerts Jannie to a dangerous shift of mood.

Mokheti shakes his head. 'I expect more from you, Detective.'

Jannie has seen this before, this bitter, sardonic scowl that Mokheti saves for the inept in his ranks. Jannie has never himself been the object of its attention and he wishes now he had not opened his mouth.

It is true. Mokheti seethes with particular rage because the dread in his stomach makes him mean. Jannie is his best man.

'Okay, forget it, sorry,' says the young detective in retreat.

'What has sorry got to do with it?' roars Mokheti.

Jannie feels the slap of those words on his cheek, the sting of them.

'You a teenage girl, Detective?'

Jannie looks at him for signs of the dry laughter that would normally follow such a comment but he does not see it.

'Now go back to work,' says the older man.

But Jannie is frozen in the glare of this fall from grace and he cannot move. He has always been this way in the face of rupture. The day his father snapped his ribs he stood there unable to move, watching his father's sadistic fury gather force. All he can think now is *I know this*.

'Go on, Detective!' Mokheti says, closer now. Jannie can feel his breath on his cheek. It is as if his whole meaning has shrunk to this staying still, this being there to look him in the eye.

When Jannie speaks it is so quiet that Mokheti has to lean forward, and he still isn't sure he has heard him correctly. 'What did you say?'

'I will do it anyway.'

'Do what, Detective?'

'Find the person who killed her.'

'That so?'

Jannie nods. 'With or without you.'

Mokheti considers his young detective, the shape of his will vivid in the see-through pink of his face.

Mokheti looks away. In truth, he loves Jannie more for his rebellion; it is unexpected and so deeply felt that it sweeps away what moments before was absolute. 'One week.' He turns his back on Jannie and so breaks the spell. 'You have one week, Detective. No noise. No fancy forensics. No case number. Just you. And if this footprint business comes to nothing, it – is – over!'

He looks at Jannie and he hisses, 'Agreed?'

'Agreed,' says Jannie, and he smiles.

'Now fuck off, Detective,' says Mokheti, and Jannie's smile widens.

CHAPTER TWENTY-FIVE

The mini-van taxi that Cheetah takes to Mercy's shebeen is so packed with people that she must hang her arm out of the window to escape the sour odour of the man sitting next to her.

Cheetah doesn't often venture this far from the pig farm. Her world has shrunk to fit its recognisable dimensions and she is grateful for that. She even prefers to buy her rations at the local *spaza* shop rather than ride a taxi to the nearest supermarket. Between that and the offerings from Klein Samuel's vegetable garden, she has enough.

Ouma's death has disrupted the discrete containment of her world, not least because she must answer the question of where her medical care will come from now. Snapping at the heels of that question comes the darker thought: *does it really matter?*

The shrill noise and human clatter of the taxi rank has always alarmed her. It's a volatile place and she is fearful of what it might ask of her. She's seen worse deprivation on her home turf of Lavender Hill, but she was young then and knew she would rise up out of its sandy wind-blown streets. She doesn't think that any more.

If she became symptomatic and lost her job, this is where she would wash up. Into whose arms and under whose protection? What would she be required to give in return? Now that Ouma is gone she is just half a month's wages away from this end. She hurries through the crowd so that no one can reach out and trap her there.

When Klein Samuel brought her to the shebeen the first time she could tell that Mercy took her for a low-rate whore. As the shebeen queen sullenly filled up her glass Cheetah felt like saying under her breath, *It takes one to know one, sister*, but she did not, for Klein Samuel's sake.

Cheetah wished, not for the first time, that she could discard the mark that chapter of her life has left on her, inside and out. Even as it was happening, she was aware that each sordid coupling showed up in her face. But how else was she to earn her crust of bread after Cassiem's death had forced her to flee from the streets of her childhood home?

She had to go far because she knew that the small boy in the big hat who had felled him was a member of the gang that would now consolidate its hold on his territory by conquering all that had been his. Cheetah knew that exorcism would leave her dead, or wishing she were, so she fled to Hillbrow, Johannesburg's sin-city. She would probably still be there had the flesh not begun to melt off her bones. Her pimp was not a bad man but he said she wasn't sexy any more.

Cheetah fled north to the pig farm and there she found Klein Samuel. To those who judged her now she wanted to say, *If you can't see who I really am, then fuck you!* But the other half of her whispered, *Love me, ag please, and if you can't, then at least treat me well.*

She shrank her life into the few acres of the pig farm where she was known and left alone. She and her paramour together made a life they could fit inside without attracting the attention of the flippant or the cruel.

Mercy's shebeen is open for business despite the early hour. When Cheetah enters the small front room where Mercy serves her clientele, she sees that it is empty apart from one solitary client in the corner with his back to her.

She is prepared for Mercy's disdain and so it comes as a surprise when the shebeen owner steps forward with her hand outstretched at the sight of her in the doorway. Then, as if an invisible thread connects her to the man in the corner, she stops short of taking Cheetah's hand and says, 'You here to drink?'

Cheetah shakes her head.

Mercy asks, 'What then?'

'You remember me?'

Mercy nods, slight.

'I'm looking for Klein Samuel,' Cheetah says.

Mercy glances at the man in the corner. Though his back remains turned to them, he pays the deepest attention to their conversation. The angle of his body suggests a looming bulk over Mercy's small child who plays on the floor at his feet.

Mercy looks at Cheetah and shakes her head.

Cheetah understands where the power in the room lies; she has an instinct for such things. She can see that Mercy is afraid.

'Please,' says Cheetah quietly.

'He was here on Sunday. He bought a bottle and then he left,' she says, and shrugs.

Cheetah can see that this is all Mercy can give her. She watches her walk over to the child on the floor and lift him, in a great swinging motion, onto her back. The child clings on, somewhat startled to find himself plucked from his solitary game. Mercy walks into the back of the house and pulls the door closed behind her.

Her sudden absence leaves Cheetah and the man in an awkward intimacy. She can see the wings of his shoulder blades and the thick flesh around his waist. She can feel his stillness and wonders idly if she should ask him if *he* knows where Klein Samuel has gone?

Before she can do that the man turns to face her. She can see his barefaced curiosity as he sums her up, as if he knows something about her that she does not know herself.

It doesn't take long. He leans back into the chair and his gaze is now the familiar *I know what you are*. He holds her there with his disdain and then hisses, 'Fugoff,' and turns back to his beer.

It would not have been more malevolent if he'd spat in her face.

She stumbles out.

The idea of getting into a taxi with its squash of human smells and the sticky heat of a stranger's skin against hers appals her, so Cheetah turns in the direction of the pig farm and begins to walk.

She doesn't see the children playing in the dust outside their shacks or the cars speeding by. It is hard enough, just then, to put one foot down and lift the other up.

She longs to lie on the green grass by the water tank with Ouma and tell her that Klein Samuel has vanished into thin air. She would even endure the *klapwoorde* one more time just to know the old lady was there to catch her when she stumbled. It takes her by surprise, this need. She knew Ouma was there to keep her alive but she did not also grasp her reliance on the old lady's custodial care.

If Cheetah had known Mokheti, she would have noticed him driving by, hunched over his steering wheel, but he passes unnoticed, and she walks towards the pig farm, moored as it is to the base of the distant blue mountain.

All the shoes that Jannie and Anriette photograph as they move from dwelling to dwelling at the pig farm would make a shoe mountain if you piled them one on top of the other and each pair would have a different story to tell.

Jannie had not expected this degree of collaboration from Anriette but when he emerged from the encounter with Mokheti at the Gathering Place she was waiting for him.

'I have a day off tomorrow . . .' she had said.

Jannie's promise to Mokheti that he would work alone with no case number and no fuss was forefront in his mind.

But Anriette kept going. '. . . and I can come along and take photos of people's shoes, as a favour, to my friend . . .'

Jannie had listened.

'. . . in my spare time.'

Jannie groaned and put his head in his hands. 'Headache.'

'What?' she said.

'Head. Ache,' he repeated and pointed at his temples.

Jannie may have broken the mould by becoming the only gay detective in the Brits police district but he did it by playing by the rules. By being more virtuous than anyone else. Anriette's plan swept through his operational rulebook like a dervish.

She prodded him sharply in the ribs. 'Well?'

'*Jislaaik!*' he snapped. There were days when Anriette's obsessive nature drove his nerves into a jangle. 'Okay! Yes. Let me just think.' And then, a moment later, he remembered himself and what she had done for him and he said, 'Sorry, Tannie.'

Anriette doesn't want to know the stories that come with each shoe because then she'll have to carry each one to her mountain hut and cast it out into the clean air, but when the time comes she can't help it. Both she and Jannie see how the workers on the pig farm and their pinched employers live.

'You want to take a photo of the underneath of my shoes?' Dumisane, the foreman at the feeding sheds, asks in some bewilderment. When Jannie nods, he opens the suitcase stored under his bed and holds up two pairs and asks, 'Which one do you like?'

'Both of them.'

'And the boots?'

Jannie notices that Dumisane has hung a blanket from the bunk above to give him some privacy. It is a small room for so many grown men. It strikes Jannie, even after this brief exposure, that there are some who will live their whole lives and will die here. And then there are others who will move on to better things. Dumisane is one of those.

As they work, others gather, curious at these strange goings on. In this way the thirty or so souls who work and sleep in this overcrowded world and whose rest is spent either with God in the Zion Christian Church meetings that take place under the wide-boughed trees on the mountain, or with the devil in the shebeens Klein Samuel frequents, offer up their footwear.

Jokes are made about which shoes may carry disease, which ones smell, which might have scorpions hiding in their toes and which might play a key role in a seduction.

There are no children on the pig farm. This farmer doesn't allow it and so the workers send their progeny home to be taken care of by relatives. Strange what that absence does to the atmosphere of a place: no playful shrieks or wails of childish conflict.

There are dogs. While those on Ouma's farm are companions to the frail humans who inhabit it, these are fighting dogs. When the baboons come down off the mountain to raid Groot Samuel's orchard, the dogs from the pig farm gather at the fence and howl and snarl in a frenzy for the full length of the primate feast.

They snap at people too. When a family member of one of the workers comes to visit, they must stand at the fence and call for an escort to the buildings or the dogs will bring them down.

That's why Delilah gets as far as the boundary and has to shout out, 'Jannie!'

Her cry whips the dogs into a frenzy, as does the cowering presence of the small white canine under her arm. 'Hey! Jannie,' she calls again.

Jannie finds her waiting at the low end of the fence. He can see she expects him to help her over and escort her to the site of the investigation and who can blame her?

But the truth is he can't allow it. He is already stretching the rules by having Anriette with him. He can hear Mokheti say, *You had a sixteen-year-old civilian do what? Shit, Jannie, and I took a chance on you.*

'She was my grandmother, Jannie, remember that,' says the girl when he tells her she must go home.

'This is an investigation now, Delilah. You can't be part of that. I'm sorry.'

As he turns to walk back to the compound he hears her say, '*Moffie.*' He turns back to see her eyes bright with fury and disappointment. 'Bloody stupid *moffie.*'

He has heard that phrase so many times that more often than not it simply slides off his carapace, but not this time.

It feels to Delilah as if someone has drawn a stick figure of her stupid, trusting self on a frosted windowpane and then watched the sun melt the ice away, and her with it. Is there not a single soul in the adult world who can be trusted?

Delilah runs away from Jannie along the fence and then under the archway that leads to Ouma's surgery. She pushes on the handle of the door, but it does not open. She pushes harder, thumps it with her hip, and the door falls open with a clatter. She gasps.

The *rinkhals* in the corner of the room pays no heed to the stumbling human who has just entered his lair.

Rinkhals. Delilah can feel the rhythm of the word fold over her tongue but she can't move. She should know what to do. God knows Ouma told her enough times. Now she can remember none of it.

The snake is in an endgame with a large frog and Delilah is not part of it. It lashes out and the frog hops back pitifully.

Delilah watches as the snake slowly, fraction by fraction, spreads its mouth round the frog. It takes a long time.

Delilah has seen this kind of inevitability before. It comes to her then that it is the misery of the adult world slowly sucking her in, her and Martinus and Jannie and her mother and her uncle and Gogo and the cows and the baboons and the jackals and all the living things in the valley. There is a sound behind her but Delilah does not respond.

Groot Samuel stands in the yard and calls out quietly, 'Delilah?'

She does not reply for fear of attracting the snake's attention but the sound of her uncle's voice reminds her of his constancy. She wonders if he could be a more reliable adult presence in her life than Jannie has turned out to be. It is not so much a conscious question as a Darwinian instinct, still forming itself.

'*Skattie* . . .?' he says.

Did she hear correctly? His use of the endearment, thus far exclusively used by her mother, startles Delilah into speech. 'What did you call me, Oom?'

'When?'

'Just now.'

He would normally walk away from such a question but there is something unsettling about her stillness in the doorway.

He says it again, awkward. '*Skattie.*'

Delilah smiles.

Groot Samuel waits for more and then he asks, 'You okay?'

'There's a big one in here, Oom. I think it lives under the desk.'

She steps aside to reveal the snake.

Before she has even taken a breath, Groot Samuel has grabbed a spade and chopped the snake in two, three, four. One of the parts contains the frog lump.

He looks at his niece. She blinks. Groot Samuel says, 'You know how it is.'

She nods. 'For every one you see there are thirty you don't.'

It would be okay with her if he chopped every last snake into pieces, as long as he remained steadfast and true.

CHAPTER TWENTY-SIX

Mokheti doesn't have time for this. God knows he's never been busier, but when his wife phones in the middle of a hectic day she will say no more than, 'Come home.'

When he asks why, with some irritation, she simply says again, 'Come home, Mokheti.'

She has never done this before, not in the thirty years of their marriage, so he gets into his car. As he drives he wonders whether she has reached the end of the road and is calling for a divorce. It would be unlike her to ask for such a thing and particularly in this way. She has long accepted her low place on the totem pole of his priorities. She knows that, at least in part, he married her out of duty. After all, she waited for him the full eight years of his term on Robben Island; transformative years, during which he earned two degrees and a place in the liberation struggle, and she worked as a domestic worker to make their collective ends meet.

She would have liked a warm and loving marriage but she is a practical woman. Mokheti has been a good provider and enabled her to raise their children with sufficient care. He never beat her; he didn't drink away his pay cheque every month. She has things to be grateful for.

The unexpected arrival of the Commissioner of Police in her living room that morning unnerves her greatly. It reminds her how opaque her husband's world is to her and how inept she is at reading its signs. She has no idea whether the great man brings tidings of good or ill.

The commissioner doesn't get up when Mokheti enters the room. Neither would Mokheti expect him to. A shared profession may bind the two men but they were also fellow prisoners for two years of Mokheti's eight-year prison sentence. They saw one another at their weakest and it gives them shared power over one another. Mokheti closes the door. He can't help but notice the commissioner's fine footwear: creamy, camel-coloured leather, buffed, and long in the toe. The shoes contrast unfavourably with Mokheti's middle-aged Hush Puppies.

The commissioner says, 'I am here about Detective Warrant Officers Bezuidenhout and Ntombela.'

Mokheti waits. He knows to do at least that much. It takes a long time.

'You will not ask them where they have been. If any charges are laid against them, they will fall foul of your overworked department, go missing, burn in a fire, whatever. You read me?'

Mokheti is silent a moment. 'Will there be charges laid against them?'

'For what they did?' says the commissioner. 'Probably. And if they go to court they will bring me down. And you, too, comrade.'

He uses the word from their struggle days to unite them, comrades in arms against the apartheid regime. Comrades now, in what?

Mokheti waits. He can tell there is more coming.

'How is Bontle?' asks the commissioner after a deep silence.

Oh, so that's it. Mokheti reels backwards onto the heels of his feet. *Bontle*, his last born, his pride and joy. Working now in the Police Service, innovative work as Mokheti understands it, on efforts to counteract the establishment of global organized crime syndicates in their young country.

'She is fine,' he says.

The commissioner nods. 'Good.' He gets slowly to his feet. 'That is very good.'

Mokheti watches him extend his hand and say, 'Give her my greetings.'

He looks down on the open-palmed hand held out to him and he tells his body to respond but it doesn't.

The commissioner looks at him, then turns and is gone.

Mokheti sinks into his chair. So it has come to this. *Just look.* Between him and *the right thing to do* is his shining child. He has been waiting a long time for this moment and now it is here.

If you had asked Anriette if she expected to find a pair of sling-back Christian Diors under a bed at the pig farm she would have laughed at you. But that is what happens. She sees it as one of the perks of the job – these pot-of-gold revelations about who someone is.

Of course Cheetah has wellington boots too, to slop out the pigs, and a pair of orange slip-slops for walking to the toilet and back, but the evening shoes have pride of place under her bed, wrapped in a nest of newspaper. She has even stuffed the toes with tin foil to keep the shape.

Anriette would never admit this to anyone but she loves shoes and so she knows that this pair is something special. She picks them up with due respect and reads the label again. *Dior!*

She looks at Cheetah's lovely face, now bearing signs of wear, and would like to ask her to explain this mystery.

Cheetah knows that look. Would Anriette believe her if she told her she once had three pairs just as good? And that the ones she now holds in her hands were her wedding shoes?

Cheetah knows that when you say the word *wedding* people think of something joyous but hers was not like that. Cassiem proposed the very day he was released from prison, his face full of slopes and hollows Cheetah had not noticed before, a hard face. It all happened as if he had a train to catch.

In the afternoon he took her to Cavendish, the Claremont shopping centre, to buy her a dress and a pair of shoes. Then they went to Muizenberg beach. It was as if he needed to remind himself of the first time he had seen Cheetah surf and knew she was the one for him.

Cheetah's father had taught her to swim in the tidal pool at St James. Who knows why he did that and not the other things fathers do. She quickly graduated to the waves on Muizenberg beach. She was there so often that one of the regulars lent her his surfboard. It didn't take her long to learn how to stay upright. The first time she rode a wave was the best moment of her short life. Her first wolf whistle came not long after and with it came trouble. No girl that good-looking stood a chance without a protector. It was another one of those things, like knife fights, or bare feet. The boys around Gracie Street never asked before taking what they wanted.

She chose Cassiem, with his walk that was really a glide, to be her protector. Or maybe it was he who chose her? Not even Cheetah thought he would make her his wife and especially not on that rainy day in July when the wind tore across the Flats and the smell of prison still lingered on his skin.

A scattering of his relations, her neighbour Tannie Hendricks, and members of his gang were the only guests at their wedding.

In one of the more bizarre twists, she was made to celebrate with Tannie Hendricks and two other women in a separate room from her betrothed, as is the way of things in a Muslim house. As Cassiem said, at least it was observant.

Beautiful shoes. Worn only once. There is a gentle knock on the door and Jannie enters Cheetah's room.

'You hear anything, Jannie?' she asks.

Jannie shakes his head. He has had two junior police officers phoning around to local hospitals to try to locate Klein Samuel but they've yielded no results.

Cheetah gnaws at her already bitten nail. 'It's been too long.'

Jannie takes his phone out of his pocket and steps outside to make the call. Who knows how seriously the junior police officers have been taking this search? There is often a sense of pointlessness about a case like this: an illegal immigrant, who is also an alcoholic, goes missing – does anyone care?

Cheetah watches Jannie through the open door. She's always wondered about the way her doorway frames the world beyond. It seems to her to make a kind of passage, quite removed from the rest of the world around it, a long, narrow slice of altered reality. Sometimes she lies on her bed, looks out and dreams of where she could get to if she just walked down the long narrow corridor made of trees and birds flying and, sometimes, silver rain.

But today it contains Jannie and his phone and she can see by the way he hunches over that he is hearing bad news. Maybe it means nothing. Policemen get bad news all the time. Then she sees him turn and glance at her, his face robbed of the playfulness he typically wears to ameliorate the world's hard knocks.

Jannie's stillness pulls her to her feet and sends her out onto the dust too. In a sudden and bewildering show of solace Jannie takes her in his arms. He just holds her and they rock. She will not ask. He will not say.

Finally Jannie manages, 'It's Klein Samuel, Cheetah.'

From the stoep of Ouma's house, Delilah, only just emerged and still in her pyjamas, sees the flurry outside Cheetah's hut. She sees Cheetah run barefoot towards Jannie's truck. She sees Jannie rouse Groot Samuel from his crouched position by the new irrigation ditch. She sees them run too.

She wants to be part of that gathered community. She wants to *know*.

The girl runs down onto the driveway below the house and calls out above the rumbling engine, 'Jannie!'

She shouts louder still, 'Wait!' and she runs a little further. 'Oom Samuel!'

Her uncle turns towards the sound of her voice but he can't seem to locate its source. He pauses only briefly and then turns and runs again. She calls again, louder now, but neither hears her as they roar up the steep slope and away.

CHAPTER TWENTY-SEVEN

Cheetah's bare, wide feet on the linoleum floor of the hospital have a kind of shocking nakedness to them. She wonders if she would have worn her wellington boots or her wedding shoes to the hospital had she had time to grab them before she ran.

She can see that the nurses and the patients who see her pass in this state of undress think her feral. The corridors leading to the wards are long and very public. She wishes she'd been wearing shoes that said she was *a somebody*.

Just as Groot Samuel wishes he could scream like Cheetah does when she sees Klein Samuel because God knows, he wants to.

The truth is Cheetah wails not for Klein Samuel but for herself. She can see that her ragged saviour has fallen: feet and legs and arms plastered at his sides, stiff wooden doll-like. And his eyes look at her. Eyes that say, *You are mine. I'm so pleased you have come*, yet are so transformed it is unclear whether he lives in her realm or the one hereafter.

Groot Samuel approaches the bed and he sits quietly beside it. He can see Klein Samuel is frightened by Cheetah's ruckus.

The farmhand looks at Groot Samuel and two teardrops fall like small stones out of his eyes and run down his cheeks, just two.

Groot Samuel says very quietly, 'The broad beans that you planted . . .' He stops, the thought that maybe, just maybe, Klein Samuel might die, makes it impossible for him to speak for a moment. '. . . are so thick on the vine now you can't even see the fence.'

Klein Samuel lets the sentence sink like grains of salt through his fear and calm it.

Klein Samuel gestures him closer and as Groot Samuel leans in he whispers, 'Gundwane?'

'Fat like a drum, and shiny.'

Klein Samuel smiles. He has lost a tooth on the right side of his mouth. He waits for more.

'Delilah found the big rinkhals in the surgery. He was slow because he had just eaten a frog. That makes how many this year?'

Klein Samuel opens his hands slowly, five fingers on one hand three on the other.

'Eight.'

Klein Samuel nods. His friend's blue eyes tether him to the earth. He wants to tell Groot Samuel what they did to him but his mouth doesn't respond to his instruction to open and form words.

If only Ouma had been alive to know that he mattered even if the man in the red T-shirt did not. She would have stopped him and his henchman from dragging him to their car. Stopped them man from pulling his belt off his waist and wrapping it round Klein Samuel's wrists, then, nonchalantly, as if he had done this many times before, fastening the belt round the chassis of the car.

Klein Samuel could make out Mercy, the shebeen queen, in the crowd of onlookers beyond. He saw her cover her mouth with her hand in horror at what she saw. He heard the doors to the cab slam closed and he wondered why they had forgotten him outside.

As they pulled off, Klein Samuel saw a diminutive Asian woman in a white pharmacist's coat begin to run after the car, screaming. A young child in the crowd hid his head under his mother's apron.

Klein Samuel heard the engine roar and then his legs were flying through the air as if weightless. His whole body lifted off to follow but the belt around his wrists brought him back to earth. Then up again, then sideways, then all the way round so he was facing the road and his arms had ripped out of their sockets. Then back round and he saw his shoes fly off one by one and he wanted to cry because they were his best shoes.

The next time Klein Samuel hit the road, he wondered if he was already dead and flying onward to the arms of his blood mother who loved him first and waited in the shadows for their reunion.

And just before he lost consciousness, Klein Samuel thought of Cheetah, of her soft, thick lips and the brown tender skin between her breasts.

'Who did this to him?' says Cheetah to Jannie when she has stopped screaming.

'I don't know,' the detective replies.

She isn't able to hold back the rush of *What about me? What about me now?* that fills her from head to toe.

Jannie sees her open her mouth to cry out, and he would like to add his voice to hers. He and Klein Samuel have never been friends. The farmhand inherited some of Groot Samuel's animosity towards the *moffie* detective, as well as carrying a good dose of his own prejudice, so they never exchanged more than a few words of greeting. Still, he remembers, almost word for word, the story of

Klein Samuel's incarceration in Weskoppies Psychiatric Hospital. The farmhand's suffering now leaves Jannie bereft. As Gogo would say, *Eish! Did they not know he is a human?*

A small sound comes from Klein Samuel's mouth. He pats the bed as if to say to Cheetah, *Come sit.*

Cheetah is uncertain.

Klein Samuel pats the bed again, more urgently. Finally Cheetah sits. He feels for her hand. When their fingers are clasped he closes his eyes and begins to cry quietly.

Dark, dark night; Groot Samuel sits on his stoep and smokes. The tip of his cigarette glows red as he pulls on it. In the lighted house beyond there is no movement but Ilse calls his name. 'Samuel.'

He does not move.

She calls again. 'Samuel?'

And then she is quiet.

Groot Samuel's inner world was always far too finely wrought to manage brutality. Even though some form of it or another filled his every day as young soldier he never got any better at it. *Bosbefok.* Fucked-by-the-bush. The phrase came to define the human wreckage in the ranks of the apartheid army. It was always Jannie's contention that Groot Samuel was *bosbefok* when he first crawled out of his two years in the army. No sensitive person would not be so after that horror.

He was not alone in this but those white colleagues who fared better were the ones who believed they were fighting something of a holy war. So the women, the children, the drunks, the pious, the innocent were all fair game.

Samuel was only eighteen years old on his first day of active service. He stood in the doorway of Ouma's surgery with his hand balled into a fist.

Ouma asked him what he was holding. Groot Samuel looked at his mother and said, 'It is hair.'

'Whose hair?'

Groot Samuel shook his head rather than tell her that it was the hair from the head of a twelve-year-old boy.

Ouma got up from her desk and walked slowly towards him. Her eyes traced the grey shadows of feeling in her son's face.

She pulled open his fingers and saw a thick wad of curly black hair lying in the white palm of his hand. Some roots still burdened with the skin and blood of the boy's scalp.

'They were all children,' whispered Groot Samuel and then he looked at his mother. He had been forced to drag the boy for twenty metres before throwing him into the police van full to bursting with others like him.

Ouma's grave face darkened further and she whispered, '*Leef hy nog?*' Is the child still alive?

Groot Samuel let his arms fall against his sides. He didn't know.

Ouma held out her hand and Groot Samuel passed the hair from his to hers. Then he sat on the floor. When his mother tried to walk away Groot Samuel wrapped his arms round her legs.

Grief rose in him like lava and all he could do was hold on so as not to be swept away. That's when she knelt down and took him in her arms and whispered, 'Stay with me.' It was the love he had longed for and which she reserved for the ruined.

He held on so tight that his eyeballs rolled back into his head with the effort. As they spun skywards Groot Samuel saw Jannie's much younger face in the doorway of his mother's surgery.

Watching him.

Blerrie moffie.

Along with everyone else and in spite of his agnosticism, Groot Samuel thanked God the day the old regime came to an end. Now he could live his life in the belief that such cruelties, too, had passed.

As he sits on his stoep looking out at the pristine night, he knows that the mother lode of brutality he thought dead has spawned a new generation of who-knows-what savagery. Klein Samuel's suffering proves it so. What is less clear to him is how to live in such a world.

Cheetah sits on her bucket in the dust outside her shack. She sips her tea. The *nagapies* rattle up in the trees on their way to the orchard. The owl makes its first liquid call of the night to wake its young. Cheetah has come to think of it as a kind companion. Now, as if her senses have been reformed somehow by events, she hears threat in the call that last night was so melodious.

She will not see Klein Samuel in her mind's eye. She will not think of him. She cannot risk it.

'Listen!' He had beckoned to her before she had left to come home that evening.

She had leant down so that her ear was closer to his mouth. 'There is a doctor.'

'What?' she said.

'For you, now that Ouma is gone.'

Cheetah looked at him a moment.

'Here, in the hospital,' he said and his eyes had lit up.

Cheetah hung her head in shame.

Even under duress, he was thinking of her.

Now, sitting on her bucket in the gathering night, she begins to weep quietly. She weeps at Klein Samuel's kindness but also because she wishes she could love him the way he deserves to be loved.

But it is too late for that. Cheetah can see he is now too diminished to be her protector. Nothing she can do about that. She knows what happens if you stick with a goner. You become one yourself.

The tread of feet on the gravel path alerts her to the presence of someone nearby. She looks up. A fellow farm worker, still in church clothes, hurries past, hand raised in perfunctory greeting. Perhaps she has not yet heard what has befallen Klein Samuel? Surely she would stop if she had? Cheetah barely responds.

She wipes the bottom of her feet with a *lappie* so as not to drag dirt into the shack. The flash of movement on the walkway a little distance away catches her attention. It comes to her as something of a surprise that she has been waiting for it. Hoping.

She gets up to see better.

It is Dumisane. She would know those broad shoulders anywhere. If she was a believer she would have given thanks under her breath but instead she straightens the scarf on her head, puts her teacup in the dust at her feet, and follows him.

If he is aware of her he makes no sign. He reaches the fence that leads onto Ouma's farm and ducks under it expertly. The ease with which he does it suggests he does this frequently. She follows him to the dam and watches as he slips off his clothes and wades into the water.

The moon is just high enough to light the gentle ripples of his silent swim. He swims gracefully, in an entirely unorthodox way. Maybe his father taught him as hers had done?

He swims from one end to another and then back again. He pulls himself onto the island and sits there, still. Somehow she knows he is dreaming of the sea.

How she wishes she could follow him into that watery solace.

PART SIX

Chapter Twenty-eight

If Anriette's husband, Francis, had been a suspicious man he would have spent many a night wondering if his wife had a lover. He knows her too well for that, so he goes to bed and expects that she will join him at some point in the night or, even more likely, at the end of the following working day.

Every morning he watches her go off to her day job as analyst in the biology section of the forensic science laboratory in Arcadia. She comes home worn from her labours, eats something and then returns to do her clandestine work for Jannie and his footprints at night. It's making her ragged. Just this morning when he asked her if she had seen his tennis shorts, she swallowed a mouthful of homemade honey muesli and snapped, 'Ja, well, blow me down . . . do I look like a maid to you, Francis?' And left the table.

Never in twenty-five years of marriage had she ever used such a phrase as *blow me down*. She sounded like someone from the Enid Blyton books they had been forced to read as children. And she never called him *Francis*; he was always *liefie* – little love – to her. He'd like to be that again.

The fruit of all this sleeplessness and domestic friction is born in the small hours of the morning when all the world, apart from those engaged in clandestine pursuits, are sleeping. Anriette places a photograph over the spoor she has made from Jannie's mould and gets a perfect match. She sits back in her chair. This feeling, of a puzzle solved and a truth revealed, is what pushes back the rising tide of chaos in Anriette's inner world. It is what she and Jannie share.

She waits for Jannie in the parking lot of the police station early the following morning. She's so sleep deprived that when she leans against the car her eyes fall closed and her head sinks down onto her chest.

It takes Jannie just a few seconds to understand her report and what it portends. Then he kisses her on the head and says, 'Bless you, Anriette le Roux,' and he runs up the steps of the police station.

If he had been outside his body he would have seen that he ran towards Mokheti's office like a cat with a prize mouse to put at the feet of his leader for approval.

He is so caught up in that mission that he doesn't at first notice the young woman who hurries past him and down the passage. Something about her gait catches his eye; he turns to watch her for a moment. Her head is bent and her shoulders pulled up to her ears. He calls out, 'Bontle!' but the young woman does not turn.

It's been years since Jannie saw Mokheti's last born, but when she was a teenager she and her siblings accepted Jannie's occasional presence in their home with grace and generosity. On one occasion when he had been beaten for looking too long at a new recruit of the same gender, they nursed him back to health. It gives them sibling status in Jannie's view.

Yet here she is, hurrying away from his greeting. Jannie walks more slowly the rest of the way to Mokheti's office and knocks on the door.

His boss is sitting at his desk and, unusually, he does not look up when Jannie enters.

Jannie has never seen Mokheti so hollowed out. His boss stretches out his hand for the photos Jannie offers him but he says nothing.

Jannie watches as he lays the prints on the desk, the one taken from the spoor, and the one from the photos gathered at the pig farm.

'His name is Dumisane Mazibuko,' says Jannie. 'He's the new foreman at the pig farm.'

Mokheti hands the photos back to Jannie and says, 'Go do your job.'

Jannie takes them. 'I saw Bontle,' he says.

'That so?'

'She didn't stop when I called her. Maybe she didn't hear me?'

Mokheti gets up out of his chair. He moves like an old man as he dismisses Jannie. 'Thank you, Detective.'

Jannie knows what Bontle's success has meant to Mokheti. He sees that when his policing life offers up human depravity that threatens to tear the joy off him in strips he thinks of her and her chance to thrive. She gives him purpose.

'Boss?' he says. 'What's going on?'

Mokheti looks at Jannie, he closes his office door then remains standing there, grave.

Jannie waits.

Mokheti shakes his head as if he himself can't quite believe what he has heard. 'She came to tell me that I am a selfish man. And that I am throwing her and her chance for a better life into my feeding bowl.'

'Your feeding bowl?'

'She says it has *Mr Right Thing To Do* written on the side.'

Mokheti glances at Jannie, but the young detective can't tell whether he wants him to leave or stay.

'She says that my insistence on it first devoured our family life and now it will eat her too.'

The words are out of Jannie's mouth before he has even thought them. 'They want you to drop the inquiry into Ntombela and Bezuidenhout or they will go for Bontle,' he says quietly.

Mokheti doesn't need to answer the question. He simply says nothing and Jannie knows that he is right.

Jannie kicks himself afterwards but all he can think to say at that moment is, 'I'm so sorry.'

Sorry – the word that made Mokheti think of him as a teenage girl when what he wanted most was to show him his strength.

The older man simply walks back to the desk and sits down.

Jannie bows out of the room so as not to add to his boss's shame by being there. The picture he takes with him of Mokheti crumpled over the big brown desk will stay with him for a long time.

CHAPTER TWENTY-NINE

Gogo's response to bad things has always been to cook. Whenever her son disappeared, or was stabbed, or stabbed someone else, she would cook for an army. The family learnt not to say anything about it because the sudden appearance of lavish quantities of food on the table almost always meant trouble was upon them.

She does not know what happened to Klein Samuel but she does know it was bad. You don't have all that screaming and shouting and cars speeding up the driveway unless it is serious.

When Gogo first came to work for Ouma she could cook only the *pap* and meat traditional to her heritage. In those days Ouma entertained frequently and Gogo's cuisine did not suit the western palates of her employer's urbane dinner guests. So, as was the way in those days, Ouma sent Gogo to *Elsbet Jansen's Cookery School*. There Gogo learnt to make recipes culled from *Huisgenoot* magazine – *bobotie*, tinned tuna pie, fish cakes, Marie-biscuit pudding and, Gogo's own favourite, milk tart. That is what the family have eaten over the ensuing years – whatever the season, whatever the event – though Gogo's *pap* and meat still has pride of place on the family table whenever they have a *braai*.

★

Delilah comes into the kitchen, sees the tuna pie in the oven and fish cakes frying in the pan.

'What's happened?' she says.

'Klein Samuel is in the hospital.'

'Why?' Delilah says, dread filling her up.

Gogo shrugs. 'I know nothing.'

Important comes trotting in behind her and sits at Gogo's feet expectantly. The old lady takes a fish cake, cooling on the paper towel, and offers it to the little dog. Important sniffs it and then delicately accepts the gift. Delilah holds out her hand for one too and says, 'Klein Samuel will prefer *pap* and gravy, Gogo.'

Gogo pauses mid gesture as if she has forgotten who she was cooking for; then in a smooth movement she scoops the *pap*-making pot off the shelf, fills it with water and puts it on the stove.

It is evening by the time Gogo seats herself beside Klein Samuel's bed and pops a ball of *stywepap* into his mouth. Klein Samuel chews with difficulty and swallowing is even harder but he does it to please Gogo. He is sitting up now and although his arms are still in casts this doesn't stop his hands from shaking.

'*Haai*, Klein Samuel. Tst tst!' Gogo says at the sight of his tremor. She has seen him go through withdrawals like this once before and knows the depth of his discomfort.

Klein Samuel beckons her closer. She leans forward and he mutters, 'Just one nip, Gogo, ag *asseblief*.'

Gogo shakes her head, '*Aikona*, Klein Samuel, let there be one good thing to come out of this terrible . . . thing.'

He looks at her, desperate.

'That poison you drink is what put you here, you stupid man,' and she pops another lump of *pap* into his mouth.

Thank goodness she didn't bring the other three dishes she had made for Klein Samuel. The poor man's stomach is like a pea. As much as she would like it to be otherwise, even Gogo can see Klein Samuel has no hunger. He's a wounded bird.

She gets up and walks into the hospital corridor in search of somewhere to rinse the plate clean. She walks past the emergency room, and into the passage leading to the outpatient wards.

She walks past glass-fronted doors full to bursting with the nation's sick and then she sees Cheetah.

Cheetah?

Gogo stops to look.

Apart from Ouma's funeral, Gogo has never seen her dressed so smartly. And she is wearing a pair of very nice shoes too.

Cheetah is in conversation with a young black doctor, who wears a white coat and has a head of lavish braids. Gogo has heard tell that some fancy, educated young girls buy someone else's hair and braid it in with their own. Over her dead body would Gogo walk around with someone else's hair on her head.

The two women talk in earnest. Cheetah holds her arm out for blood to be taken. She laughs. The doctor smiles. Gogo wonders if she made a good joke.

The catering lady moves Gogo out of the doorway so she can get in with her laden trolley. It is only then that Gogo sees the sign above the door, *Ward 17*. In recent years she has heard talk of this place amongst the workers at the pig farm and those mothers in her church who have HIV-positive children. Sometimes, when asked where they are going they answer simply, '17.' It's shorthand, stops people asking any further questions.

Gogo has never been able to reconcile the suffering and loss of life caused by AIDS-related illness with her faith in God. In her annual visits home to Qalabotjha in the Free State she has seen homesteads led by scatterings of almost feral children, their adult carers all taken by this scourge.

In fact she lived with the worry that her son carried the same in his veins. That he was cut down in a knife fight spared her the task of answering the question but she did wonder often what made him so thin.

How could the Almighty stand by and look while his people fell like *mielies* in a hailstorm?

Gogo sighs. She turns once again to Cheetah. Like everyone else, Gogo has heard tales of Cheetah's days in the Cape mixed up with the gangs.

Ouma had always claimed that had she come from better beginnings, Cheetah could have been a doctor, she was that clever.

Gogo used to say, '*Haai*, rubbish, Ouma, she brings trouble with her that one.'

'How do you know that, Gogo?' Ouma would shake her head and say. 'Don't decide somebody's story. The truth is always more surprising than anything you can make up.'

'*Gah!*' Gogo said. 'Ouma, you just look for the good in everybody.'

Gogo remembers how Ouma stood up then and crossed to the kettle to put it on for tea. She stood looking out of the kitchen window and when she spoke it was to nobody but herself. 'I look for their reasons. That's all.'

*

That night Cheetah cooks enough for two. It is the first time she has thought about food in a long time. She picks spinach from Klein Samuel's vegetable patch and cooks it with meat and onion.

When she sees Dumisane pass her doorway on his way to his evening swim, she puts a plate over one of the two bowls to keep it warm.

She waits for him to come back from the dam, then steps into the path and hands him the bowl of food.

He takes it with both hands and bobs low to show his gratitude and respect.

'*Ngiyabonga, sisi.*'

'Ja,' she says, turns to go back into her shack, and then remembers. 'It might need salt.'

CHAPTER THIRTY

A full night of sleep has come and gone but Delilah still does not open her eyes. She can't risk it. Lucky then that she and her small canine companion have a limitless capacity for slumber.

The story of Klein Samuel's ordeal, as told her by Gogo the night before, has settled on her like ash after a veld fire. Whatever further horror the world offers up she, for one, will not be conscious to see it.

On occasion, when she does open her eyes, Delilah looks down on the slumbering Important and wonders if Ouma would find her *medemenslikheid* sufficient today. Then she closes her eyes again.

Sometimes she wakes to find her mother watching her sleep. She doesn't mind her vigil; it goes some way to making up for her prior absence.

Gogo is there too, cleaning the windowpanes; her keeping of order is comforting in a skin-tingling kind of way. If asked to describe it further, Delilah would say it is like being rocked in a huge benign hand to have Gogo near. One time, she finds a tray with food at the foot of her bed and Important with his nose in the milk jug.

She wishes Jannie would come with news of the investigation but knows it is unlikely after she insulted him so.

Towards late afternoon, she wakes again, to find her mother sitting on the end of her bed. Delilah smiles at her but she doesn't smile back. Instead, her mother says, 'You must promise me something, *skattie* . . .'

'What?'

'That you'll get away . . .' her ma says '. . . go to university, do something good . . .'

She doesn't go on but Delilah knows what she would have said next, *Promise me that nothing will happen to diminish you.*

'Martinus?' asks the girl.

Her mother nods. 'Pa says he sleeps all the time when he's not working. He calls the mine "the dark".'

Delilah looks at her mother and she longs to be asleep again. Her waking hours are made ragged by these revelations about those she cares for and is powerless to help.

'That shining boy,' says her mother, and then she looks up and says again, 'Promise me.'

Delilah feels her mother's fear blossom. It catches on her person like a plastic bag snagged on a fence by the wind.

'What about you, Ma?' Delilah snaps in reply.

Her mother looks alarmed. 'What about me?'

Before she can stop herself Delilah says, 'What are you going to promise?'

Aletta blinks.

Delilah lies back on the bed and says, 'Don't ask me to promise you anything if you can't promise me you'll do it too.'

As Jannie approaches the farm he waits for the quickening of his heart rate that normally accompanies the moment of closing in on someone. But he has none of that feeling as he follows directions to the pig sheds where he is told he will find Dumisane. He is aware of many eyes watching him as he walks.

He finds him beside the truck overseeing the loading of the baby pigs into crates for their trip to the abattoir. The creatures scream as if they know that their end has come. Jannie watches Dumisane shuffle them all into the beaten-up truck while their mothers in the sheds wail and the piglets shriek. It spooks him how human they sound. He can see that Dumisane feels it too because he stops for a moment and covers his ears even as he keeps the traffic of piglets and workers moving.

Jannie remembers his lovely face from the day he and Anriette photographed the shoes at the pig farm. He had been struck then by how little Dumisane owned, even less than most, and yet his station was neat, his bed carefully made.

Dumisane shows no fear when Jannie steps forward to shake his hand. Jannie shows him the match of his shoes and the treads. 'Yes, of course they are mine. I go to the dam every night. When there is water.'

'You go to the dam?'

'I go there every night.'

'For what?'

'To swim.'

Jannie looks at the man's wide, handsome face, and finds no malice there.

'You swim in the dam?'

'I swim at night so I don't disturb anyone. I don't mean trouble.'

'Is it nice?' Jannie doesn't know where the question comes from but he finds himself longing for the young man to say how sweet and cool the dam water is. Perhaps he wants to imagine Ouma being held there in a kind embrace.

Dumisane considers the young detective. He can see the shadows around his eyes and senses the density of feeling in his question. 'It is not the sea,' he says and he looks away.

As he must, Jannie goes through the routine of taking a statement from Dumisane but he knows the man has nothing to hide.

He stays longer than he might because he finds the young man so beguiling. How a life as hard as this could be lived by such a promising person gives him a sense of foreboding new to the backpack of alarm he already carries around with him.

Jannie leaves reluctantly. As he turns his truck towards the driveway he notices the world caught somewhere between day and night, golden, yet made solemn by the approach of dark. His headlights capture Cheetah as she steps into the driveway ahead. She has something to say. He has come to half expect these stolen conversations with her on his way in and out. She has become something of a gatekeeper, sensitive to the movement of people on both the pig farm and Ouma's land. He slows down and winds down the window. '*Ja-nee*, Cheetah,' he says.

She does not return his greeting, she merely tells him what he needs to know. 'I've seen him there these past many nights, swimming.'

Jannie looks at her face and wonders if she finds Dumisane as captivating as he does. 'That so?' he says.

'He says he grew up by the sea.'

'Ja, so I hear.'

She steps out of the beam of his headlights and says, 'He's a good swimmer.'

'Thank you, Cheetah,' Jannie calls out of his window but she does not acknowledge him as she slips away into the bush.

Jannie finds himself driving very fast through the gathering dark. Will Mokheti now shut him down as he threatened to do if the footprint lead came to nothing? Doubt about what he will propose they do next, if given the chance, takes up all the free space in the car.

Jannie doesn't doubt that his boss will investigate Ntombela and Bezuidenhout. After all, he is *Mr Right Thing To Do*, but it will cost him his comfort. Life is not often kind to the whistleblowers of this world and pursuing an investigation into the two police officers' wrongdoing will weaken Mokheti's place in the department. It will weaken Jannie too.

The separate question of why Jannie did not save Ouma's life, as she had his, joins the community of regrets he contemplates as he drives. What kind of useless detective is he?

He lifts his two hands off the steering wheel but he doesn't slow down. He'd like to take off and feel bits of him come away as he flies through the air until all of him is gone. In the absence of that outcome, he slams his two fists brick-hard against his ears. The force makes his eyes roll back into his head.

Dumisane's innocence may mark a dead end in their trail but Anriette will have none of it. She hears Jannie out, brews a pot of rooibos tea and, without ceremony, begins to bake a cake.

'A cake?' asks her husband.

'Don't talk to me, Francis,' she says for the second time that day. When she pulls the cake out of the oven she sprinkles icing sugar over its fragrant, nutty surface. Then she packs it into a basket, picks her keys off the entrance hall table and walks out of the house.

'Have you ever seen a freckled nightjar, Jannie?' asks Francis as he stands at the door and watches his wife drive off into the evening.

'I have,' says Jannie, alert.

'There's a family of them nesting in the rocks behind our cabin.'

'That so?'

'Anriette loves them because they can be sitting on the rock right in front of you and you won't see them until one of them moves and then suddenly there they are, five beautiful birds.'

Jannie can feel Francis's alarm.

'She's like that. My Anriette.'

Jannie says, 'She's just tired.'

'She's done enough, Jannie.'

'Enough of what?'

'This case.'

'It's not over yet.'

Francis shakes his head. 'I want my wife back, Jannie. Before she loses the thing most precious to her.'

'The nightjars?' says Jannie; he knows what her retirement to the wild mountains means to her.

'No,' says her husband. He looks at Jannie and he says, 'Her camouflage.'

Anriette doesn't drive to her place of work, but rather follows a well-remembered route into the suburbs of Brits. She pulls up in the driveway of a small house in the heart of town. It is only when faced with its closed curtains and overgrown lawn that she pauses, and understands the full measure of its neglect.

There is no answer when she knocks on the door. She tries again, and then sets off down the side of the building.

She finds the man of the house in the back garden surrounded by a constellation of plastic containers, all sprouting red Barberton daisies. It is this sight that floors Anriette. She knows how much Ouma loved this bloom and she sees the labour that it must have taken for him to produce so many.

'Hello, Pieter,' she says quietly.

He looks at her and sighs. 'You know, you are too well behaved to be a renegade, Anriette.'

'How so?' she asks. Her lips are paper dry.

'My friend at the lab —' he sees her flinch — 'yes, you know, *nothing* happens that I don't know about,' he continues. 'My friend tells me that not only did you do clandestine night work for Jannie, but you signed in and out every time you did it!'

Anriette blushes. 'It's important work, Pieter.'

'Yes, but it is not *your* work,' he says and he sways slightly on his feet. She sees that he's had a little too much to drink.

'You grow these for her, Pieter?' she asks, looking at the riot of potted plants.

'Who else?' he snaps. 'What else?'

Anriette is one of the few people who knew about his long love affair with Ouma. He had told her, early on, when he was certain he and Ouma would marry. He is grateful that she has kept his secret so steadfastly but even more so that she never asked him when the great day would be.

Anriette says, 'I know you miss her.'

Pieter turns on her and he says, 'Enough!'

'Sorry?'

'Let her be, Anriette.'

'We need to know how she died, Pieter.'

'Go home, go home, go home. God knows you are asking for trouble.'

She nods her head. 'I would, except I baked you a hazelnut cake.'

He sits back on his haunches and says, '*Jy het nie.*'

'Ja,' she says.

He shakes his head and mutters, 'Shameless.'

She sits on the stone step and surveys the back yard. 'You need to mow your grass.'

She takes the cake out of the basket and hands it to him. He smells it and says, '*Heerlik.*'

'And you need to give me and Jannie access to Ouma's autopsy report.'

He puts the cake on the step beside him and looks at her. 'Death by drowning. No criminal act suspected.'

'You sure about that?'

'Anriette, hear me well. If you don't let this go, I will have no choice but to tell your boss what you've been doing night after night and it is a firing offence. You understand?'

'She didn't slip, Pieter,' Anriette says.

He shouts then, halfway upright and beside himself, 'You know nothing! *Niks nie.*'

She gets to her feet. 'Pieter . . .'

'Get out!' he bellows, loud enough to send the swifts that nest in the eaves of his roof flapping off into the evening sky.

Before she ducks down the side of the house, Anriette looks back to see the old pathologist crumpled on the stone step, surrounded by Barberton daisies, his head in his hands.

Had Anriette been passing Mokheti's living-room window at that moment she would have seen him in the same position. He has been like this for hours, wracked by indecision. At first, his wife offered him solace in the form of food and drink but he would have neither.

Now, she walks into the room and stands directly in front of him, knees touching his. It has been so long that they had this kind of proximity to one another that he looks up at her in surprise.

She takes his hand and pulls him to his feet. Then she leads him to the bedroom. She unbuttons his shirt and pulls it off his body. He sits on the edge of the bed and she kneels down to remove his shoes and socks and then his trousers. She selects a clean pair of perfectly ironed pyjamas and offers them to him.

She gently guides him to the pillow. When he is under the covers, she pulls her own dress off her thick body. She folds it carefully on the chair in readiness for tomorrow and gets into bed beside him.

Chapter Thirty-one

The table groans with the usual suspects: tinned tuna pie, *bobotie*, and fish cakes. In spite of many years spent cooking these very dishes, Gogo has never mastered how to combine the different elements of a meal so they complement one another.

The family goes with the flow. Some simply ladle it all onto one plate and let the warring parties find a kind of gastric peace but others, like Delilah, take one dish at time. And so the meal takes longer.

Tonight the table is fuller than usual. They have been called together by Groot Samuel for the purpose of reading Ouma's will. Jannie has been included at Ouma's request. He is not surprised. She spoke often of her intention to bequeath him her collection of first edition Elisabeth Eybers books dating back to the beginning of her oeuvre. Jannie was humbled by her generosity and vowed to take good care of them.

Groot Samuel is at the head of the table and Frans at the foot. Aletta and Ilse on one side, Delilah and Jannie on the other.

Dogs from both houses and, of course, Suffering, are spread all over the floor. Gogo negotiates her way around them with some complaint as she comes and goes with the food.

Groot Samuel eats almost nothing. Gogo puts a plate of pureed gem squash with butter and sugar on the place in front of him. He is grateful.

Frans lifts his glass, 'To Ouma.'

Everyone looks at him.

Groot Samuel says, 'Later, Frans.'

'I wish she was here,' says Delilah.

'Her, yes, but not her cooking,' mumbles Groot Samuel. And he giggles, a hiss of relief.

'*Haai*, she couldn't even cook a potato, that one,' says Gogo as she picks the gravy boat off one end of the table and takes it to the other to flavour Groot Samuel's simple fare.

'She couldn't sing either,' says Frans.

'Shame. Not even "Thula Baba",'says Aletta.

Howls of laughter.

Delilah says quietly, 'I liked that song.'

'Not the way she sang it,' says Frans.

'I liked the way she sang it.'

Aletta's voice rings out,

'*Hippe, hippe perdjie*
Bonte, bonte stertjie
Tjoef tjaf val hy af
Tjoef tjaf klim hy op
Hippe, hippe perdjie!'

It is the Afrikaans nursery rhyme that Ouma occasionally sang when they were small children. She would hold them on her lap and, when they least expected it she would open her knees and the children would fall through, screeching.

Tjoef tjaf val hy af
Tjoef tjaf klim hy op
Hippe, hippe perdjie

Now it renders the siblings and Gogo helpless with laughter. The irreverence of it startles Delilah, who asks quietly, 'When are we going home, Ma?'

Aletta sucks in a breath and turns to face her child. 'I don't know.'

'School starts next week,' says the teenager, anxious.

Aletta gets up and begins to fill the water glasses. She avoids all of their eyes.

Delilah watches her mother like a hawk. She knows there is more coming.

Aletta finally glances at Delilah's waiting face and says, 'There's nothing to go back to now, *skattie*.'

Jannie knows he should not be witnessing this. That this is the province of those bound by blood.

'What?' says Delilah.

Aletta fills Groot Samuel's glass right to the brim, then sets down the jug. 'The landlord took back the bakery.' She looks directly at her daughter again and says quietly, 'I'm sorry.'

The child blinks at her mother as this new and devastating fact makes its way through her body. *What will she be without her crumbling house, the river, the reeds, and the flash floods . . .*

She watches her mother sit, then look up at Groot Samuel and Gogo and say, 'Can we stay in Ouma's house until we find work up here, *boet*?'

. . . the swimming hole in the river that Martinus-the-brave threw himself into from the overhanging tree branch, the stoep from which she watched the world go by . . .

The words tumble out of Delilah's mouth much too loud, 'What about Martinus? And Pa?'

Aletta snaps, 'Them, too, Delilah. Of course they would come too.'

There is silence. All eyes turn to look at Groot Samuel. He says, 'You want the whole family to move here?'

Aletta nods.

Delilah looks at her mother. 'What about the Nanjis?'

'What about them, Delilah?'

'What about the Nanjis, Ma?'

Aletta shouts, 'What? What about them?'

What comes out of Delilah's mouth is, 'They had a gold sofa!' The girl looks at her mother's anxious face, then she leans forward. 'I wanted to sit on it one day.'

Aletta takes a deep breath and says, 'They've gone, Delilah, just like everyone else. There's just us left now.'

Delilah blinks at her mother. 'They've gone?'

'They left their gold sofa behind on the pavement. I thought about pulling it into the living room for you but it didn't look as good up close as it did through the window so I let the rubbish collectors take it away.'

Frans closes his eyes and Gogo can see he finds his sister's despair gratifying. *Nothing came of her.*

Aletta speaks to reassure herself as much as any of them. 'Tertius will try to get a job at a big bakery, or at a school. I can teach music.'

Delilah turns away from her mother and says quietly, 'The rubbish collectors took it . . .'

'Delilah, please.'

'Tertius?' says Frans.

'My husband.'

'Ah. The baker.' *Nothing came of him either.*

She repeats the words. 'My husband, Tertius.'

'Ah yes,' says Frans.

Delilah sees the colour rising in her mother's cheeks.

Groot Samuel looks at his sister and says, 'This is your home, Aletta. You, and your family.'

She looks up at him. '*Dankie.*' Relief washes over her face.

Gogo reaches for Aletta's hand and holds it. Without thinking, Delilah reaches for Jannie's; he receives it gratefully. *Of course he should be here.*

Frans sits up abruptly. 'You can't make it work here, Samuel. It will be the same story as Aletta's bakery in fucking Pilalo.'

'The bakery is in Pongola.'

He hisses at her, ugly, 'You mean *was*, my sister. *Was.*'

'We'll make a plan,' says Groot Samuel quietly.

Frans looks into his brother's steady blue eyes and says, 'Ouma made the plan. Without the income from the surgery you'd have lost this place long ago.'

Gogo says under her breath, 'Slowly now, Frans.'

He turns to look at the old woman. He does not need to tell her he is serious – she can smell it on his skin. She always has been able to tell when he was bluffing and when he was about to cause harm.

Ilse, silent until now, surprises everyone with her quiet vehemence. 'It wasn't Ouma. She long ago forgot about money and what it meant.' She looks at them without rancour. 'You would have known that if you'd come to visit.'

Aletta looks away.

'It was him.' Ilse looks at her husband. 'He worked from before the sun came up to long past dark. *Dis hy wie die land winsgewende gemaak het.*'

'She speaks the truth,' says Gogo.

Ilse looks at her hands and says, 'Samuel made this land profitable.'

Groot Samuel looks at his wife and his gaze shows his gratitude to her for speaking up on his behalf even though he wouldn't be able to say it.

Frans takes a sip of water. 'Well, it's my home too, *julle*,' he says, 'and I want to sell it.'

Jannie feels the skin on the back of his neck prickle.

'There are four of us now, Frans,' mumbles Groot Samuel under his breath, 'and I doubt any one of us will have the money to buy your share.'

'Four?'

'Us three, Gogo is the fourth.'

Frans looks at Groot Samuel. The sudden slackness of his face reveals his shock.

Gogo looks from one face to another. She is bewildered by what they are saying and why they have mentioned her name.

'When did that happen?' asks Frans.

Groot Samuel shrugs.

'When the fuck did that happen?' Frans asks so his voice hits the back wall and bounces back to wash over them a second time. 'When? *When?*'

Groot Samuel shouts back, 'I don't know!'

He throws a document across the table. It knocks over a water glass in its path. Delilah raises a hand to stop Gogo reaching for a rag and she soaks the water up with paper serviettes.

Frans picks up the document and reads. The whole room falls silent.

Gogo watches Frans struggle to understand the words, his brow furrowed. When he reaches the end he closes it and looks up at them all. It is the hurt on his face that makes the moment so shocking. Not a single one of them knows what to say or what to do.

'She even saw to Aletta's young ones,' says Frans, more to himself than to them.

Aletta looks at Groot Samuel and says, 'What?'

'She left some money, sissie, for Delilah and Martinus to go to university.'

Aletta and Delilah exchange a look. After a fleeting moment of relief and wonder, the young girl sees shame rise up in her mother's eyes. Aletta would, from this moment, be compelled to honour her imperfect mother for fulfilling a duty to her children that she herself had failed to do.

Delilah smiles at her mother. *Never mind that*, her look seems to say; be grateful that our doctor/philosopher can come up from 'the dark' underground. Delilah holds her mother's gaze until the shadow passes and she is able to smile back.

'She left nothing *just for me*,' says Frans to himself. The truth is he has dreamed all these years that his mother would one day realize the error of her parental ways and make amends. This would be the time. She would take this chance to make *him* the chosen one.

And she did not.

CHAPTER THIRTY-TWO

As her final task of the night, Gogo folds down the bed in Ouma's room where Aletta sleeps. She does this every night and always has done.

She's there when Frans comes into the bedroom. Ouma's watch lies on the bedside table where Delilah laid it down. Frans scoops it up and slips it into his pocket. Gogo can see that he does this without thinking; it is an automatic act, and so thoughtlessly predatory that even he would be shocked by its callousness if he could see it.

He opens the wardrobe. Gogo sees that his image in the mirror that hangs on the inside door could as well be reflecting his child-self: the matted hair, the bites and scratches on his skin, the dirty and broken nails – but more than all of that she can see his continuing need.

Gogo sits on the bed. She did her best with him when he was a child but, unlike the other two, Frans could never accept her as proxy for his absent mother.

The contents of the wardrobe are so Spartan that Frans pauses a moment and then kneels down to sort through the collection of broken shoes that lie on the bottom. There isn't a single pristine pair. Gogo sees him falter. Nothing of value here.

'She didn't care any more, child. She didn't mind if the rain seeped through the soles of her shoes. Or what she wore to keep warm,' says Gogo softly.

When they lived in the grand house in Pretoria Ouma was a dresser; she turned heads. The move to the farm meant she stopped shopping for clothes. 'Who is going to see me here?' she asked. She dressed warm if it was cold and light if it was hot.

'But where are her things?' Frans asks.

Gogo shakes her head. 'She gave them all away.'

She remembers the day Ouma closed her eyes and said, 'I feel it here, behind my eyes, Gogo,' and when she opened them again she spread her arms out to encompass the whole valley. 'Too much to carry.'

Gogo saw then that she was lightening her load for her next journey. There was no logic in how she went about it. She gave things away even if they didn't belong to her. Each casting off rendered her a little freer.

'She was getting ready for the end, child,' says Gogo.

'What about those she left behind?' he says. 'Did she not think about what we needed?'

Gogo shakes her head and she says, 'Towards the end I think maybe she forgot.'

'Yes.'

'That we were beautiful.'

'She never thought it in the first place.'

'What?'

'That I was beautiful.'

Gogo saw that he spoke the truth.

★

Frans was never much part of Ouma's life after he left home except when he needed cash. Ouma would see his silver car come sailing down the long driveway and she would call out to Gogo, 'He's coming, Gogo,' and Gogo would take her hand and remind her, 'Not a penny, Ouma.'

The old lady would nod and grit her teeth, for her firstborn had already talked her into handing over a portion of her dwindling resources. Sometimes, when she looked at her bank statements and she saw a cheque in his name, she whimpered because she didn't remember giving it to him.

'Stay near me, Gogo,' she would say. 'Please.'

'It is hot for June,' Ouma said for want of something better as Frans sat in the garden chair and she weeded the lawn.

'It's hot when it should be cold, and dry when it should be wet,' he said.

'Ja,' Ouma sighed. Her fingers were busy as she plucked the invader shoots out of her Kikuyu lawn. She knew what was coming and she was fearful of it.

Gogo hung the sheets on the nearby washing line so as to be close.

'I swear this country is going to the dogs,' he would say. 'No water bill for eight months and then one for sixty thousand rand. It's either pay it or brush my teeth in the fishpond.'

As was her wont, Gogo said, 'Frans *wena*, don't make your mother tired with these questions.'

But this time Ouma raised her head and, as if a new thought had occurred to her, she said to Frans, 'I will do a trade with you, my son.'

Gogo had not heard such certainty in Ouma's voice for a long time. The old lady had glanced at Gogo and said, 'Gogo, I am very thirsty.'

'It's the heat,' said Frans.

Gogo saw that they were conspiring to dismiss her. She never found mixed messages easy to manage. She wanted to stand there with her hands on her hips and say, 'Hey, Ouma, do you want me here or not?'

Instead, she turned and began to walk across the grass to the house. She made as if she was going to the kitchen but slipped, instead, behind the tree ferns and made her way back under their cover to within earshot of their conversation. She heard Ouma say, 'I don't have much, but I will give you what I can.'

'And what do you want from me?' Frans asked his mother.

'I want to die, my son.'

Silence. Gogo sank onto the grass and if she had been free to, she would've moaned. To hear such words, spoken by her companion of so many years, made the line of hills behind the house, on which she had always counted for her bearings, uncertain. Her outrage followed swiftly. Did Ouma not know how wrong it was in God's eyes to say such a thing?

But Frans did not seem, from where Gogo sat, to be at all shocked by his mother's request. Perhaps his kind knew the longing that all people have now and then to bring difficult things to an end.

He had seen a lot of death and could help his mother to her end so easily. Why then did he not seize the moment? That thought made Gogo fume afresh. *To pay him to end her life, surely Ouma would land in hell.*

Then Gogo heard Frans say, 'You don't have enough to pay me for that, Ma.'

There was a silence and then Ouma said, 'I will give you everything.'

'No,' he said.

Gogo found herself rocking to and fro where she sat. She could
hear that Frans was seizing the chance to show his mother what it
was to be that forgotten boy with scratches on his legs and dirt on
his face.

There was more value in that for him than all the money his
mother could give him.

Gogo saw him get up. He looked down on his mother and said,
'You are a doctor. Do it yourself.'

'Too weak,' Ouma had replied.

Gogo could see it gave him joy to hear that phrase and that he
would have liked to lift up his head and crow.

Ouma spoke as if what she said was shameful. 'I need someone to
be there to see me out.'

'Selfish,' said her son, 'as always.'

'No, my child. Just human.'

Frans turned and sauntered across the lawn to his car. Gogo had
not seen such a jaunty step in years.

She waited for his car to edge up the driveway and then she got
up and walked over to where Ouma sat. The old woman did not
acknowledge her. She was defeated, so Gogo took her two gnarled,
long-fingered hands into her own and said, 'Your life is not yours
alone, Ouma. It belongs a little bit to everyone who loves you.'

Ouma lifted her head and Gogo saw that there were tears flowing
down her cheeks.

'And to God,' added Gogo in case Ouma needed to hear that.

Ouma looked down at her hands, so wrinkled and misshapen, and said nothing. She couldn't speak for the sadness that occupied her.

'Did you give him anything, Ouma?' Gogo asked gently.

The old lady shook her head and said in an old person's voice, 'I never could, could I, Gogo? I didn't know how.'

CHAPTER THIRTY-THREE

Alone on the stoep of Ouma's house, Delilah wonders how she will fill her teenage hours. Where are the Nanjis to watch from her balcony and the passers-by to wave to as they carry home their shopping balanced on their heads? Where are the people?

Delilah knows the reprieve offered her and Martinus by Ouma's legacy has made the future a much less odious place. But it is the present that vexes her still. What school will she now attend? One with broken windows and sixty in a class that she has heard about? Or will she be forced into one on a local farm with surly boys who twitch in their seats and long for the open bush?

If only it were day, then she might be able to go for a long walk over the back of the mountain where she can sit and watch the cars moving swift and silent along the long thin strip of tar that spans the plateau below.

When the time comes for Frans to leave, Groot Samuel walks with him to his car. He stretches out his hand to express sympathy for his brother's disappointment, but Frans does not take it.

Groot Samuel stands on the front lawn long after the lights from

Frans's silver Mercedes have climbed up the hill and disappeared into the dark night.

He feels something in his mouth give way. He reaches in with his fingers and removes . . . a tooth. It rests in his palm like a pearl.

It does not surprise him. He slips it into the pocket of his short-sleeved shirt.

On most nights and especially in the winter, Jannie likes a cup of hot milk before he goes to bed. It is something of a ritual, this moment, when he leans his back against the cool fridge and watches the foam begin to form on the surface of the milk. He is always secretly amazed by the moment when it hisses and swells upwards, when it demands his urgent action to avoid a flood of white all over the stovetop.

He doesn't bother with hot milk tonight.

The chill light of his computer makes him appear old and, in truth, he does feel the weight of the past days filled to the brim as they have been with hardship and uneasy revelation.

He is surprised by how many references to Frans come up when he types in his name. Most are newspaper articles from the local De Wildt newspaper. There are several celebrating his victory in local swimming galas. One of him on his wedding day, where he is thin and grinning, with a doll-like blonde woman on his arm; he knows it was a brief union, based more on lust than a match of character.

Jannie and Ouma used to joke about being beyond sex, and the two of them did, at times, seem like aesthetes, pecking at being physical creatures. Now he wonders if it was wise, this cashing in of his sexual self to remain unharmed, to ensure he didn't end up once again upside down in the acacia tree with blood thumping in his head. Was it worth it to have to live so frugally? Today, he thinks not.

Jannie waits for the results of the credit check he has run in Frans's name. It's standard procedure and he does it without much expectation but within seconds pages and pages of bad debt begin to scroll up his screen.

The familiar glow of Groot Samuel's cigarette in the dark night is the only sign of his wakefulness but he is not the only one who is having trouble sleeping.

Groot Samuel hears the door to Gogo's small house open. The old woman steps out in her pink pyjamas with a *doek* wound tightly around her head.

Groot Samuel can see she looks across to his house and so he calls out softly, 'Yebo, Gogo.'

'Groot Samuel.'

She says no more but heads out across the green grass towards him. As she does so she prays that she will not encounter the nocturnal snakes that she knows slither this way and that as they hunt. She knows them to be vastly superior predators than she and impossible to see in the dark. She also hopes that Ilse has baked a new batch of buttermilk rusks; she could do with the comfort they bring.

Groot Samuel and Gogo sit side by side on the stoep and drink rooibos tea. Gogo softens the dry rusk by dipping it into her tea and then chews it noisily.

Groot Samuel waits for her to finish. He knows not to hurry her. Finally the old woman asks, 'What was that you said at dinner, child?'

'About what, Gogo?'

'You said my name.'

Groot Samuel pauses for a moment. 'Ouma didn't tell you?'

'Tell me what?'

'She left part of the farm to you.'

'Me?'

'Aletta, Frans, me and you.'

Gogo whispers to herself, 'Me.'

Groot Samuel nods his head and grimaces. 'It's not worth too much split into four and dry like this.'

'But you say a small piece of it is mine?'

'It will be worth something one day, when the suburbs have been built right up to the gate, and they are looking for more land,' says Groot Samuel.

When she was a child, Gogo's father told her stories of her great-great-grandfather's land on the banks of the Lekwa river. The tales of his herds and his many wives seemed to her to be myth, so different were they from how they lived. The inhumanity of the 1913 Land Act, making it illegal for a black person to own land, was the most oft repeated of her father's stories. And it was always told with anger and sadness as it marked the beginning of the decline of her proud clan into servitude.

And now. Here she is, *wa bona,* a landowner. It is this fact that she braved the snakes to confirm. Just look how different it has made her, if only inside her own skin, in the way she views herself.

Chapter Thirty-four

If Jannie had had his wits about him, he would have cancelled his February book club meeting. He has barely woken from a rare but necessary afternoon nap when the first member is knocking on his door.

Suffering greets each visitor lavishly. In the normal course of events Jannie would have baked something delicious, the house would be spotless, there would be flowers in a vase.

Today it is mayhem.

What is even worse is that one of their members has brought along a new addition to the group. Jannie is so flustered that all he sees of the new poetry lover is his startlingly warm, acorn-coloured eyes and his mellow brown skin. More striking than the sight of him is the sound of his name. Its musicality finds a quiet place in Jannie's chest. *Cornelius Coetzee*. It is a beautiful name.

Jannie's friends seem to sense his shaky ill preparedness on this sunny Sunday afternoon and take over his function as host. One makes tea. The other has brought a cake. Jannie retreats into the bedroom and prepares a hurried Elisabeth outfit.

Then the readings begin. After all these years the poet still has the power to calm him.

The final poem in her 1982 collection, *Bestand*, is only four lines long. He would have liked to say it to Ouma.

As he listens to Cornelius Coetzee read it aloud, it seems as if he does just that, as if Ouma has risen from the dead and offered this lovely man her ear.

> *Sal jy nooit wys word nie? Jy het hulle lief*
> *ewe voorwaardeloos en primitief*
> *en ryp vir elke pyn asof hulle uit*
> *jou eie verwaande ingewande spruit*

> Will you never be the wiser? You who ever give
> unmitigated love, and primitive,
> and ripe for every pang
> as if it was from your proud belly that they sprang

And so she did. Ouma loved them all. All the wretched and wounded souls living in her corner of the earth. She loved them imperfectly and primitively, as the poet had her own grandchildren.

Jannie used to wonder if Ouma was seeking redemption for her sins or perhaps those of her fathers.

In this very singular moment he sees that it was the sins performed in the name of the soil, ancient and profane, which Ouma sought to redeem.

The doorbell rings and all ten members of the Elisabeth Eybers book club freeze in mid gesture. Suffering heads for the door but

Jannie sees Cornelius stop him with a sweet, sharp whistle.

Suffering trots over to him and allows him to pat the top of his head. Cornelius leans down to whisper in his ear. The dog licks his hand. Jannie wonders how Suffering knows he is one to trust.

The doorbell rings again. Of course, it falls to Jannie to open it. He wishes he had not done so because standing before him is Pieter, the pathologist.

He looks at Jannie in his Elisabeth attire and mutters, 'Oh my good heavens.'

Jannie blushes red and stumbles, 'You want . . . would you like . . . to come in?'

'Not on your life,' Pieter says, shaking his head.

Jannie runs his fingers through his hair and slips off his earrings. 'It's my book club . . . the Elisabeth Eybers book club.'

'For which you have to wear a dress.'

Jannie shuffles in his shoes and mumbles, 'Actually it's optional . . . but some of us do it.'

Piet raises his hands to stop him talking. 'I need two minutes.'

Jannie steps into the front yard, not unaware of the spectacle he makes.

'Jannie, you've got to stop her.'

'You mean?'

'Anriette's boss phoned me today. He found her at the lab matching footprints to treads. I presume it's for you?'

'Yes,' says Jannie, worried.

'Well, she's not going to find anything. She's tired, she's sick and she's going to lose her job.'

'He wouldn't do that.'

'Watch him.'

The two men look at one another, deadly serious.

Jannie says, 'Is there a full autopsy report on file, Pieter?'

Pieter looks at Jannie and says, 'Of course. We are pathologists, Jannie. It is our job to determine the cause of death.'

'And?'

'How many times do you need to hear it?' Pieter asks, exasperated. 'Death by drowning. No criminal act suspected.'

Jannie watches Pieter walk away towards his parked car and he calls out, 'Because I know someone did it.'

Pieter swings round to look at him. 'I wouldn't be too sure about that.'

Jannie looks at his feet. 'I know it.'

'I've got nothing for you, Jannie.' He turns to walk back to his car and says over his shoulder, 'Just leave it alone now.'

Jannie calls after him, 'You sure about that? I mean, just one small thing?'

The pathologist doesn't even turn this time. 'She slipped, Jannie. She just bloody slipped.'

Jannie shouts, 'I saw you at the funeral.'

'Ja, and so?'

'Did you know her, Pieter?'

Now the pathologist does stop and turns around. He considers Jannie's face. 'I did.'

'How?'

'Think you had her all to yourself, my friend?'

Jannie is taken by surprise by the fierce light that shines out of Pieter's eyes. 'She was mine once a month for thirty years, from ten pm to four am. I wish it could've have been every day and every night.'

Ouma's secret hits Jannie somewhere in his stomach.

'But that was all she could give me.'

Pieter turns and walks towards his car.

Jannie sees that he is an old man. 'I'm sorry for your loss,' he calls out.

'And I for yours,' says Pieter as he deactivates the car alarm.

'There was something under the nails on the right hand, Pieter,' says Jannie.

Pieter stops moving but does not look back this time.

'Send the sample to forensics for testing. Please,' says the young detective.

The pathologist is still for a moment, then he throws his hands up in the air and says, 'I will not spend another taxpayer cent on this debacle.'

Pieter opens his car door and says, 'And for God's sake get some proper clothes on.'

Jannie looks up to see the neighbour's five-year-old staring at him from the driveway.

He waves at the boy.

The child blinks at him for a moment and then darts into the house.

Pieter turns on his ignition and watches Jannie make his way back into his house. Then he rests his head on the steering wheel.

Age has diminished him in many ways but the one that causes him the greatest discomfort is this uncontrollable opening of the tap on his feelings.

The first time Ouma unbuttoned her shirt to reveal her fine, knife-bone ribs, the two small peaks of her hips and her high breasts, he remembers wondering how such discreet architecture could contain such enormous heat.

He worried that he was too heavy, too hungry, too much, but oh my how succulent she was. He came to know her body well, but he could never anticipate the rebellious ingenuity her mind would offer up in matters of love.

The years passed and when his concerned parents asked him if he was ever going to marry, he would smile and say, 'Perhaps.'

He always wanted more than she could give. And as the years passed he wanted it more.

It was not until she asked him to help her die that he felt the full extent of his ire at her refusal to make a life with him. It gave him a perverse pleasure to say, 'This is the kind of thing only a husband would do for a wife, Susanne.'

She looked at him, and said, 'I am that for you, aren't I?'

'When did we go to church together?' he had snapped.

'I'm not a believer,' she had said.

'Or walk down the street together, or fight in the supermarket or watch each other eat breakfast?' And as he said these things he realised how long the desire for them had sat in him.

She rested her head on his shoulder then and he knew she was offering herself to him. She did that when she wanted something.

Pieter had loved her through her cancer. He had seen her lose one breast and then the other. He had expected that his longing for her would fade at these losses but her desire came from a deeper source than skin and bone. She showed no shame at her changed body and he found none. He wanted her easily, like he always had.

'Touch me,' she said, on this strange night.

'I will not,' he said, although his hunger for her was roused and he longed to. 'If I touch you, I will agree. I always have.'

She hit her hand against his chest and said, 'Every day I am *less*, Pieter.'

He shook his head. He had come to rely on her presence in his life, albeit an insufficient one. The years of longing for more had made that condition part of who he was and it was far too late for him to love another way. He could not let her go.

Had he been a different kind of man he might, then, have asked the question that had haunted his every day, *but what about me?*

He left burdened with a terrible sense of foreboding because he knew that when she decided something she would find a way to make it happen. She always did.

He grieved, in anticipation.

Pieter can barely see out of the window as he drives away from Jannie's house.

He unlocks his office door, switches on his computer and finds himself typing *Susanne Aletta Delilah De la Rey* into the search engine. It is an old machine, and slow.

When the file appears on the screen he sees the now familiar phrase at the top of the page: *Death by drowning. No criminal act suspected.* Then he clicks on the word *Findings.*

He reads slowly. *Skin fragments belonging to the deceased found under the nails of the right hand.*

Pieter walks to the window and he wonders, for the first time, if this is correct?

As he gives himself over to the question, he picks up the phone and dials a number. The phone rings for a long time before someone answers,

'Hello, Brigadier,' says Pieter. 'Ag sorry to phone you at home – is it supper time? Ja, it's just that I have a favour to ask.'

CHAPTER THIRTY-FIVE

Delilah is a devoted Beyoncé fan. Before her mother put her on the train to send her to Ouma, she gave Delilah the old earphones and music player she wore when she baked bread.

'Don't tease me, Ma,' Delilah remembers saying. 'You need this.'

Her mother's eyes had welled up. She didn't answer or couldn't answer and so she stuffed the apparatus into Delilah's pocket and kissed her so hard on the forehead that the girl knew she'd have a golf ball bruise there the next time she looked in the mirror.

Funny thing was, Delilah hadn't used the earphones since. Not once.

It was only last night that she came upon them again and stuck them in her ears.

They are still there when Important's empty belly rouses them just before dawn. The two of them pad to the kitchen only to find the other hounds have cleaned out the dog food. They will have to refill the plastic container from the large barrel in the storeroom.

The very early light outside is dense with moisture. Important follows Delilah across the grass and through the small gate that leads to the garage.

Delilah makes her way through the bags of feed and hosepipes and drills and all the rest of the equipment necessary to the lives of the two Samuels.

In the corner she sees the oil drum that contains the dog food. She fills the plastic container and then, as she is about to leave, she sees a pile of soft fabric on the top of Gogo's collection of rags in the corner.

Her body responds to the sight of it before her mind. Ouma's dress! Last seen when it was wet and sodden around her grandmother's dead body.

Delilah feels it with her fingers to make sure. *Oh God.*

She runs back to the house. Important keeps close to her heels. She picks up the phone and wakes Jannie up with her call.

Delilah saves her warmest greeting for Suffering, who receives her attentions with ease and familiarity.

She hands Jannie Ouma's dress in silence. In spite of the rapprochement at the will reading, an awkwardness remains between them. They both stand on the grass for a moment, considering the dress.

Neither finds it shocking that Delilah found it in the rag box. Gogo never throws anything away. She washed it, yes, and then added it to the container of material she uses for rags. But Jannie does wonder why she was wearing it at all.

'I never saw it on her before,' says Delilah.

Jannie says, 'It's a going-out dress.' And everyone knows that Ouma never went out.

They look at one another. Neither wants to be the one to say it, yet it occurs to both of them equally powerfully. *Did Ouma take her own life?*

The conscious choice of a 'special' dress on an ordinary day might suggest such a thing. Jannie sits on the stone step leading up to the stoep. The idea clatters around in his head uncomfortably.

Standing on the step beside him, Delilah wonders if he would be comforted if she kissed the top of his head. Such an intimacy would startle them both. 'It wasn't her way, Jannie,' she says.

The detective lets out a breath of air. 'No.'

'Not her,' says Delilah.

'No,' he says again, but the question stays with him as he folds the dress and pushes it into the evidence bag he has brought with him.

Delilah watches him write a number on the evidence bag and zip it shut.

'Go find him, Jannie Claassens,' says Delilah quietly.

The detective gets to his feet and says, 'Yes, ma'am.'

Jannie runs up the steps of the police station and into the building. He passes Beauty in the corridor on his way to Mokheti's office.

'He's not here, Jannie,' she says in passing.

'Where?'

'They say he's sick.'

'He never gets sick.'

She shrugs. 'Tea, two sugars on your desk.'

'I don't take sugar, Beauty. Never have.'

She pushes her tea trolley on and says, 'You do today, if you want a cup of tea, *wena*,' and she swishes down the passage.

Jannie hurries on. As he passes the window to the courtyard, he sees two familiar silhouettes at the far end of the lawn.

He stops to look more closely. They begin to walk across the grass and Jannie sees that it is the missing detectives, Ntombela and Bezuidenhout.

They walk with an easy swagger. There is nothing tentative or ambivalent about the way they exchange greetings with others as they pass.

Jannie watches them until they have swung open the double doors leading into the building. He tries to understand what circumstances would have brought them to this place and with such ease. He stops short each time his logic brings him to Mokheti. No, he would never agree to this. After all, he is *Mr Right Thing To Do*.

Jannie finds Mokheti in the small back garden of his house. He is sitting on a paint can in the sun, wearing his pyjamas and a dark blue dressing gown.

'They're back,' says Jannie breathlessly without bothering with a greeting.

'Who is that?'

Jannie sees that Mokheti hasn't slept.

'Ntombela and Bezuidenhout.'

'Ja.'

'Where've they been?'

'I don't know.'

'What?'

'I didn't ask.'

Jannie sees the wear and tear of that decision is his boss's blood-shot eyes.

'Nothing to say for themselves?'

Mokheti shakes his head.

'And you?' asks Jannie.

'What about me?'

'You have anything to say?'

'About what?'

Jannie looks at his boss and a word arrives unbidden in his mouth. *Waste*. Ouma's word for Aletta and her wasted promise. Now it belongs to Mokheti. What a waste of a good man.

Mokheti will not look at him. Jannie notices that his hair has gathered into small clumps on his head, there is grey stubble on his cheeks. It is as if a storm has blown its way through his body and taken his *binnegoed* with it as it moved on.

'They found Ouma's dress,' says Jannie quietly.

'What?'

'The one she died in.'

Mokheti shakes his head. 'Jesus, Jannie, just forget it.'

'I will not,' says the young detective quietly.

And now, finally, Mokheti raises his eyes and looks at him. 'You are full of shit, Jannie. *Gogo* and *Sissie* and *Boetie* and whoever the fuck else there is in your little family. Have you investigated them?'

Jannie looks at him for a moment, then shakes his head. 'No, sir.'

Mokheti's eyes narrow. 'And you want me to put myself on the line?'

Jannie looks at his commanding officer and speaks slowly. 'You are already on the line, sir.'

Mokheti sucks in air. 'You blackmailing me, Detective?'

'I'm just trying to do my job.'

'Then do it right, Detective,' snaps Mokheti.

Jannie looks up at Mokheti and nods his head. 'Ask the prosecutor to open the criminal case docket, so that I can.'

*

When Jannie presents Anriette with Ouma's dress in its official specimen plastic bag, she smiles at him over her glasses and says, 'At least you aren't wearing it, hey?'

Jannie blushes. 'Pieter told you.'

Anriette laughs. 'It was a first for him.'

Jannie wishes Cornelius Coetzee was there to make a quip with his wide smile and his quick tongue. All he can say is, 'Ja, well, next time he can join in.'

'Where did you find it?' asks Anriette of the dress.

'Delilah found it in the garage in a box of rags.' Jannie hesitates before saying, 'I'm going to test the family, see if there's a match with what you find on that.' He indicates the dress.

'Who says?'

'Mokheti. He's asking the magistrate to open a criminal docket.'

Anriette sighs. She can tell Jannie is waiting for her to tell him that this line of inquiry will, of course, come to nothing but she's too pedantic for that. In her experience it is a mistake to assume anything at all about who might do what to whom. The only thing you can be certain of in this life is the beauty of nature and the perversity of human beings.

The ritual of Sunday lunch with his mother has been a constant in Jannie's life. He knows how important it is to her so he makes sure he is there, even on book club days.

When Ouma was alive, he would first walk with her on the koppie behind the house in the cool of the morning, tea would follow on the stoep with Gogo and Ouma, and then he would drive over to his mother for lunch.

This morning he finds himself, as usual, reaching for his hiking shoes. Only then does he wonder if he and his investigation will be welcome on the farm. Perhaps not.

That realization sends him back to the comfort of his bed. He doesn't seem to be able to galvanize himself, even when Suffering stands at the foot of it and whines. He phones his mother and asks if he can come for supper instead.

He wonders, as they eat the frugal fare she has clearly prepared for lunchtime and is now dry from too many hours in the oven, what it would be like to have Cornelius Coetzee at the table with them.

He would introduce him as a friend from the Elisabeth Eybers book club and then, over time, he would become an assumed presence in all the corners of Jannie's life. The idea sits well with him.

Jannie and Cornelius.

His sexuality is never mentioned between he and his mother. It is his secret belief that she tolerates it only because it has spared her the experience of being replaced by another woman.

He and his mother share a leftover piece of cake for pudding and then Jannie lowers his head for his goodbye kiss.

The last thing Jannie expects as he arrives home is a visitor. This is an early-to-bed world and, although it is only 9 o'clock, all the farmers of the district are asleep.

At first glance he can't see who the person is who waits at his front gate as he pulls his truck into his garage. It's only when he gets closer that the sweet face of Cornelius emerges from the dark.

As he steps towards him, Jannie sees he has a book in his hand. 'I found a first edition of *Kruis of Munt*,' he says, shy.

Jannie's face lights up. 'That's been out of print for years,' he says.

'Ja. I was lucky.'

'You were.'

'It's for you,' says Cornelius and hands him the book.

Jannie looks at his fellow poetry lover as he takes the offering. He sees the soft tuck of skin around Cornelius's eyes crinkle and a bubble of anticipation makes its way up his back.

Suffering greets Cornelius like an old friend.

Jannie is again surprised by the communion the dog and Cornelius have with one another. 'Have you got a dog?' he asks his visitor.

Cornelius smiles. 'Her name is Bokkie and she only has three legs.'

'Good name,' says Jannie.

'Suffering . . . now that is a name!' says Cornelius, and he grins.

Jannie's heart lurches when it dawns on him that Cornelius is flirting with him and that this is what he longs for. He opens his mouth to ask him in, but he finds that he can't bend his tongue around the sounds, neither can he open his heart to this beautiful man for fear of the hurt he might find waiting there.

Cornelius steps away. 'Well, goodnight,' he says, and he waves awkwardly. Then he turns and hurries back towards his car.

Jannie looks down at the book in his hand. He opens it to find a small card sitting in the fold. It contains Cornelius's address and phone number. He closes the book with a snap.

CHAPTER THIRTY-SIX

Jannie lays the sealed packets out on the kitchen table in Groot Samuel's house. He was early enough to catch Ilse before she leaves for work and now she sits at the table in her white uniform, long greying hair tied back in a ponytail.

Jannie cuts the packet and removes the flat lollipop swab from its plastic casing.

'Open,' he says, and she opens her mouth.

He rubs one side of the swab against her left cheek and the other side against the right cheek. He puts the swab back into the plastic case.

As he works he visualizes the epithelial cells attaching themselves to the FTA paper inside the case. He imagines the cutting that will be made at the lab and how the cells will look under the microscope. It never fails to thrill him that such a thing is possible.

He is aware, as he fills in Ilse's particulars on the label, of a hot feeling building behind his eyes. It's a bewildering sensation.

As he lay in bed the previous night, he saw them all: Groot Samuel, Gogo, Cheetah, Delilah, Klein Samuel and Ilse. But it was Ilse who bubbled to the top of his list. He knows it could not have been simple to live in the shadow of Ouma's declining capacity. That Ilse couldn't find it in her to love the old lady in her declining years makes him hate her momentarily.

It wasn't always so. In spite of his feelings for Groot Samuel, Jannie was pleased when Ilse first turned up in the farmer's life. Both he and Ouma could see that she lightened Groot Samuel's load and even brought him moments of happiness.

Ouma and Ilse's clash over the younger woman's *shoot first* response to Tobias Mhlangu's visit to the farm that first morning, might have ended so differently had Groot Samuel been there to kiss each of his women on the cheek and say, '*Let it go now. Come, I'll make tea.*'

After Ouma had turned her back on her, Ilse took refuge in the garden, and the vegetables, shrubs and indigenous trees flourished. She put in nesting logs for birds and established feeding trays in the trees for the monkeys. She coaxed nature into responding to her hand, but the people remained aloof.

She would walk past Klein Samuel and he would simply nod his head as if she were an itinerant stranger. Cheetah didn't even look up. Gogo had to obey her instructions but Gogo barely said good morning to her. Even Groot Samuel began to leave the house before she was out of bed in order to avoid her. She thought that once they were married it would be better but it wasn't. All of this isolation and loneliness she laid at Ouma's door.

Then a gift came Ilse's way.

Ouma began to have her watch-less days. When the old lady held her plate out for a slice of milk tart, Ilse got up and put the remainder of the sweet custard pie in the fridge, remarking that the old lady had had two already. She thrilled at the flash of confusion that lit up Ouma's face.

'Did I?' the old lady asked.

The first time Groot Samuel witnessed this cruelty he stood up for his mother.

'Give her a piece.'

'Too sweet for an old person.'

'Give it to her.'

Ilse threw the entire cake in the dustbin and put the empty plate in front of Ouma.

Groot Samuel stood up from the table. He took his mother's arm and the two of them walked out of the house. They strolled slowly across the lawn to the old farmhouse. Ilse watched them stop to watch the cloud of moths gathered around the outside light. They looked as if they were on a tour of the garden.

They looked complete.

Ilse sat down at the dining-room table and wept at how cruel she had become when cruelty was not part of her nature.

Delilah's arrival from Pongola, with her small suitcase of worn clothes and her grief, gave Ouma a new lease of life.

Ilse looked on as Ouma and Delilah walked on the hill behind the house and lay in the canoe for hours, talking. The frail old woman and the fine-as-silk child communed until they knew all the backwards and forwards of one another's lives.

Delilah's presence took the sting out of the evenings too and for that they were all grateful.

Ouma dug a word game out of the old game cupboard and a nightly after-supper tournament began on the stoep. Gogo would catch up with her ironing in the corner. Now and then she'd offer up suggestions and if they were wrong she would laugh into her hand

and say, '*Wa bona*. My father should have kept me in school for one more year.'

She had only had two years of education before poverty drove her to take up her first job as a servant on the farm where her father laboured.

On the nights that Jannie drove over from town the game took on a particular intensity. He wondered if he were the only one who could feel the drums of Ouma and Ilse's war beating quietly beneath the pleasantries.

Their game called Cheetah from her shack. She never joined in, but she liked to watch from the surrounding bush. Sometimes she and Klein Samuel sat there together, rolled a joint and smoked their way through the contest. Sometimes Cheetah said the answer to herself before anyone else.

Suffering always slept on Ouma's lap as they played, his head tucked right into the hot warmth of the old lady's armpit. The noisier the contestants were, the deeper he burrowed.

They played to win.

Groot Samuel turned the egg timer over and shouted at Delilah, 'Go!'

The teenager's eyes shone and she flapped her hands in excitement. 'Okay, it's a word for someone, a woman, that you are in love with.'

Ouma said, 'Latin?'

'Yeah. Latin.'

Ouma's eyes flashed as she raced through the word files in her head. Then Jannie saw her falter. As if there were no files. Suddenly. No words.

Groot Samuel leant forward to ask, 'You okay, Ma?'

Ouma turned to look at her son and there was panic in her eyes. Both Jannie and Groot Samuel saw it. Gogo stopped ironing.

Ouma turned to Delilah. 'Tell me again, child.'

'A true love. In Latin. A woman.'

Ouma blinked.

Ilse muttered, 'We will get old waiting for this word.'

Groot Samuel looked at his wife and he thought how hard the set of her jaw looked in this light.

'Inamorata!' bellowed Ouma out of the blue.

Delilah shouted, 'Yes! Oh God, yes.' She hurried on to the next card. 'It's a word for a large family of frogs.'

'Ranidae.'

'We say this when someone is economical with words.'

Ouma gestured for more.

'Um. Sounds like someone who drinks too much.'

'Laconic!'

'Yes!' shouted Delilah. 'Another word for a sermon.'

'Homily.'

'A duck with a crested head. Eats fish.'

Ouma hesitated.

Groot Samuel and Gogo held their breath. Delilah whispered, 'Come on, Ouma.'

And she came back.

'Merganser!'

Roar of victory. Gogo smiled from the safety of the ironing board. Five out of five and time to spare! Ouma grinned from ear to ear.

Groot Samuel leant forward. 'Want to go to bed, Ma?'

'What? In this, my finest hour?' she said, and she grinned wider.

Still Groot Samuel's craggy face was troubled. He was grateful for the pleasure Ouma took from these moments but the erratic nature of her memory meant that it was always a good idea to stop while she was ahead.

She leant forward to whisper, 'Smile, my boy.'

He did his best.

She shrugged. 'What's the worst that can happen?' And she ran her hand across his cheek.

Jannie remembers Ilse's face as she witnessed this intimacy. Truth was, she would not have minded it so much had there been more of it in her own life.

Groot Samuel turned the egg timer over and said to Jannie, 'Okay, go!'

He read, 'It means stubborn. Resistant.'

Before Ilse could open her mouth Ouma shouted out, 'Obdurate!'

'It's not your turn, Ouma,' said Delilah.

'Ma . . .' murmured Groot Samuel in warning.

'Sorry,' said Ouma.

Jannie continued, 'Small beetle . . . sometimes found in flour.'

This time Ilse and Ouma shouted in absolute unison, 'WEEVIL.'

Jannie will never forget how Ouma laughed then and clapped her hands.

Ilse didn't laugh.

Groot Samuel turned away. He did not like where this was leading.

Cheetah, still watching from the bushes, giggled quietly to herself.

Jannie could see trouble brewing on Ilse's face. He tried to keep things moving with the next clue. 'A model or pattern of excellence . . .'

But Ilse ignored him. 'Oh my God, what is that smell?'

Her words snatched the laughter right out of Ouma's mouth.

Groot Samuel turned to see his mother poised like a bird on her chair, her face sucked dry by sudden anxiety.

Gogo moved from the ironing board to Ouma's side. '*Dis niks nie,* Ouma. It's nothing.'

Ilse took a deep breath and hissed, 'It's not nothing. It's *her*.'

And she pointed at Ouma.

Groot Samuel got up from his chair and said quietly, 'Want to go to bed, Ma?'

Ouma roused Suffering from his place on her lap. The dog licked her cheek as if he could sense her disquiet and then he jumped onto the floor. She got up slowly. Gogo reached for her arm to help her.

Ouma snapped, 'Leave me.' Then she turned to go and, with as much dignity as she could muster, she walked slowly across the grass in her stained pants. As she reached the fishpond she called back, 'The word is *paragon*.'

Jannie said quietly, 'So it is.'

They watched her go. Silence settled on them like snow.

Gogo picked up the stained pillow on which Ouma had been sitting and went inside.

Delilah got up to follow Gogo.

Groot Samuel walked off the stoep and into the thick night beyond. Ilse called after him, 'Where are you going, Samuel?'

He did not answer. When he was out of sight of the house Groot Samuel lit a cigarette and sucked the smoke in deep.

His women. At war.

Jannie wondered where it would all end.

Ouma wondered the same thing as she sat on the edge of her small bathtub. The only light from the room beyond cast her face into inky shadow.

The water washed over her feet. Her old naked legs thin as sticks.

She sank against the wall for support and closed her eyes.

No more *krag*.

The question shocks Jannie as much as it does Ilse when he hears it come out of his mouth, 'Did you want her dead, Ilse?'

She sweeps the sample packets off the table, eyes blazing and spits, 'You talk rubbish when you open your mouth, Jannie.'

'Ag, now look. I'm going to have to start all over again,' he says and he very methodically cuts open a new plastic bag and takes out another swab. 'Open,' he says.

She does not.

'Open up.'

She will not.

'Open!'

She obeys and he inserts another swab into one side of her cheek. He chooses the cruellest moment, when she is at her most exposed, to speak. 'If you'd waited a few years, nature would have taken its course.'

This time Ilse hits him hard across his face and he hits her back harder still.

He is not a detective any more but a grieving son. If he'd had a partner there working with him, he or she would have pulled Jannie back, taken him outside and told him to take a deep breath. He or she would've known he was a danger to Ilse and to the rule of law.

'Out!' screams Ilse from the pit of her self. 'Out of my house!'

Jannie is aware in that moment that he's got it in him to push her to the ground and stand on her windpipe.

He holds his head and whispers, 'Sorry. So sorry, Ilse.'

'What's happening here?' says a voice from behind him.

Jannie looks up to see Groot Samuel come out of the kitchen carrying a tea tray. Why the sight of him with his tray of tea should remind Jannie so acutely of all the years of his unrequited love is bewildering to him.

There is a delicacy to the way the farmer waits; he could almost be a butler. But it's not that, it's his bewilderment, the hurt gathering in the crow's feet at the edges of his eyes that moves Jannie the most.

'I need to take DNA samples from everybody, Samuel.'

'What do you mean?' Groot Samuel looks at him. He is lost. The tea is forgotten but he is frozen in the gesture of holding it.

Jannie steps forward to put his hand on the bewildered man's shoulder. Groot Samuel pulls away from his touch and puts the tea tray down on the table.

For the third time that morning Jannie cuts open a bag and removes a swab. 'Open, please,' he says and he rubs the swab inside Groot Samuel's cheek, first on one side, then the other. It brings them face to face and Jannie is struck once again by the bright blue of Samuel's eyes.

'Ja, Jannie,' says Groot Samuel, 'you have always wanted to *know*.'

CHAPTER THIRTY-SEVEN

Gogo sits on the small single bed that Ouma insisted on after her husband's death. The bed in which she slept with Pieter on their nights together and from whence he was dispatched before the sun came up.

Gogo knows Jannie will find her here. She saw him enter Groot Samuel's house that morning and she heard the shouting that followed. She vows that whatever he has come for she will give to him without all that noise.

Out of the bedroom window Gogo sees Delilah walk up the path from her morning outing to the dam with Important. She wears the maroon and white school uniform that she and her mother drove into Pretoria to buy a few days earlier. Today is to be her first day at the Brits Hoërskool.

The girl doesn't see or hear Jannie on the path ahead of her because she has Beyoncé blasting in her ears and she's interested in the pattern the soles of her new shoes leave in the fine red dust as she walks.

Jannie waits for her on the path and wonders whether she'll notice him before they collide. It's his shadow that alerts her. Delilah pulls the earphones out of her ears.

'School!' says Jannie

'Ja, well, wish me luck,' she says. 'What're you doing here, Jannie?'

He digs in his bag and hands Delilah a swab.

'What's your DNA going to tell us, Delilah?' he asks.

'That I'm really Beyoncé,' she says.

'That so?' He smiles.

She grins, hits him on the arm, and says, 'Yes!' She says it without irony. 'My insides are anyway – even Ouma said that.'

Gogo watches Jannie straighten her school tie, then take his leave of Delilah. He turns on to the path to the pig farm and steps over the fence to knock on Cheetah's door. There is no answer. He knocks again. The door opens a crack and when she sees who it is Cheetah opens it wider to allow him in.

Gogo takes in the two paintings on the wall of Ouma's bedroom. They are the only objects in the room without utilitarian purpose, as if, after a life full of fine things, Ouma had turned her back on beauty.

The paintings had hung in the old house and were once surrounded by African tribal art. Ndebele aprons, Zulu beadwork and God knows what from the north of the continent. When Gogo challenged her choices, Ouma had explained the place of decorative granary doors from the northern Dogon civilization. Still Gogo wanted to know if Ouma was aware that to combine them so indiscriminately was like putting chickens in the cattle kraal? Ugly chickens at that.

The masks were the worst. When she was cleaning in the living room Gogo turned them to face the wall. Why should those northern mediums have ringside seats in Gogo's southern life? When she forgot to return them to their right orientation, Ouma would shake her head and say, '*Julle mense!* You people know nothing about art.'

When Jannie eventually comes to find Gogo she doesn't ask any questions as he swabs her mouth but she does slowly rub the knuckles of her right hand.

Jannie can see that her arthritis aches. It does that when she is cold or anxious.

'I know what you are thinking Jannie but you are wrong,' she says quietly.

'Is that so, Gogo?' he says as he replaces the swab in its plastic case. He wants to know more, yet he must wait for her to be ready to tell him. This is the way Gogo is.

She takes out her pot of snuff. Jannie wants to say, *Spit it out!* but he has had enough fury for one day so he waits while she goes through the ritual of laying the brown powder on the side of her hand and snorting into one nostril and then the other. He waits for the sneeze he knows will follow and then he waits for her to blow her nose.

It is only when she tucks the hanky back into her bra that she says, 'It is true that Cheetah knows how people die . . .'

His face shows his surprise.

'Yes – Cheetah,' she continues. 'But she would never have hurt Ouma.'

'Why is that?'

'Because the old lady stood between her and a terrible sickness.'

Jannie considers the old woman who was so sworn against Cheetah in times past.

'Cheetah needed her,' says Gogo quietly and she claps her hands quietly together as if to say she has made her case and now she is washing her hands of the matter. Such is her certainty.

By the time Jannie gets to the hospital, lunch has been served and then cleared away. Klein Samuel is asleep in his bed at the far end of the ward. Jannie approaches the bed and looks down at the farmhand's sleeping face.

'Did you ever hear about *Gukurahundi*, Ouma?' Klein Samuel had asked Ouma as the two worked in the vegetable garden and Jannie picked beans to take to his ma for Sunday lunch. It had rained and the earth was a dark red.

'No, child, what is that?' said Ouma.

'The Shona people call it the early rain which washes away the chaff before the big rain comes.' He had sighed and then said, 'Twenty thousand people fell to Mugabe's *Gukurahundi*.'

Ouma stopped tying up the tomato vine and listened. Jannie worked quietly beyond them.

The *Gukurahundi*, or soldiers of Mugabe's fifth brigade, stole young boys away from their villages and split their heads open with rocks so the Ndebele rebels would have no soldiers to confront Mugabe's power. They burnt the fields and slaughtered the cattle and within months the people of Matabeleland were lining up with plastic buckets for handouts to stave off the swollen bellies of starvation.

'Ag, Klein Samuel, people can be so cruel,' Ouma had said and she sat down on the oil drum in the corner of the vegetable garden.

'My children were crying from hunger,' said Klein Samuel.

And he told her how he stole onto a cattle truck that was crossing the border and hid amongst the cow legs, ducking low to avoid the horns. After many hardships he heard that there was a job going at the pig farm.

'God was watching over me that day, Ouma,' he said with a small smile.

'Why is that, Klein Samuel?' she asked.

'Because I opened the wrong gate, and it brought me here.'

Ouma watched him plant the seeds in the furrows and she said, 'You have blessed us, Klein Samuel.'

He had laughed and looked into her eyes. But Jannie and Klein Samuel saw that hers were very grave.

Klein Samuel's arms are still bound to his chest, so he can only sleep on his back but he has tipped to one side in an effort to find comfort.

Jannie contemplates prodding the wounded man to wakefulness to take his swab, but the truth is he can't bring himself to consider this man a suspect in spite of Mokheti's insistence that he look amongst those closest.

Jannie puts the swabs away, gets up and walks slowly out of the ward.

Chapter Thirty-eight

The sun hangs directly overhead as Jannie sets out for his last mission of the day. He is grateful for the quiet of a long, solitary drive.

Frans lives on a rented smallholding just outside the northern city of Polokwane. Although Jannie has his address, he must stop for directions because the roads don't connect in the normal way. The smallholding is in the marginal no-man's land between the town and the wide-open farmlands that begin a little way out. *Too small to farm and too big to garden* – but, unlike Groot Samuel's place, this land is clearly not worked by two ardent souls.

'Hello,' calls Jannie into the deserted air. No response comes from the farmhouse. He hears music and follows this to the back of the house. He pushes open what he takes to be the kitchen door, 'Hello,' he calls out again.

No answer. He continues inside; the kitchen contains only a single table and no chairs, a kettle, a two-ringed hotplate and a box of tea bags. Through the doorway he can see Frans lying on a sofa. A burst of laughter and Jannie sees a young black woman sit at the feet of the prone man.

A fine-boned white man sits on the floor beyond them with his back against the wall. 'You a policeman?' he asks as Jannie pauses in the doorway.

Jannie doesn't answer.

'Because you look like a policeman to me.'

'Jannie!' says Frans. 'That's Jannie.'

'Who are you, sir?' Jannie asks the man on the floor.

'D'you mean that in the existential sense or do you want my name and passport number?'

'A philosopher!' announces Frans with a grin and a slur in his voice.

Jannie turns away from him and says, 'Or a fool.'

'Or both,' says the young man and he smiles. 'I teach at the university.'

'Where?'

The young man points towards the door. 'But the students are on strike already, even though classes only start next month. They're always on strike . . . about something . . .'

'That so?' says Jannie.

'What do you want here?' asks the man on the floor.

Jannie looks at Frans and says, 'A sample from him.'

'He means my spit,' says Frans.

The man laughs and rests his head against the wall. 'Now that's a first.'

Jannie takes him in, him and Frans: the *once were* elites, washed up at the fringes of a more egalitarian world. Not good enough to compete but raised with the entitlements of a prior age. He wonders what other expressions of their harried despair these walls have seen.

'Bring it on, Jannie,' says Frans and waves him over.

Jannie hands him the swab and watches as Frans wipes it on the inside of both cheeks. As Jannie waits, the young woman on the sofa reaches over provocatively and puts her hand on Jannie's arm.

Frans smiles at her and says, 'He's not one for you, my dear.'

'*Tssss*,' a long drawn-out sound of disdain meaning *oh, one of those*, and the young woman stands up and walks over to the man on the floor.

Jannie replaces the swab in its case and says, 'Thank you.'

Frans salutes him from his sofa but makes no move to get up. Jannie wonders if he even can. As he turns to leave the room, he catches a glimpse of the young woman squatting beside the man in the corner. He hears her say, 'Fifty for you, my brother, because it's your birthday.' He sees the young man offer her his belt to undo.

Daylight ends abruptly as Jannie turns onto the busy road back to Brits. *Where are all these people going*, he asks himself. The drivers move with such intent, as if there were a loved one calling out to each. He opens all his windows and puts on some music to blast out the trace Frans and his world have left on his skin. He cannot escape it fast enough.

He stops off to drop the swabs at the near-deserted lab. The only person crazy enough to be there at this late hour would be Anriette, and even she is home in bed tonight.

Instead of driving home Jannie comes to a stop outside a small neat house on the outskirts of town. The first thing he sees as he opens his car door is the small birdhouse hanging in the tree in the front yard. It is built to look like a miniature human homestead and it says *Welkom* above its front door.

The night is still-still, the street empty. Jannie opens the gate and walks up the path. Then he hesitates. He can smell the lavish odour of honeysuckle growing somewhere near.

The curtains have yet to be drawn and so Jannie can see into the small living room. The shelves are stacked with books. Simple furniture, a chair draped with embroidered Islamic inscription. Jannie wonders if it says *God is Great*, and which side of Cornelius's heritage is Muslim.

It occurs to Jannie that they would make a real concoction, he and Cornelius, and that's before you include Elisabeth, their cultural ancestor of choice, into the mix.

Cornelius himself comes into the room. He wears running shorts, a T-shirt and a pair of reading glasses.

Jannie watches him curl up on the couch and open his book.

As a small boy, Jannie's mother read him Hans Christian Andersen's 'The Little Match Girl'. There was a time when he asked for that story every night: *in this cold and darkness there went along the street a poor little girl, bareheaded, and with naked feet . . .*

What captivated Jannie the most were the visions she saw as she sat in the snow and struck her matches – of a warm fire, a roast goose, a Christmas tree.

Cornelius is all of those, and Jannie the small girl striking the match.

He steps away from the door. Like The Little Match Girl it is too far a distance from where he is to where he longs to be.

PART SEVEN

Chapter Thirty-nine

Groot Samuel's white truck comes down the driveway very slowly. The suspension has been unreliable since the police returned it to him a few days after Klein Samuel's disappearance, but at least he didn't have to buy a whole new vehicle. He doesn't pull up in his usual spot but turns and stops outside Klein Samuel's shack.

Groot Samuel helps Klein Samuel to get gingerly out of the passenger door and hands him a pair of crutches.

Klein Samuel is much thinner, almost a boy in size and heft. Groot Samuel finds it hard to watch him as he swings forward on his crutches.

He doesn't go to his room, but turns towards Cheetah's shack. Groot Samuel says gently, 'She knocks off at five, Samuel.'

The farmhand stops and, with some difficulty, turns and heads towards Ouma's house.

Groot Samuel is aware that the pace of their progress across the lawn is pitifully slow. It makes him conscious of how briskly he usually moves, called as he is from one task to another.

He rarely stops to look at the verdant trees around the dam and the blooming tree orchid clinging to the trunk of the stinkwood tree. Now they stop and consider it all.

The dense, hot, saturated green of leaf and grass threatens to overwhelm the small farmhand. He has lain for so long deprived of smell and sight that they come at him now, so densely intertwined that he reaches out for Groot Samuel's arm to steady him.

He sees this old, familiar place in a new way. It is not only that Ouma's absence makes it changed; it is that he can see himself in it all for the first time. His *binnegoed* lies here just as deeply and painfully as does Groot Samuel's, yet what does he have to show for it?

He has never allowed himself this question before. What can he offer Cheetah to seal her into a life with him? Only the hand-to-mouth of their daily grind and there is nothing to be done about it.

No wonder he has fled to the comfort of the bottle in times past. He would do the same today if he could, if only to contain the anger that erupts in his insides at the unfairness of it. It lands where it lands, on the grass he seeded, the trees he planted and the farmer to whom he is bound.

Klein Samuel lets go of Groot Samuel's arm and turns to make his way towards Ouma's stoep. He climbs the shallow steps and lowers himself into Ouma's straw chair.

Groot Samuel, ever discreet, and convinced of man's ultimate aloneness, leaves Klein Samuel to his thoughts.

It is not a creature from the world of men who softens Klein Samuel's re-entry here but the sound of Gundwane's rumbling call. It seems to say *Hey, have you forgotten me?* It brings a flicker of a smile to Klein Samuel's eyes and he returns the call.

Groot Samuel hears their communion as he opens the gate of the vegetable garden and steps inside.

The wall of green beans weighs down the stakes with its plenty. The tomato plants, the spinach, and his personal favourite, not to eat but to touch and to look at, the silky purple eggplant.

He kneels down to pick some tomatoes. He knows Klein Samuel loves these cooked with onion and spinach. He will leave some at Cheetah's shack for her to prepare for his supper. His hands fill quickly, so he pulls out his shirt and its tails become his basket. As he works, he hears a raucous bellowing at Gundwane's kraal and looks up to see Klein Samuel and his bull with their foreheads touching — the one taking strength from the other.

Groot Samuel gives silent thanks that Klein Samuel is back and breathing, still.

The five o'clock bell at the pig farm sets Cheetah free. She sees Groot Samuel's car parked at Klein Samuel's shack and calls his name. No answer. She turns to walk towards the farm in her wellington boots and her overalls. She is slick with mud from feet to knee.

Klein Samuel, resting on a pile of bricks beside the kraal, sees her coming and gets up to meet her. He tucks his crutches under his arms and waits for her to stop in front of him. He touches her cheek.

'I stink,' she says.

'Not to me.'

They look at one another. It strikes Klein Samuel that he has become old and she young in the time that he has been away. That he has taken strides towards his end and she has dodged out of the path of her looming affliction towards a life of possibility. All this he can see in her face. He brushes away the thought and takes her hand.

The two of them make their way slowly towards Klein Samuel's place. Like Cheetah, the workers from the pig farm have knocked off for the day and their laughter rings out in the clear evening air.

Dumisane walks past on the pig farm side of the fence, his towel over his shoulder, clean face, clean hands, clean back. Klein Samuel does not know who he is but there is something about the way the young man looks at him that gives him a flicker of unease.

Cheetah too can see his declamatory presence as he stops at the fence to watch their approach.

She helps Klein Samuel onto his bed and she puts a pot of water onto the primus stove to cook the vegetables Groot Samuel has left at her door.

Klein Samuel pats the bed beside him. She pretends not to notice. He calls out gently, 'I'm not hungry.' He pats the bed again.

She reluctantly sits beside him.

He holds her hand but she slips it free and asks brightly, 'You better?'

He nods, but his hand shakes as it lies on the sheets, like an old man's hands. 'You?'

She shrugs. 'The doctor is good. She's good to me.'

Klein Samuel reaches for her. She turns away; her whole body goes rigid at his touch.

He is not unaware. 'It's okay. Just lie with me,' he says and he leans back on the bed.

The truth is that he appals her. He is ancient, small, withered.

She lies beside him and closes her eyes. He takes her hand again.

There is silence for a moment and then he whispers, broken, '*Unontlori*. A ruin. I am a stick insect.' And he begins to cry.

'No, no, it's not that,' she says.

But he does not believe her. He cries quietly. She wipes the wet of his tears off her bare arm and by way of explanation she says, 'I'm dirty, I smell, I'm tired.'

He does not speak but turns towards the wall, away from her.

'Sleep,' she whispers.

And, eventually, his eyes begin to close and he does.

She extracts her hand from his. It takes a long time, it is so tightly held. She covers him up with his blanket and heads for the door.

The moon is full.

She pauses at the doorway for a moment and then hurries to her shack. Before she goes inside she turns to look in the direction of Dumisane's abode. He is standing in the doorway, waiting.

He does not wave. He simply points at her and so claims ownership of her whole being with the simplest of gestures.

She waves. Then she turns to go inside her shack and closes the door.

CHAPTER FORTY

The forensic lab in Arcadia is a hive of activity. The Biology section is housed here, two floors of administrative offices and open-plan laboratories where samples for DNA profiling go through their labyrinthian processes.

It is crime investigation on a grand scale and every time Jannie sees it he finds the fact that so many minds are applied to *finding out*, to establishing truths, comforting to him.

The lab is not without its own dark history; rumours still abound of the theft of a large cache of drugs tested here and stored for safe-keeping, then sold by an insider for an untold amount of money. If you asked Anriette about it she would shrug and say, 'Ag, such is the way of the world. You have to choose your battles.'

Now that Mokheti has, however reluctantly, asked the prosecutor to open a criminal case docket, Anriette has been able to formally delegate the examination of different parts of Ouma's dress to other forensic analysts.

In spite of characteristic rigour on all their parts, and more than two weeks of work, the results come back negative. There is nothing to be found, not a trace, not a smudge against which to compare Jannie's DNA samples.

Anriette is as disappointed as Jannie when he stops by to hear the findings. 'Ask any one of them to test it again, Jannie. And you will get the same bloody answer. I'm sorry.'

She can see the despair in Jannie's eyes, the *what now?* moment that all seekers find so frightening. She invites him home for supper but Jannie shakes his head. 'Thank you for asking, Anriette, but no.'

There is only one place he wants to be; not at his own childhood farm but on the land he thinks of as his place of origin, as if he's one of a weird species that could only have sprung from that soil. He sighs at how pompous it sounds, but also how true it is.

Once again, Jannie swings his truck between the rusting poles of the gate to Ouma's farm. It feels like coming home. As he drives down the steep driveway towards the house, he wonders if he will still be welcomed here as a son.

He finds Gogo at tea on the stoep and after a moment's hesitation she says, '*Haai*, Jannie, come, let us drink tea and shut up,' and she eases herself into the chair with the laden tea tray in front of her.

'Thank you,' says Jannie, and he feels a softening of his insides.

As Gogo pours the tea, Delilah and Aletta emerge from the house to join them. 'Get two more cups, child,' says Gogo to the girl.

They sip their tea in companionable silence. A bumper crop of apricots from the tree in the orchard inspired Gogo to make both apricot upsin-down cake, as she calls it, and apricot crumble.

'Did you put cinnamon in here, Gogo?' says Jannie of the crumble.

'I always do, child.'

'I know you do for the apple but I wasn't sure about the apricot . . .'

And so it goes. Nothing of import happens, nothing meaningful is said, and still none of those around the table can bring themselves to leave.

The sun has begun its slow downward journey when Groot Samuel's truck pulls up in front of the farmhouse. He nods a greeting to Jannie as he gets out of the car.

'Ja, Jannie.'

Delilah goes to greet her uncle. Groot Samuel turns to see her and smiles. Jannie sees Delilah stop in her tracks.

There is a wide gaping space in his mouth.

Delilah pulls back, wary. Groot Samuel has no teeth.

Aletta gets up from her chair on the stoep and joins her daughter. Both of them stare at Groot Samuel. Their attention makes him squirm.

Jannie wishes he wasn't there to witness this moment because the sight of him so diminished grinds his insides.

'Hey, *boet*, who stole your teeth?' says his sister, trying to keep it light.

Groot Samuel covers his mouth with his hands and turns away.

'Hey, hey wait,' says Aletta and comes closer.

Groot Samuel looks at his feet. 'They took them out.'

'Why?'

He shrugs.

'But why?'

'I got a disease.'

'How?'

'Too many cigarettes.'

'I don't understand?'

He shrugs. 'That's what they say. Gum disease.'

Jannie watches Gogo turn silently away.

Delilah doesn't know what to do.

Aletta's eyes fill with sudden tears and before she can stop herself she asks, 'What has happened to you, my brother?'

It is a question so shocking that it stops time.

Groot Samuel looks at her and says, 'Nothing.'

And he shrugs again.

'Nothing has happened to me.' He hovers there, mouth gaping.

Aletta cries.

'Why are you crying?' he asks quietly.

'Because you'll never be able to eat a mango again, like we used to do it, with the juice dripping down our arms and the strings in our teeth.'

Then to the profound surprise of everybody there Groot Samuel begins to cry too. His tender face crumples. His bare gums shine.

Delilah steps forward and takes his hand. He allows her to lead him towards his house.

As they walk she says, 'It must have hurt.'

He doesn't answer.

'I bet you were brave when they took them out.'

Groot Samuel has lost his heart to this girl. He shakes his head. 'No. Not brave. Stupid.'

Other people are brave. He knows them. The ones that do not give up the names of their friends, even when they feel the cold hand of death reach across the River Styx.

He knows them.

When Ilse sees her toothless husband enter the living room, hand in hand with his niece, she gets out of her chair very slowly and then she says, 'I will make soup for supper.'

Groot Samuel waves that idea away with a brisk sweep of his arm. He takes his leave of Delilah and heads for the bedroom.

CHAPTER FORTY-ONE

The late afternoon is as hot as if it were midday. Jannie leaves work early, takes a cool bath and then dresses in a clean shirt and shiny shoes. Fine beads of sweat sprinkle his nose and upper lip within minutes of getting out of the water. He combs his hair.

The annual dance at the Jopie Fourie terrain has always caused Jannie sleepless nights. Some think the event should be a source of pride to him because, although now distant, some of the selfsame blood runs in his and Jopie Fourie's veins. But Jannie has chosen another Afrikaans hero to honour and wishes he could be at home reading her poetry with Suffering on his lap and Cornelius by his side.

Before his father died, his parents were the main organizers of tonight's event and he has served it at every age and stage of his rocky road to adulthood.

Now, the dutiful son once again picks up his mother, dressed in her faded blue party dress, and sets out to drive her to the dance.

Klein Samuel stands at the door of the barn shaking a bucket full of grass pellets, a crutch under one arm. A gust of wind brings the scent of food to the bull's nostrils. Gundwane turns his body and lumbers towards the barn. The bull breaks into a trot. As he stuffs his dark nose into the bucket, Klein Samuel scratches him on his neck.

The laughter that comes from the pig farm has a Friday late-afternoon timbre to it. A *no-work-tomorrow* kind of laughter. It has a drink in its hand and it calls to Klein Samuel most keenly.

Perhaps Cheetah will cook for him tonight and then they can sit in the dust outside her shack and listen to the radio like an old married couple. Klein Samuel and Cheetah.

Samuel. The sound of it is suddenly foreign. The first white farmer he worked for christened him thus and so replaced his Ndebele birth name, Sifiye.

Cheetah and Sifiye.

He wonders if she will do any better than the white farmer when she comes to speak it.

Someone has set up a radio outside and the local music station spits its dispiriting fare into the coming dark. Klein Samuel buries his head in Gundwane's neck and breathes in.

The bonfire is roaring when Jannie and his mother arrive at the Jopie Fourie terrain dance. The *braai* laden with cooking meat, the tables heavy with salads and *stywepap* and *tamatie bredie*. A modest band plays a mixture of old pop tunes and *boere tiekiedraai*. The darkness gives the teenagers in the crowd courage and they jostle one another along as they mill around the food tables.

The music reaches Delilah on the stoep of Ouma's house but it's the hum of distant conversation that beckons to her most. The sound of people choosing to be together reminds her of her isolation. Then a new song begins that lights up her face. It's 'One Plus One' by her heroine Beyoncé.

She begins to dance on the green lawn in the failing light. Her long skinny legs give her a young-doe kind of grace. The child has not learnt to dance while comparing herself to others, so she brings something entirely original to the way she moves.

In the clearing outside her hut Cheetah dances to the same song. She is closer to the sound than Delilah. It envelops her.

She does not dance for Klein Samuel who sits in the dust to watch her. She dances for Dumisane who waits in the bush beyond.

Klein Samuel is not aware of his competitor in the bushes, but he is alert to the other workers who have crept up to edge of the bush to watch Cheetah twist and gyrate.

Cheetah learned to dance listening to the radio in her father's flat in Lavender Hill. She was forced to relearn it when she washed up in the brothels of Hillbrow where dance was always a flagrant simulation of sex. Her pimp put her in a revealing lemon yellow nightie but it only made her sordid. Her black hair was dyed bright peroxide orange like that of the other girls who waited at the door for their johns. There were no windows in her room; the sheets on her miserly bed were always dirty.

But there was something stuck on the wall in her small bedroom that saved Cheetah from despair. It was a drawing she had made of a surfer. Not any surfer, but Cheetah herself, riding the waves. The black charcoal shape of her tell-tale pigtails, crude and out of proportion, but unmistakably her. Often, when she lay beneath her squalid patrons she would look at that drawing and think *That is what I am, not what you would make me.*

Klein Samuel doesn't like the way the pig-farm workers look at Cheetah as she dances. He stands up and says, 'Come inside.'

She barely hears him and chooses not to respond.

He repeats himself, 'Inside, Cheetah.'

'It's nice here.'

'*Haai wena!*' he shouts. 'Inside!'

She stops dancing and looks at him. 'Shit. I was just dancing.'

'The boys are watching.'

Cheetah turns to look at the workers, now melting away into the night, and she says, 'Who cares?'

He mumbles, 'They are no good.'

'Ag, what's good? You tell me that,' says Cheetah. She gathers up her headscarf. 'Me? Am I good?' and she looks at him.

His eyes say that she is. They burden her with their faith.

Klein Samuel says quietly, 'I am good.'

Cheetah looks at him and she stops herself from saying, *Ag but you are not enough, Klein Samuel, not by miles.*

He holds out his hand and says, 'Come.'

She shakes her head. 'Not tonight.'

He looks at his feet. He wants to beg her. To say he is sorry for his poverty and for being a stick insect, but he does not.

He just watches as she turns away from him and begins to make her way back towards her shack. Then he goes inside his meagre shelter and shuts the door.

Cheetah wonders if her new love is still out there or whether

Klein Samuel's cloying attention has driven him away. She stops on the road to listen.

A man steps onto the path ahead of her. Cheetah's heart begins to beat. It is he.

She hurries towards him. She takes his hand and whispers his name, 'Dumisane.'

He answers in a murmur, 'Yebo, Cheetah.'

Cheetah leads him silently, step by quiet step, to her small house nestled under the trees.

Groot Samuel and Ilse sit at the table on the stoep of the farmhouse. It is dark now and the moon has yet to rise.

Groot Samuel looks at his wife as he sips his fresh tomato soup.

Ilse watches him. 'Would you prefer soft peas? Or I can make some gem squash.'

Groot Samuel shakes his head. 'You've done enough.' He looks at her and says gently, '*Dankie.*'

She smiles, a fleeting show of white. He leans back in his chair. The music from the pig farm is at full volume now.

'Is Gogo eating?' he asks.

'I don't know.'

'Oh.'

Ilse puts down her fork. 'Maybe we don't need Gogo so much now that Ouma is gone.'

He glances up at her. She doesn't see his alarm. 'A younger person would be better.'

Groot Samuel listens.

'She can hardly bend to do the polishing any more and the dust on the kitchen cupboards is thick as my fing–'

He raises his hand to compel her to stop talking. When she does so he says, 'Thank you.'

Then he gets slowly to his feet and walks out into the night.

The moon has begun its descent when Delilah walks up to the fence separating the farm from the Jopie Fourie terrain. A mellowness has come over the late-night revellers.

Delilah sees Jannie sitting amongst the older generation of women and their gossip; it is as if he and the birdlike woman holding court in the middle of the knot of like ladies share the same oxygen. She has Jannie's face.

A petite woman with long dark hair watches the dancers from the edge of the dance floor. Her face is alight with longing to be among them. She turns and Delilah realises, with shock, that it is Ilse. Someone pulls her in and she begins to dance. She is happy, mischievous even. And she can dance. Delilah wonders how someone can be so changed.

Just then Jannie looks up and sees Delilah at the fence. He hopes no one else will do the same. This community was never welcoming to Ouma. They found her a traitor to the ways of their people. They blamed it on Ouma's upbringing in the city where, they believed, burgeoning intellectuals had led them astray and watered down traditional Boer values.

They didn't like change here. A homemade bomb had been found on a farm in the valley a few years ago. When asked about its intended target, the farmer had muttered, 'The Xhosa bastard.' He meant Nelson Mandela. And that farmer went to jail.

What will they now make of Ouma's granddaughter, Jannie

wonders. He is relieved to see Delilah turn away from the fence and walk off into the night.

Dumisane pauses as he and Cheetah enter the clearing in front of Cheetah's room. He senses something there. Trouble. He puts his finger to his lips and gestures that she follows him.

He walks through the veld to the dam. Cheetah has watched the jackals walk like this when they come down from the hill to sniff around in the rubbish bins. He makes absolutely no sound.

The dam is full from the rain and the water a thick, inky black. The lovers pause on the bank. The still reflection of the moon's yellow glow invites disruption.

Dumisane pulls off his shirt and steps out of his trousers. He slips into the water like a seal. He uses a smooth self-taught stroke that keeps him moving forward, silently, out to the centre of the dam. He gestures for her to follow. She shakes her head. The music from the Jopie Fourie terrain fills the night.

She pulls off her dress but she doesn't enter the dam.

He treads water, waiting. She shakes her head. *Can't*, she seems to be saying and then he understands. He can see that Ouma's death in these waters means that this pleasure is denied her. He swims back and pulls himself up on the bank where she waits and spits something out of his mouth onto the stone. She picks it up. It is a condom. She smiles, shy as a virgin. He leads her into a clearing in the bush.

Groot Samuel sees Delilah standing on the lawn below Ouma's house long before she is aware of him. She turns to him as he approaches.

'Did you eat already, Delilah?'

She shakes her head. 'Not hungry.'

'What is it, child?' he asks.

'Something . . .' She looks at him but says nothing more. How does she tell him that her *piep en tjank* keeps her there. That the music doesn't even sound like music to her any more.

Groot Samuel stands beside her. Eventually, softly, he murmurs, 'We've had our share, Delilah. Even terrible times come to an end.'

The music from the party plays only for Cheetah and Dumisane now. Dumisane stands wet and slippery as a seal, and he begins, very slowly, to dance.

His body is strong, thick legged, wide shouldered. And young. Not only in years but in vigour.

Cheetah has never seen anyone so full of a future before. No small boy with a gun and a hat on his head in this man's story. No servitude to hold him down.

His feet hit the stone *ka, kakaka*. And then he lifts his one leg, like a crane and hovers for a moment, then his feet again *kaaah, kakaka*.

As she watches him, desire of an entirely different sort takes occupation of her. It has to do with wanting him. Her. Wanting. Him.

She reaches out her hand and touches his leg. He stops moving. She pauses. He moves slowly again. She moves her fingers up higher. He feels her travel up his calf to his knee. She trembles.

He breathes like a springbok, quick, in and out, so as not to interrupt the journey her fingers make.

She kneels and brushes the skin between his legs. He turns towards her. He lifts her to her feet as if she were plain air. Places his two palms under her buttocks and lifts her further.

She tears open the condom packet with her teeth.

He dances, joined with her. It is a deeper rhythm than either has ever found before. She holds the wide mountain range of his back and she finds that she can dance too.

A quickening and in one swift movement his hands find the bottom of her feet. She stands in his palms and is free to tug and suck at him, ever faster.

Argh. A falling – he to his knees and she to her back. A thrust raises them up and burns all other intimacies to nothingness.

They lie on the rock until the music from the dance has stopped and the night crickets have slowed to a murmur.

Then they begin to talk. Cheetah learns that he is working at the pig farm to prepare for something better. He hopes he can be an engineer one day.

She wonders if he will take her with him when he leaves, but she doesn't ask him that. Instead she tells him how the surf off Muizenberg beach swells when the spring tides come in.

'You surf?' he asks.

She smiles and a flutter of hope whispers in her chest. She and Klein Samuel never talked about the sea. Some years into their relationship she realised he had never seen it. Maybe this time she can tell her story.

She doesn't start with Cassiem; maybe she never will tell that tale of heartbreak. Instead, she tells him about how often she sat on her board in the evening, beyond where the water breaks, and watched the sun go down behind the mountain and the lights come on one by one. And how she wondered who was turning them on and if she would ever know them.

Their sparse exchange continues on and off for a long time until it's indistinguishable from the breeze that rustles the reeds.

CHAPTER FORTY-TWO

Klein Samuel lights his kerosene stove early in the morning. He puts the kettle on the flame. When it boils he pours the hot water into one cup and then another. He shares one tea bag between two cups. Then he spoons sugar into each.

The chilled grass crunches under his feet as he makes his way from his shack to Cheetah's. He knocks gently on the door as he always does and says, '*Kho, kho.*'

There is no answer. He pushes the door open. It is very dark inside and it takes a moment for his eyes to adjust.

Then he sees them.

She is lying in her bed, almost naked, the sheets in disarray, and the man beside her is fast asleep. She looks at Klein Samuel with a steady gaze. Then she lifts her finger to her lips and says, 'Sshsh.'

It is that gesture, that concern to preserve the slumber of the stranger in the bed beside her, which snaps Klein Samuel's reason.

The sound that comes out of his mouth has not been heard in these parts before. It gets Cheetah to her feet in terror and Dumisane grasping for his clothes.

The young man makes a run for the door, his height and weight aimed full speed towards escape. But in his hurry he has failed to scan the floor and he falls, face first, over the small primus stove forgotten there.

Klein Samuel seizes the opportunity offered by his rival's fall: he grabs Cheetah's kitchen knife and points it upwards. Dumisane's own weight and vigour drives him onto the blade. It leaves a bloody hole in his chest. The depth and suddenness of the wound robs Dumisane of his capacity. He blinks. This brutality, after his tender, entwined sleep is too extreme a difference for him to manage.

The young man falls to the floor. Klein Samuel's veins swell with conquest. The blood from the wound in Dumisane's chest pumps thick red onto the mud floor. The light is fading in his eyes. He gasps for breath yet makes one more effort to escape his frail assailant.

Klein Samuel, confident of victory now, allows the boy to pull himself as far as the dust outside Cheetah's hut. He stands above him and stabs him again, this time into his back. He does not stop stabbing.

Through it all Cheetah watches silently with her hand stuffed into her mouth. She wants to scream at Klein Samuel to stop but there are no words that can halt this madness.

Dumisane rolls over one last time and locks eyes with his assailant only briefly, before the light goes out. In that glance he recognises Klein Samuel as Cheetah's former lover. It does not surprise him that the man would feel this way.

Klein Samuel steps away from Dumisane only when he feels the last wisp of life leave his body.

★

Cheetah turns and walks away across the grass towards the farm-house. It is only when she is halfway there that she begins to cry, small mewing cries that frighten rather than comfort her.

Groot Samuel comes running out of the house with his jeans pulled over his pyjamas.

He glances back to see Gogo, Aletta and Delilah emerge from Ouma's farmhouse beyond. He turns and screams, 'Keep her inside, Gogo! Close the door.'

Gogo takes the child's hand and leads her back into the house.

Delilah follows, mute. Aletta bolts the door from the inside.

Delilah tries desperately to shut out the certainty that there has been another life lost. It shames her but she is only too relieved that this time it is not her that sees it first.

Groot Samuel runs into Cheetah's small yard. He sees his old com-panion turned to stone with shock and soaked in blood. He sees how he stares down at the man lying at his feet.

Groot Samuel waves away the scattering of workers drawn to the scene by Dumisane's cries. 'Go home!' he tells them. '*Voetsak!*'

Klein Samuel turns to look at Groot Samuel. He says nothing. Does nothing. Then he turns and walks away towards his room.

Groot Samuel watches him go.

Klein Samuel fills a bucket with water. He notices that the bucket is new. Cheetah must have bought it. It has splashes of mud on its outer rim.

He dips the washcloth in the water and begins to clean himself. First his face. Then his neck. Finally his hands. The water in the bucket goes a deep red. Then black.

He hears Groot Samuel shouting in the garage beyond but he doesn't know what he's saying.

Groot Samuel drives up to the door of Klein Samuel's room. '*Maak gou!*' he shouts. 'Hurry.'

But Klein Samuel does not move.

Groot Samuel gets out of the car and runs into the shack. He begins to shove Klein Samuel's sparse possessions into his trunk.

He carries the trunk out and puts it on the back of the truck. He returns to get the bicycle. And puts that on too.

Then he emerges with a shirt. A clean shirt. He holds it open. '*Kom.*'

This time Klein Samuel stands up slowly and slips his arm into the sleeve.

Groot Samuel steps to the other side and holds up the other arm. And so he dresses him, garment by garment, until Klein Samuel looks just like a migrant worker returning to his family.

They climb into the cabin of the truck and they drive up the hill and out of the gate.

PART EIGHT

CHAPTER FORTY-THREE

The farmhouse is dark; its walls barely contain Delilah and her dread. She lies prone on the bed with Important and listens to the sounds of her mother and Gogo moving around the house.

'Let Groot Samuel deal with it, Gogo. The child must stay inside,' she hears her mother say. She hears Gogo murmur her assent. Delilah sighs. At least she'll be spared a day at school with its blur of faces peering at the new girl.

The familiar smells of baking tuna pie and frying fish cakes waft out of the kitchen and settle on them all. None will find an appetite when the time comes to sit and eat, not even Gogo.

True, there are always hungry souls who will benefit from this food, but it is the close ones Gogo wishes to comfort and their stomachs have rebelled.

Delilah listens to her mother talk on the phone with her father; they confer on the myriad decisions that come with disassembling a lifetime lived in one house: 'No! Give it away, Tertius. It's broken. Ag *nee*, listen, throw the bloody thing away . . . but bring the blue bookshelf! Just in case.'

Delilah covers her head with a pillow so as not to have to hear and therefore imagine the universe of her childhood being separated from its very own air and light. When she closes her eyes she sees the contents of her house spinning in space like planets.

It is late afternoon when Jannie's truck comes down the steep driveway. All Gogo's cell phone message said was, 'Please come.'

Cheetah sits beside Dumisane's body in the bloody dust outside her shack. She has covered him with her red blanket now turned black with blood in places.

The flies have gathered.

Jannie kneels down beside her. They are silent for a long time. Then he says, 'Who is it, Cheetah?'

'Dumisane.'

Jannie reels.

'Dumisane who likes to swim?' he asks, thick lipped with dread.

'Yes.'

Jannie gets up and lifts the blanket off the body. He has seen many fallen but it is worse than cruel, this death. Finally he says, 'He's been dead for a long time.'

Cheetah nods. In a distant sort of way she is grateful that the pig farmer and his wife are away and that she was spared from having to explain.

'You know who did it?'

She nods.

'And he is gone?'

She nods.

'Where did he go?'

'They told Gogo not to tell you until they had a chance to reach the border.'

'Groot Samuel said that?'

She nods.

'Who did it, Cheetah?'

She looks at him and she whispers, 'Me.'

He can see that she believes it utterly. He shakes his head and asks again, 'Who did it?'

She says nothing.

Jannie snaps, 'Jesus, Cheetah, say it!'

She takes a breath. 'Klein Samuel did it.'

Jannie sits back onto the dust. And he puts his head in his hands.

The sun is caught on the lip of the earth. It glows red but gives little light. It is still hot. Feels to Delilah like it always will be like this, the air still and thick.

Air! She has to have air and smell the green. She pulls open the front door and all activity stops. Gogo darts into the living room from her kitchen to see who has breached the security of their enclave. Her mother puts down her phone and blinks at her. Delilah regards them both for a moment and then she turns and walks out of the door.

Once out of the confines of the farmhouse she finds herself moving quickly across the green lawn. She doesn't know where she is going exactly but she must move her jumpy limbs to dissipate some of the dread trapped inside her muscles.

She runs up the steep driveway. The dogs come from nowhere to join her and form eddies around her moving legs. Suddenly one of them stops; is there a mole under the earth or a snake on top? The dog is rigid on one spot, tail straight as a die. On a normal day Delilah would stop and find out but today she's got another task and she must keep going to locate it.

She finds herself drawn to Cheetah's shack. She stops at the fence and sees her sitting in the dust, so still. Even from here she can see that her body may be there but her insides have dived down like a whale does when harpooned, defensively. Even if she shouted her name, she can see Cheetah would not have the capacity to respond.

Delilah can smell the dark mark on the sand beside Cheetah. Blood. She closes her eyes against the sight of it. The smell fills in what her eyes have forbidden her to see. In this way she learns the shape and weight of the life that was lost. Then she tiptoes away.

The night settles into its darkest hours and still Cheetah does not move from her drenched patch of dust. She barely breathes.

Chapter Forty-four

The old white four-wheel drive truck does not have much speed on the open road. The rattles and clanks of the vehicle so familiar to Groot and Klein Samuel exacerbate the sudden intimacy between them, marooned as they are inside the cabin.

Trucks taking food, petrol and milk to Zimbabwe barrel past, making it seem as if the truck is held in a stationary position by a force field of fate.

Klein Samuel does not respond when Groot Samuel offers him a cigarette. The farmer lights up. Thank God none of his women are present to forbid him this most essential comfort.

Klein Samuel unbuttons the clean shirt Groot Samuel dressed him in and then removes it entirely. He folds it carefully and lays it on the seat beside him.

Groot Samuel wants to ask him what he's doing but he is aware that words may be beyond Klein Samuel, and he fears his own may emerge from his mouth in a jumble of hisses and clucks.

Had he asked, Klein Samuel would have told him that his mother taught him to always keep his clothes clean and at that moment he can feel that his flesh is in revolt.

The farmhand's near skeletal torso shocks Groot Samuel into a deeper quiet. Where did this frail body find the strength to perform its butchery?

Klein Samuel winds down his window. The smell of blood seems to fill every particle of space, every tiny blowhole.

He thrusts his head out of the window and retches bile and sorrow into the air. It catches in the wind and is split into an infinite number of separate parts. Then he rolls the window up again and puts his shirt back on.

Not a word passes between them. Not a sound. Groot Samuel keeps his eyes on the road ahead.

The two Samuels pass the night hours that it takes to reach the Zimbabwe border in complete silence. They stop only to fill up with petrol and buy a cold drink. They drive the long, straight, black roads of the plains. They climb the moonlit Soutpansberg mountains; they see their first baobab tree. Under different circumstances Groot Samuel would have loved to see the dark semi-desert opening before him.

A long time ago Klein Samuel would have thrilled at the prospect of home. For the first few years he returned annually to his wife and growing family with money in his pocket. His heart would begin to beat in his chest when he caught sight of the Limpopo because it meant he was close.

But he stopped visiting so long ago he can barely remember when he was last here. His new home was made in Cheetah's fiery chest and now that too is gone.

As they approach the border post, Klein Samuel indicates with a mute raising of his hand that they should turn off the main road and travel along a two-track farm road. The truck tyres sink into soft sand.

They approach a man on a bicycle illuminated by their headlights. He wobbles off to the yet softer sand on the side of the tracks to let them pass.

The bicyclist and Klein Samuel exchange a look, the one asks a silent question, the other answers with a nod. Much later Groot Samuel marvels at the subtlety of that exchange because he knows it determined their next step.

Since Klein Samuel was last here, fences have been erected on the South African side of the river to stem the rising tide of immigrants like him. If he could muster the energy he would be afraid.

A four-wheel drive truck looms in the road ahead. A ruddy-faced white farmer in a wide hat pulls up beside them. Groot Samuel rolls down his window. He speaks a different kind of Afrikaans than Klein Samuel has heard before. It is full of shared bravado. '*Nee, boet, I'm here to buy an Nguni bull from the farmer on the far side.*'

Groot Samuel understands that it doesn't matter what he says; it matters only that the farmer knows they are of the same tribe. The man takes off his hat and warns Groot Samuel that gangs of traffickers operate on this border, violent bands of thugs looking for people to sell and others to ravage. 'It's the bloody "Wild West",' says the farmer before he drives off.

Some miles on, Groot Samuel draws to a stop and both men get out.

The sun is rising.

Groot Samuel holds the bike still while Klein Samuel ties his bag onto the back. They do not speak. When all is ready Groot Samuel extends his hand.

'Good luck,' he whispers.

Klein Samuel will not look at him. How is it that his life, so firmly attached to that slim piece of land and to Groot Samuel, Cheetah and Ouma, has slipped away? How is it that he has lost it all and in such a short space of time?

He wonders through the blur of his grief how one says goodbye to someone forever. *Vir ewig.* For all time. How does a person do that when the other is part of the life inside you?

It is the burden of the years and the intimacies they have shared that make it impossible for the two men to take their leave in a proper way.

So Klein Samuel simply turns and pushes his bike down a thin track that leads to the Limpopo river. He will avoid the crocodiles that await him there. He will avoid the thugs that roam the banks, but he knows, as he takes his leave, that he will not live long here. The awkward tenderness of the farewell between the two men tells us that Groot Samuel thinks so too.

CHAPTER FORTY-FIVE

When the morning sun hits the side of Cheetah's face she gets up from her place of vigil on the dust. Her limbs have tightened during the night and she walks bent to where she might be safe.

She finds herself at the door to Ouma's surgery; the abandoned condition of the building settles on her slowly, once again detail by detail. Cheetah turns and follows the path that leads to Ouma's house. The dogs sleeping on the dusty driveway lift their heads but do not bark. There is nothing threatening about the wraith who slips into the shady spot under the wild gardenia. She seems immediately to be part of the mute things growing there.

Ilse watches her through the kitchen window and sighs as she rinses her tea cup under the tap. There is such a *giving up* to Cheetah's broken presence there that Ilse wishes she had not seen it. It makes her want to crouch on her kitchen floor with her head in her hands. She hopes Cheetah will soon realise there is no one to save her here and move on somewhere else.

★

It is almost midday and the heat hangs in the farm air when an elderly man walks slowly up the driveway. The dogs yap as he nears the house but he has no fear of them. He walks burdened by his thoughts, until he has reached the top of the driveway.

As if he senses her there, the old man turns to see Cheetah in her shade. She rises to her feet with a gasp for she sees Dumisane in the old man's face; it is his wide cheekbones and his vivacious mouth.

The old man and the farm girl see one another's devastation.

Without the exchange of a single word, Cheetah leads him down the driveway to the fence that surrounds the pig farm. She holds the wire down for him so he can climb over it easily and she shows him the way to Dumisane's room. The father opens the door and steps in.

Cheetah does not follow, but through the open door she watches him pack up his son's meagre life. Carefully and diligently he wraps his two pairs of shoes in newspaper, then folds the overalls, wipes down the wellington boots, and finally he cushions his son's radio with his drying towel and adds it to the bag.

Then Dumisane's grieving father sits, depleted, on the bed.

Ilse looks out of the kitchen window as she prepares the evening meal and she sees Cheetah back in her position under the wild gardenia tree. Cheetah and her misery. Is there nowhere Ilse can be without seeing this need?

And God knows a devouring compassion is necessary to pay witness to a life like the one Cheetah has lived.

Is it wrong for her to want to walk with her husband in the evening light and observe how well the baby yellowwood saplings are faring without this *pain*? Is it wrong, after so many years, to want that discrete peace?

'Hello, Cheetah,' she says as she walks over to the tree.

The girl looks up at her with her skull face.

'You can't sit here all day and all night,' says Ilse.

Cheetah looks at her but doesn't seem to know what to say.

Is it wrong for Ilse to want to look out of her kitchen window and see nothing but the trees and veld? The thought occurs to her that perhaps, in such a world, it is.

'*Miesies*?' whispers Cheetah but she doesn't move. She says it like a hiccup, a sound without meaning. Everyone knows Ilse isn't her *miesies*.

'It will get cold soon, and then how will you sleep?' asks Ilse.

Cheetah simply looks at her.

'Would it not be more comfortable at your own place?'

Cheetah shakes her head. She has no words to explain the horror that lives there now.

If Ilse had felt less beleaguered by Cheetah's presence, she would have seen that the girl was not laying the duty of care at *her* door.

The truth is that she is there for Gogo, for the steadiness of the old woman's presence and the bowls of food she shares with her.

Right now, Gogo is ironing the bed linen in the laundry room alongside the house. She can see Ilse through the doorway and hear every word.

'Go on now, Cheetah,' says Ilse again, gently, 'please.'

Cheetah does not move.

Gogo puts down her iron and waits. She prays that Ilse will give up and walk away.

But she does not. Instead, in her helplessness and her panic, she speaks as she would to her animals. 'Come, come, now, Cheetah, up!'

That is too much for Gogo. She sighs, carefully turns her iron off at the switch and walks slowly into the sun towards the two women. 'Let her rest here a little longer, *asseblief, miesies*.' Her plea is in Afrikaans to better appease Ilse.

But the younger woman is now frightened by the unresponsive wraith on the ground before her. Might she not lie down under the tree in the night and just slip away? She seems close enough to that crossing. '*Kom nou*, Cheetah! *Loop!*' she snaps.

The solid earth of caution that has held Gogo up all these years gives way to something much more volatile. 'She is not a dog,' she says quietly. 'She is a somebody.'

Later, Cheetah would tell Delilah that the birds stopped singing at that moment; even the cicadas went silent. And that when Ilse hit Gogo, they shrieked in chorus, bird and insect together. Deafening. At least that was how it seemed to her.

Gogo does nothing.

'Tell her I say she must go,' says Ilse, shaky voiced.

If she had known Gogo better, she would have seen the stillness settle on the old lady and run back into the house as quickly as she could. Cheetah recognises it. She has felt the brunt of its power more than once. But something further has been added to that already potent personhood. Does Ilse not realise that the old lady is now a landowner? Word of Gogo's good fortune has spread fast amongst the workers at the pig farm. It elevated her in their eyes.

Cheetah whimpers and buries her head in her lap. She can see trouble coming.

'Did you hear me?' hisses Ilse. 'Tell her!'

Gogo's blow knocks the breath out of Ilse's body. The younger woman caves inward and releases a whistle of air.

It is at this moment that Groot Samuel's battered truck turns into the homestead and comes to a stop.

CHAPTER FORTY-SIX

In some ways it would have been much better if Groot Samuel had raged against the fighting women. But he simply stood looking down on them, silent, his face folded closed in defence.

This final rupture in the weave of his life made its way through his body and soul unimpeded by surprise or outrage. It simply stacked itself on top of the long list of Groot Samuel's other wounds.

Die waarheid kwaak 'n karige geluid.

If Jannie were there he would have recognised the meagreness of the long-avoided truth that revealed itself that hot summer evening.

'Cheetah said if you closed your eyes it sounded like hippos fighting. They didn't sound like people,' Delilah had told the young detective on the phone.

When it was over Groot Samuel followed his wife into the house and Cheetah rested her head against the tree and closed her eyes.

It wasn't long before Groot Samuel emerged with the first box of Ilse's things. Then the second, then the suitcase, then the sleeping basket for the large ridgeback, then the ridgeback himself. Delilah told Jannie how eagerly Ilse came out of the house and got into her car and followed Groot Samuel and his loaded truck over the hill to her family seat.

It was only much later, when time and tenderness had brought Ilse and Groot Samuel together as friends, that Ilse said how sure she was that day that it would be no better between them now that Ouma was gone. It was not only the old lady who stood in the way of her special relationship after all. It was the land and those who washed up on it. There would always be someone who needed the refuge it offered.

'She was nearly running, Jannie, that's how much she wanted to be gone,' said Delilah.

And, as she said it, Delilah realised how unhappy Ilse must have been.

How trapped by duty were both she and her husband, and how even the dutiful ones can reach the end of their tether.

The following morning, as soon as Groot Samuel is sure Gogo is awake and dressed, he knocks on the door of her small house.

'*Koh, koh,*' he says.

'*Ehe,*' says Gogo and she pulls open the door. A suitcase is on the floor beside Gogo's high bed. The room is impeccable. Embroidered cloths on the pillows, every last item put away so as not to clutter the small space. Groot Samuel knows every inch of this world; he has searched it out for nurture ever since he could walk.

Gogo can see him remembering and she asks, 'Tea?'

He nods his head.

They sit outside to drink it. Groot Samuel on the same red plastic chair he has always sat on, Gogo on the wicker one Ouma gave her for Christmas more than twenty-five years ago. They sip their tea in silence until both cups are empty. Groot Samuel lights a cigarette. Gogo has never admonished him for this habit. She knows the comfort it gives him and as far as she is concerned, when your time comes, it comes, whatever you do to hasten its arrival.

She opens her snuff pot and snorts the powder into one nostril. She waits and then sneezes.

'We will need someone to help with the land,' says Groot Samuel.

Gogo is silent for a moment. Then she says, 'Maybe Tobias from the tree-fern nursery?'

'He is a fine worker.'

'I will ask him,' says Gogo.

'Thank you,' says Groot Samuel and he gets to his feet.

'You need peace, child,' murmurs Gogo.

'We all need that,' he says as he walks a few steps and then remembers. 'Delilah's brother Martinus and her father arrive today.'

Gogo looks at him. 'I will make the beds.'

He is about to turn away again when he says, 'Are you hurt?'

She shakes her head, 'Bruises only,' and she pats her body with the flat of her hand.

'Good,' he says and he walks away into the hot morning.

Gogo watches until he has disappeared and then she gets up, opens her suitcase and begins to unpack her things.

Gogo knew that her day would come. From the moment she had witnessed Frans's refusal to help his mother die, she knew she would be next. She vowed to herself that she would flee from the request, even before the sentence was out of Ouma's mouth.

Even as she said that to herself, she knew she was making up a story. Ouma was too clever and indeed too desperate to give her that chance.

If tea last thing at night was Gogo's favourite ritual, the early morning cup on the stoep was Ouma's.

'Do you see that the gardenia has its first buds, Gogo?' she says.

'*Ehe*, Ouma,' said Gogo and she took a sip of the sweet, hot liquid.

'And the crested barbet has had chicks?'

Gogo had nodded and said, 'A bird is a bird, Ouma.'

'And what about me?' said Ouma seamlessly, as if she were asking Gogo to pass the sugar.

'What about you?' asked Gogo, still softened by the sweet routine of the morning.

'Do you see that I am *less*?'

Gogo sat up straight. She would need her wits about her. She looked at Ouma and shook her head. 'A loved somebody is never *less*.'

'Until they are nothing,' said Ouma.

Gogo got to her feet. There it was, see. She thought it was their routine morning tea to start the day but the question was already on the table.

'Tell me,' said Ouma, 'how will you know when there is nothing left of me?'

'Ag no, Ouma, don't start.'

'When I don't know my own name?' the old doctor asked.

Gogo looked at her. 'Stop it, Ouma.'

'When I can't save anyone? That's coming soon.'

'*Haai*, Ouma, enough.'

But they both knew that it was true. Just the day before Ouma had failed in the middle of an emergency birth.

'Run, Gogo!' Ouma had shouted when she saw the woman

pushing the wheelbarrow down the drive and the two women ran to meet it.

A young woman, a girl really, was curled up embryo-like in the barrow. Deep grey pallor dulled her black skin.

The trail of red that marked the concrete driveway was like cookie crumbs left by Hansel and Gretel indicating where she had come from. It came out of a small hole at the bottom of the wheelbarrow and it was blood.

Beneath the young girl, in the scoop of the wheelbarrow, was a pool of the same.

'Take the other handle, Gogo,' shouted Ouma and together they pushed the young woman to the surgery.

They lifted her onto the examination table. 'Cut off her dress,' said Ouma.

Gogo did her bidding and she saw that the girl was hugely pregnant, her limbs waving beetle-like on either side of her pot belly.

'And now?' she asked Ouma, as the blood pumped over the examination table and onto the floor.

Ouma didn't answer.

'Ouma!' shouted Gogo.

But Ouma just stood there with her arms by her side and her eyes blank as a dead person's. She turned to Gogo and said, '*Ek kannie*, Gogo. I can't do this.'

The young woman's eyes rolled into the back of her head so only the white was showing.

Gogo shouted, 'Ouma?'

Gogo saw then that her friend had no idea what to do. The part of her mind that contained the *doctor* had slipped away.

'Hey, Ouma, you did it with me, remember?'

Ouma looked at her.

'Remember?'

Ouma's eyes blink.

'Remember!'

Ouma looked up. 'Your boy?'

'My boy. There was no harder birth than my boy.'

And so it had been. Gogo's baby rampaged his way out of her body. When it was over and Ouma handed him over to Gogo she saw he had a cleft palate. Ouma said, 'In a few months we can fix that.' And she had.

Gogo didn't weep when she saw the gap of her child's upper lip but whispered, 'Thanks be to God,' because she knew it could have been worse.

She had met her child's father late. He didn't stay long enough to see the baby born.

It was Ouma who dragged that reluctant baby out alive. Her strong Boer arms wrapped around Gogo's body, urging her to push through the pain.

'Stay with me . . .'

And when that baby was a fully grown good for nothing, Ouma sewed him up, time after time, and sent him back out into the world for another day. Until that last meaningless squabble over a woman at the pig farm when he was shot down for good and ever, *ka mehla* – for always.

That same Boer grip insisted that Gogo remain in this world without her son. In this way, the birth and eventual death of her only child was eased by this old woman.

'Do it now, otherwise she will die,' shouted Gogo.

And then she did. The skill returned to Ouma through her hands rather than her mind and she took command.

Gogo and Ouma sit silent for a moment. They each take a sip of tea. Gogo breathes a sigh of relief. Perhaps the old lady has forgotten her question.

'When I can't tell the difference between my pyjamas and my day clothes? What about that?' asked Ouma.

'Nobody will care about that.'

'When I have no watch-days?'

'Ouma!'

'So, when, Gogo?'

'Stop!'

'When? Just say when?'

Gogo gets to her feet. 'When you can no longer remember the name of your child.'

'That is it. Thank you, Gogo,' says Ouma quietly.

There it was. No one said anything about living or dying – but they had made a solemn vow and they both knew it.

Gogo could only pray that it would never happen.

But it did.

And she was a woman of her word.

CHAPTER FORTY-SEVEN

The sight of the battered blue truck that comes down the driveway carrying Delilah's father and brother could not be more sobering. A web of different coloured ropes holds their modest possessions in place. None of the adults watching it approach is unaware that its arrival adds a new burden to the too-small-to-be-a-farm on which they all depend.

Delilah and her mother have been watching out for the truck for hours.

Cheetah sees their hovering anticipation from her shade under the wild gardenia until the wife of the pig farmer comes up the drive to call her back to work.

It is not a magnanimous gesture but the queen sow in pen number two has refused to eat or, more importantly, to offer her services to the prime male breeding pig they have to pay for by the hour. The farmer suspects that Cheetah is the only one who can restore the sow's spirits. For that service he promises her a different room and an increase in her wages.

Out of concern for Tannie Hendricks, Cheetah stands up out of the dust and follows the farmer's wife back to the pig farm.

★

Delilah can see that the truck her father drives is burdened with things that are not worth having. The thin-as-paper sheets she grew up with and the Little Mermaid pyjamas.

It brings her father, who emerges from the truck and, after embracing Delilah, falls into his wife's arms.

Delilah watches her parents' reunion with surprise. Her mother's face tucked deep into her pa's neck, his teeth around her ear. Their relief, plain and simple, at being in one another's arms again, brings a kind of ordinary glow to their faces. It does not erase any of the hardship or the years accumulated in both but it does quiet a murmuring worry in Delilah that the exhausted, bread-baking, defeated parents of her recent memory would split apart from the weight of their suffering.

At least this one piece of the adult world to which she is shackled contains the small grace of true affection. It is while she is so engaged watching her parents that Delilah hears a soft, 'Hello, sissie,' behind her. She turns.

It is Martinus's face but the sparkle in his eye is dulled. His once strong body is close to skeletal, his limbs implausibly long and stick thin. Is it possible that time has speeded up and left her brother old and emptied out?

Delilah knows the cause of this transformation to be the sudden absence of a promising future and she doesn't know how to respond to that.

Her mother steps forward to intervene but Delilah's father holds her back. '*Wag net*,' he says and, amazingly, Aletta obeys and steps back to allow the siblings to find their way.

'Hello,' says Delilah to her brother finally. Since when was she the more powerful one, she wonders. The thought slips into her mind that she herself might be able to take on the challenge of the gold sofa and its attendant comforts. Something blooms there in the vertiginous space that Martinus's ambition, now broken, once occupied.

'Come,' she says, and the two of them walk away from the grown-up world and down the path towards the dam.

Delilah shows him the frogspawn in the water below the bank. Martinus gathers it gently in his hands and looks at it intently before replacing it on the surface of the water, unharmed.

Delilah turns the canoe upside down to drain it of the rainwater that has collected there since she and Ouma last used it. She shows Martinus how to climb into it without upsetting the balance and then the two of them glide across the water. Her brother's face lights up at the silent swish of their passage. Delilah guides them with her paddle towards the island at the centre of the dam.

When their small craft reaches the water below the weaver bird nests, Delilah lies back in the bottom of the canoe, just as she did with her Ouma. She watches the small yellow birds with the black bandit band across their eyes swoop in and out. Martinus wordlessly follows her lead. They are silent for a long time and then Martinus laughs. The sound bounces over the water like a skipping stone.

Chapter Forty-eight

The dark has yet to lift from the huts around Klein Samuel's homestead. The birds are busy and already, in neighbouring homesteads, one can hear the sounds of early risers. It is cool but the promise of heat to come is in the air.

Klein Samuel pulls open the flap of tattered animal hide that covers his doorway and steps out into the morning. He sits on his haunches beside the small cooking fire and stokes the coals back to modest life. The sky begins to lighten. He takes in the familiar smell of dust, thatch and bitter spinach from the simple meal his wife cooked him the night before.

When he first arrived, she had greeted him as if he were a stranger. She stopped her work and watched his approach across the sandy compound. It was only when the familiarity of his features consolidated into the face of *husband* that she got slowly to her feet.

Husband – who should have been here to help her farm the fields and raise the children. Who should have been here to help hide them from the Gukurahundi soldiers when they came to do their slaughter. The one who should have been here to touch her hand when she buried their lost ones.

She was not steady on her feet, so thin.

Klein Samuel saw in her face only the shadow of his young bride. How could she be so transformed? In her eyes he saw the shock of his own transformation.

'*Is it you?*' she whispered.

'*It is me.*'

Longing for Cheetah's youth and beauty turned in Klein Samuel's gut then, a wish to be gazing at someone with a life still to be lived.

There was no question of a conjugal reunion between husband and wife as they lay side by side. Klein Samuel closed his eyes and said to himself, *Stick insects, both.* And he fell into a bruised sleep.

Now, in the morning light, his wife watches him enter the far hut. She is already up and at her post against the wall of the far hut. She sees him emerge with the hoe and walk across the dusty homestead towards the kraal that once protected his cows from the jackals and hyenas that stalked the night.

He enters the kraal and the smell and bulk of Gundwane comes back to Klein Samuel in a rush. How he nursed that beast to adulthood, then back again from death when the drought hit. How he loved him. Had he remained here, he might have nursed his very own cattle in that way. It is an idle question and full of dreaming. He knows full well that it was his family's empty stomachs that drove him south for work.

He walks past the cattle kraal to the enclosure beyond it. He lifts off the long pole that acts as a gate and steps inside. There were once sheaves of corn here, ragged from the winds that whipped them and the modest water that nature bestowed on this dry world. But they fed his family and their cattle too when the grass dried up.

The sun begins to show itself over the horizon. He lifts the hoe. When did the implement he knows so well become so heavy?

He brings it down. It splits the earth open, revealing deep cracks that run down, down. How far do they go before they hit the deep water guarded jealously by middle earth?

Too far for him.

Klein Samuel works, sweat pouring, until the sun is high. Never does he find the easy rhythm that attended this labour when he was a young man. His sweat tastes to him like blood. Then he stops.

What will happen to the seed that he will scatter here? Will it merely lie on these rock-hard clumps of earth until the wind comes up to blow it away? The earth heats up and makes him an uncertain shifting shape in the haze.

It is no good. He lets the hoe fall useless by his side and he walks out of the gate. He does not replace the gate-pole. There is nothing here to protect.

He takes the single-track path that leads him to the small mud hut that has housed the local village shop since his father was a young man.

With the money given to him by Groot Samuel he buys a bottle of moonshine. Too eager to wait until he reaches home, Klein Samuel sits on the steps of the small shop and lifts the bottle to his lips.

He sips it slowly, as is his wont. A man passes leading a donkey burdened with a load of firewood but Klein Samuel does not notice. When the bottle is finished he lies on the earthen floor and closes his eyes.

The sun moves from morning to afternoon and then to almost night. The birds gather in the trees near the shop and shriek. At closing time the shopkeeper rouses Klein Samuel from his slumber. He can see, by the time it takes Klein Samuel to sit up, that the final sleep of this returning son of the soil he knows by the true name of Sifiye Khumalo is not far away.

The doorbell's insistent ring the following morning wakes Jannie from his restless slumber.

Much to his surprise Pieter the pathologist steps into his entrance hall and momentarily rests his head, forehead first, on Jannie's shoulder.

The young detective shows Pieter into the garden.

Pieter takes an envelope out of his jacket pocket and rests it on his lap.

'Tea?'

'No.'

They sit in silence.

'What can I do for you, Pieter?' says Jannie finally. He'd like to dig in the garden a little bit to calm the jitters Pieter has brought into his house.

Pieter bows his head. 'Nothing.' He looks up at Jannie. 'Thank you.'

There have only been a few moments in Jannie's life when he can remember feeling something like Delilah's *piep en tjank*, but he feels it now, and its attendant dread.

'I have bad news, Jannie,' says Pieter quietly.

Jannie says nothing.

'We found traces of skin under Ouma's fingernails,' says Pieter regretfully, 'like you said, on the right hand.'

'I see,' says Jannie

Pieter sighs. 'It belongs to the girl from the pig farm.'

Jannie tips forward in his chair. 'Cheetah?'

Pieter stands up. 'If it were up to me, I would put the findings back in the file and mark it closed.'

Jannie can barely breathe.

'But I'm afraid the genie is out of the bottle.'

Jannie struggles to follow his train of thought; he is still back at the beginning of the conversation. *Cheetah*?

Pieter doesn't want to speak ill of Anriette, his *seenuweeagtige* friend and colleague of twenty years, but he wishes he had not shared the findings with her the night before. It felt like a heavy load to carry on his own.

'It is the law!' Anriette had shouted at him.

'The law is not always right, Anriette.'

'But it is all we have,' she said, 'to show us how to be,' and then she had wept.

They could not have had more divergent views. Pieter is grateful to have the question of who finally helped Ouma leave this world answered, but he would much rather now let it lie. After all, it was Ouma's wish that it be so.

'The one with the Diors . . . I liked her,' said Anriette regretfully.

But the law was the law. There was a proper way to do things and she would see it done, even if he would not.

Now Jannie looks into Pieter's craggy face.

'I'm sorry,' says Pieter and he takes a deep breath, because he has a further revelation.

'She is not the only one, Jannie. I found skin from the old lady too. Gogo's skin.'

Jannie is suddenly nostalgic for the moments before this singular fact was made known to him, when his life and the world he lived in were more or less steady on their course.

Cheetah maybe but not Gogo! Surely not?

He sways a moment and when Pieter steps forward to steady him he brushes away his arm and sits on the garden chair.

PART NINE

CHAPTER FORTY-NINE

Beauty Sephamla thinks there should be a union for tea ladies and its first rule should be that no one, not even sad *moffies*, should be allowed to mess with her kitchen.

'*Phuma*,' she says gently to Jannie as he soaks his rooibos tea bag for the second time that morning.

The detective shuffles out with his head down.

Beauty prepares her tea trolley and sets out on her morning rounds.

In the course of his frantic morning, Mokheti catches sight of Jannie as he prepares for the arrest with his customary thoroughness. The warrant is in order, the search warrant made out in case it should be needed. And yet Jannie still doesn't order their departure.

He runs to get Suffering from under his desk and put him on the seat in the van. Then he thinks better of it and returns him to his spot under the desk.

Beauty clatters into Mokheti's office with her tea trolley and pours dark tea into a mug; she adds milk and three sugars. He doesn't look up or greet her as he normally would. *Tsk*. In Beauty's view, he's a crocodile with a headache. She adds one more sugar to his tea.

If he had asked her what she was doing, she would have said, 'Maybe it will make you sweeter,' and would thereby let him know that he was a little too *kwaai* today for her liking. But he doesn't ask.

An email has just come into Mokheti's mailbox and in the subject line is written, *I don want truble plse. Do wat is rite in gods eye.*

What the hell could that be? Mokheti has been told never to open unknown attachments without sending them to head office for checking, but who has the time for that? *I don want truble plse. Do wat is rite in gods eye.*

He clicks on it.

Anriette finds Jannie on the steps outside the police station with the sun pounding down on his head. She sits beside him.

'Hello,' she says.

'Ja, hello.'

They sit in silence on the step, then Anriette says, 'You know it doesn't have to be you to bring them in.'

He looks up at her. 'It must be me.'

'Ag, *boetie*, then it won't get any easier if you wait.'

He is pale as chalk but he stands up and walks over to the police van. A small nod to the arresting officer waiting there and they are gone.

Cheetah is in the pen with Mrs Hendricks when she sees the police van make its way down the steep driveway. It moves very slowly as if the driver is reluctant to arrive. If she half closes her eyes, she can make it seem toy size, but not for long.

She knows what it has come for and she sighs and gets to her feet. She has been waiting, she realises, for this moment. Now she wonders, with a distant kind of musing, if she would care more if Dumisane was alive? It burns unbearably bright, this longing for him. Her own grows dimmer in its glare. If he were alive she would run away from this police van. Through the bush, bent double, with sweat dripping into her mouth. She would care about getting away.

You would never know it but Gogo has been waiting for the arrival of the police van too.

She polishes the red stoep. It has been weeks since she paid it this attention and it is dull and sun dried. She has, as is her habit, wads of newspaper tied to each knee that *swish, swish, swish* as she moves.

The members of Gogo's choir group laugh at her doing her polishing this way. Their employers long ago switched to automatic polishers but she never asked Ouma for an automatic. How would they talk together with that loud noise interrupting their words?

Right now she would like to tell Ouma a thing or two about the arrival of the police van. She has a lot to say about the why and wherefore that led to that event.

But there is no one to tell. Now there is only her fate to meet. She gets very slowly to her feet.

Groot Samuel is halfway up the hill behind the house fixing the leak in the water tank. He loves the view of the farm from this height; it disguises all the mess and flaws and struggle that are evident close up.

All one sees from here is verdant lawn, a vegetable garden containing Tobias, recently of the tree-fern nursery, as he prepares the earth for planting. A herd of fat cattle, and a dam full to the brim with water. It looks almost possible from up here.

Groot Samuel sees the slow approach of the police van and he wishes it were not part of the picture. He reluctantly climbs down the ladder and packs away his tools.

Inside the farmhouse Delilah and her mother unpack their final few boxes. The emergence of the Little Mermaid pyjamas and the thin-as-paper sheets gives the child only momentary pause. She throws them onto a pile of give-aways in the hope that her mother doesn't see and haul them out again for another decade of use.

'*Skattie*, can you still fit into this?' says her mother and Delilah sees her hold up a bright yellow nylon dress.

'No,' snaps Delilah. 'I mean, it might fit, but who would wear that yellow?'

Her mother looks at her and wonders if this opinionated teenager was born out of the trauma of recent events or just out of nature's perversity.

Then they hear the whine of the police van. Delilah looks out to see it draw to a stop in front of the house.

No one gets out of the van and no one approaches to see what they might want.

From Jannie's perspective in the driver's seat it looks as if the whole world has packed up and left. Though he knows it unlikely, he prays that it is the case.

He opens his door and gets out. The silence quickly reasserts itself. The hiss of the cicadas only adds to the emptiness.

And then they come.

Cheetah is the first to emerge from the bush, spectrally thin to

Jannie's view. Then Groot Samuel from the hill. Gogo from the stoep with newspapers still attached to her knees with rubber bands.

Delilah and Aletta are last to join them. No one speaks. It is as if they have all lost the means.

Jannie's dread makes him thick headed. He is aware that he should speak but his tongue feels too wide for his mouth.

The arresting officer shuffles impatiently at his side. Delilah looks at him quizzically; he can see the alarm building in her eyes.

Only then does he say, 'I have a warrant for the arrest of Itumeleng Mokatsane and Cheetah Solomon.'

For a moment Delilah asks herself who Itumeleng Mokatsane is and then she sees Gogo's stricken face and she knows.

Cheetah lowers her head and shuffles wordlessly sideways until she and Gogo are standing side by side. The old woman reaches blindly for Cheetah's hand and the two of them lock fingers.

Jannie does not look up as he says, 'You are both charged with the murder of Susanne Aletta Delilah De la Rey.'

Delilah's *piep en tjank* rushes into her bones so hot and furious that she has to bend over to be able to breathe. It's a shrieking ambulance siren given physical shape. She looks around her at the adult faces. They are not surprised. Knowing faces, all of them.

Delilah reaches for Jannie's hand because he shares her thin-lipped shock. She grips tight because they have to hang on to this blasted moment long enough to understand – just long enough for that.

CHAPTER FIFTY

There were evenings on Ouma's farm as close to perfection as you could come. The wind blew the smell from the pig farm away and the sweet wild gardenia took its place. The birdsong was contented and the sunset luminous.

On nights like this Groot Samuel would light the *braai* and, hand in hand, he and Ilse would watch the flames burn down to glowing coals. Gogo would make her special *pap* and *bredie* with fresh tomatoes from the vegetable garden. And soon the odour of sizzling *boerewors* and rosemary-scented lamb chops would soften the struggles of the day.

On this particularly lovely night, Jannie joined their table. He brought a bottle of wine and a bunch of dahlias from his garden. He was proud of having conjured the modest blooms out of the unlikely sand of his back yard.

They sat down to eat. After all these years Gogo still didn't easily sit at table with the family but tonight Delilah made place beside her and said, 'Gogo, come.'

'Please sit,' added Groot Samuel, and so Gogo sat.

Ouma picked at her food. She chewed slowly, choosing the more delicate vegetable flavours over the meat. In the normal course of events it was the sweet things she loved the most, but not tonight.

When the plates had been stacked and the dessert bowls set Gogo brought out Ouma's favourite ice cream and said, 'One scoop or two, Ouma?'

Ouma looked up and smiled, 'Not for me, thank you.'

Gogo looked at her and said, 'This is the first time I have heard such a thing. No ice cream?'

'My parents will be coming to pick me up soon,' said Ouma by way of explanation.

Gogo and Delilah glanced at one another.

Ouma sat unusually upright in her chair, a hand on each of the armrests, alight with anticipation. 'Shortly . . .' she whispered.

They didn't say parents, they said ma and pa, and they didn't speak that pert, Enid Blyton English.

Delilah looked at her grandmother. '*Wat sê Ouma nou?*' She spoke in Afrikaans to call back the woman she knew.

'Your ma and pa are coming here?' asked Ilse, confused.

Ouma looked at her daughter-in-law with shining eyes. 'My mother Susanne and her beau, Ebenezer.'

She used the old-fashioned word *beau*, like her mother would have done. It was as if she had slipped inside another skin, halfway between one era and another.

Groot Samuel didn't like it. 'You are tired, Ouma.'

'No,' she said and turned to look at him. His face was familiar to her and yet not. She searched its nooks and crannies and then said lightly, 'You can come too.'

He looked at her earnest face and he said very quietly, 'Where are you going?'

'To visit Samuel.'

Groot Samuel held her gaze, willing her to make sense.

'My son.'

Gogo stared down into the tub of ice cream, melting now into a soup of white.

Delilah looked from one face to another, trying to understand. Jannie saw the dread rise up in Groot Samuel's eyes.

Silent tears streamed down Gogo's face. She wiped them away with one hand, careful not to spill the ice cream she held in the other. Groot Samuel got up and walked out into the night. This time, not even Ilse tried to call him back.

Groot Samuel and Gogo sat together on the stoep as the first sliver of dawn light appeared on the horizon. Neither spoke. The baboons came down from the mountain to strip the avocado and litchi trees in the orchard. They sauntered from tree to tree, goading the dogs at the fence into shrill hysteria.

Their barking roused Ouma and she shuffled into the living room and then stood in the doorway to the stoep, one shoe on and one shoe off.

Gogo got up from her contemplation and approached the old lady. Both she and Groot Samuel saw the small dribble of urine run down Ouma's leg and form a puddle at her feet.

Groot Samuel put his head in his hands.

'I know what we must do,' said the old lady quietly.

'About what Ouma?' asked Gogo.

'The people.'

'And what is that?'

'We must find them.'

'And then?' asked Gogo.

Ouma looked at her as if she couldn't credit that she would need to ask such a question and she said, 'Then we must tell them that they are not alone.'

There was no pity in her statement, no urge to save anyone, just a certain knowledge of how it was *out there* and *in here* and what must be done about it.

Groot Samuel got up and walked slowly into Ouma's bedroom. He gently scooped Suffering off her bed and into his arms. The little dog licked his face.

He took him to Ilse, who lay sleepless in her bed in the other house. He sat beside her and said, 'Can you do something for me, Ilse?'

She sat up. 'What?'

'Take Suffering to your mother's for a few hours. Ouma had a bad night; she needs to sleep.'

Ilse was about to ask all the questions you would normally ask under these circumstances, but Groot Samuel raised his fingers to his lips and the absolute imperative in his gesture silenced her.

When Cheetah got up to prepare for the early shift at the pig farm she took care not to wake Klein Samuel.

As usual, she ate nothing; she just climbed into her overalls four sizes too big and tied a belt round her waist. She pulled on her wellington boots and walked through the just-awake world of birds and scurrying creatures.

She opened the door to Tannie Hendricks's pen and leant down to breathe in the pig's calming, earthy smell. A car engine broke the peace of their communion. She looked over the half wall just in time to see Ilse drive by with Suffering on the passenger seat beside her.

Ilse swore under her breath as she drove up the steepest part of the hill. 'Fuck!' It was a word so foreign to her vocabulary it sounded as if some delinquent spook had uttered it in her place. All night her husband had sat moping on the stoep with Gogo and now he asked *this* of her so his mother could sleep?

'*Fuck!*' The dog in the seat beside her began to whine. The compassionate soul in her wanted to stop and stroke his yellow coat until he licked her face and wagged his tail. But *Fuck that too*, she thought. He was Ouma's dog. And in that toxic moment she was no longer the woman who made it her business to protect living things from harm. Her mother would have said the devil was in the car with her that morning.

She drove up to the brim of the hill. She turned into the road and drove away from her family seat.

Gogo gave Ouma a cup of tea and almost-burnt marmalade toast as she always did at breakfast time. Ouma chewed on the right side of her mouth as she always did so as to avoid the painful gum on her left.

Gogo combed Ouma's hair until it was smooth and tucked behind her ears. If it weren't for the lines of laughter around her eyes she would seem more child than old person.

'The best dress, Ouma?' Gogo had asked her, and the old lady nodded. In truth, it was the only dress in her wardrobe but Gogo held it out for Ouma's approval anyway.

Ouma smiled. '*Mooi*,' she said.

'The flowers are nice,' said Gogo.

She put Ouma's hat on her head and the two women walked hand in hand across the grass and onto the path leading to the dam, one birdlike skin and bone, the other, plentifully round.

Groot Samuel stood on the path ahead, waiting for them. Gogo could see that his body was weighed down with grief.

As they drew near, Ouma let go of Gogo's hand and walked the few steps to Groot Samuel on her own.

She stood in front of him and looked up into his face. 'You are a man for the ages, Samuel,' she said and she ran her hand across his cheek.

Practised as he was at mastering his feeling Groot Samuel had to clench his jaw to stop the trembling of his chin as he leant down and kissed her, first on her cheek and then on her forehead.

He watched her turn away and it was as if part of her had already stopped *being*. He could see that her mission to wholly complete that conversion was so much part of her that to separate her from it would bring her to her end.

Still, it took the strength of Samson for him not to stop her from walking towards the dam.

The water was very low. Gogo laid a blanket on a patch of cracked mud and the two women settled onto it like they were going to have a picnic. Ouma smoothed her skirt over her legs.

The pearl-spotted owl chicks crowded the entrance to the wooden nest on the tree in the centre of the island. Ouma looked up to see the small forest of their wide-open mouths screeching to be fed, and she smiled.

'Ready?' asked Gogo softly.

Ouma nodded.

Groot Samuel turned on the tap, and water thundered into the dam. Soon, a thin slick of it reached their stretched-out legs. It felt cool against their skin.

The water rose.

'You remember when I bought the tombstone for my son, Ouma?' said Gogo.

Ouma smiled. 'The biggest one. And marble.'

'Ja, red marble.'

Gogo shifted in the rising water.

'Remember how I went every Saturday for twenty years to pay Mr Vosloo there in the funeral yard my twenty-five rand?'

'I remember.'

'Then one day, by that time the grass had long grown over the grave and the red stone was pink from the sun, I went there and again handed Mr Vosloo my money. I remember he looked at me and said, "*Gogo, you are paid in full.*"'

Ouma was very still, as she waited, in peace, for the next words.

Gogo whispered, 'You are paid in full, Ouma.'

Ouma's eyes closed and she smiled.

The water rose and Ouma reached for Gogo's hand. She turned to look at Gogo and said, '*Ke a leboha.*'

'Goodbye, *sisi*,' whispered Gogo.

Ouma brushed her cheek with her hand and then she slipped, without fuss or comment, under the water.

When it was done, Gogo slowly raised herself upright. As she turned to half swim, half wade towards the bank, something stopped her progress. Was she caught on a stick hidden below the water?

The understanding of what held her there arrived slowly. Gogo tried to pull free but she felt fingernails dig deep into her flesh. It was Ouma's hand.

She called out in panic to Groot Samuel who waited on the bank but it was not he who stormed into the water.

It was Cheetah.

Gogo will never forget how she looked, the brown girl, as she splashed, long-limbed, towards her.

Gogo thought she could be either angel or devil in the predatory, opened-winged way she dived into the water. Certainly she was not fully human.

Cheetah pulled Ouma's hand from Gogo's ankle and then held Ouma's head down. Every sinew of the young woman's small body shook as the duck's feathers and the muck filled Ouma's nostrils and her body stopped asking for more life.

Cheetah knew. She had seen it before, the will that lay in the primitive underlay of a person's mind.

The part of Ouma that now insisted on living was that which was banal about her: the reflex of her lungs for another gulp of air, her heart to pump, her teeth to grind. But not, Cheetah knew, her sly wit, her skill and her *medemenslikheid*.

Ouma was on her way to becoming a wraith, and she for one could not abide the suffering that came with it.

Gogo waited in the shallows for Cheetah to emerge from under the water.

Groot Samuel stood on the bank of the dam, expectant. Although time had long since become unreliable to him, he somehow knew the water had been still for too long.

There was no thought about what he did next. It came to him

as naturally as the air he breathed. He waded into the mud. The level of the water as he approached the middle required him to half swim and he did so with strong strokes, urgent. He dived under the surface of the water twice before he found her. Cheetah fought him for only a few seconds before going limp in his arms.

They emerged, an eight-limbed creature, trailing algae and mud.

Gogo waded out of the dam with a stumbling stride, no strength left in her limbs and foreboding at what Cheetah had done in her chest.

Groot Samuel did not let Cheetah go when he reached the bank but held her as she vomited out the water she had invited into her lungs. She had shown his mother such mercy.

When she was still, he put her down on the sand. Then he lay nearby, face down, and wept.

CHAPTER FIFTY-ONE

The rain clouds hook on the mountain behind the farm and swell above the small gathering of humans on the dust in front of Ouma's house.

Delilah looks at them one by one – her mother, her uncle, Gogo, Cheetah and Jannie – but none of them returns her gaze.

It is not the first time she has had to look outside of the family for her education, and she has stored this teacher in her mind since she was five. She remembers it precisely because it was her birthday when she stumbled on the man with the panga in the reeds on the edge of the river.

She asked him what his panga was for and he said for cutting sugarcane and then she asked him what he was doing in the reeds and he said, 'I am waiting, in the shade.'

'What for?'

'For my death,' he had said, and he showed her the fang marks on his ankle. He knew the kind. There was nothing to be done. The child nodded. She knew it too. It made unsentimental sense to the five-year-old Delilah that he would be there, doing that.

She knows that there is nothing to be done here either. She says, softly and to no one in particular, 'It was too hard for her to be alive.'

And so the teenager, unshackled by the way it should be, steps lightly into the way it is.

And it does make pure, shining sense to her that the woman she knew, so denuded by the watch-less days, would want to end her life in this way.

She remembers now how Ouma leant over to whisper into her reluctant mother's ear during her visit to Pongola two years before. It was a question that rendered the ensuing years *Ouma-less* and the mystery of it had plagued her. Until now.

Groot Samuel looks at Jannie and says, 'She asked us to help her die, Jannie.'

It is as if a thick layer of new snow has fallen on Jannie's insides. He has seen it only once in his life and he remembers the attendant muffled quiet acutely. And he wonders, in the quiet of that moment, why it was that Ouma didn't ask *him*?

It is a thought so painful that it ruptures Jannie's fragile inner peace. He turns to Groot Samuel and says softly, 'Your mother . . .?'

There is silence.

'Did you hold her down?'

Groot Samuel looks away.

'Did you?' hisses Jannie. He is aware of an ache building in his jaw. It is hard to manage his thoughts in the face of its painful advance.

'No,' says a voice to his left and he turns to see Cheetah looking at him. 'I did,' says Cheetah.

Jannie says to his young policeman, quietly, 'Arrest her.'

The young man removes the handcuffs from his belt, uncertain.

Gogo steps between Cheetah and the policeman. 'And I did,' she says.

Jannie lifts his finger and points at Gogo and he mumbles, 'And her.'

'Jannie Claassens!' says Delilah and her voice gives him pause.

Her face has the too-red apple cheeks he knows come from distress.

'Did you think Ouma slipped?' she asks.

Jannie stares at her.

'Did you?' she asks again.

'At first,' he says.

'And I showed you otherwise.'

He nods his head. 'It doesn't matter now.'

'It matters because I was wrong.' She looks at him and the regret in her gaze traps him in its glare, 'Now look at what you are doing. *Kyk net.*'

No one moves, or speaks.

Jannie lowers his eyes and everyone can see his heart is breaking.

Finally, Groot Samuel says, 'Ouma knew it wouldn't be fair to ask you.'

He looks into Groot Samuel's eyes and says, 'I would have done it for her.' It is true. He would have broken every rule in the book to be her chosen one.

Cheetah says, 'She would not have loved you any more for it.'

She speaks from experience. He can see the shadow left on her face for having been the one to do it.

To escape the truth of that, and the pity he sees in the dark gaze of his one-time love, Jannie mumbles to his subordinate, 'Come.' Then he turns away and stumbles over to the police van.

The small posse watch in silence as he slams the door and starts the engine.

The *rooigras* is thick on either side of the driveway. Jannie wonders how he didn't notice that before. It will provide good grazing for the cattle. How many seasons has he watched this grass change from green to red and then fade to yellow clumps in the driest months only to bounce back when the first rains come – green, red, yellow.

Chapter Fifty-two

Mokheti hits play on his computer. A shaky image fills the screen. He watches it with a bruised, morbid dread. It is clear that he has done so many times already.

A crowd gathered on a pavement, shouts of alarm, people shuffling in front of the lens to get a better view. A man shouts the refrain of all terrified men in these parts. '*Asseblief, my baas . . . please, my master, be merciful.*'

Mokheti doesn't know that the man being beaten on the ground is Klein Samuel but he does recognize his abuser.

He watches as the man in the red T-shirt wraps his belt around Klein Samuel's hands and then ties them to the chassis of a car.

A white man gets out of the driver's seat and then turns to face the crowd. Mokheti knows him too. Someone in the distance begins to cry.

With no great fanfare the man in the red T-shirt climbs into the driver's side of the car and starts the engine.

The white man tests that the belt round Klein Samuel's wrists is secure, then he jumps into the passenger's seat and the car pulls off.

A young child in the crowd hides his head under his mother's apron.

Mokheti pauses the video. He hangs his head. He is deadly still.

He gets up out of his chair and walks quickly to his office door. 'Jannie!' he shouts.

He shouts so loudly that even Beauty in her small kitchen looks up from her magazine.

Mokheti waits for Jannie to pull his chair close to the screen, and then, without saying anything else, he presses play on his computer once more.

Klein Samuel's body bounces into the air when the car hits the first bump in the potholed road.

Jannie half stands at the sight of it. He sees how the belt round Klein Samuel's wrists brings him back to earth. He sees how he tries to keep his feet from being torn off when they drag along the road.

How he twists round to face the earth and then the sky, helplessly. And again.

He watches the car speed up. A petite Asian woman in a white pharmacist's coat runs out of the crowd and onto the road.

He sees Klein Samuel's shoes fly off, first one and then the other.

As the car pauses at the intersection the pharmacist pounds on the roof and shouts, 'Stop! Stop this bloody madness.'

Nothing happens for a moment and then the driver emerges from the car.

Jannie gasps. He knows him too. He watches in horror as the man undoes the belt that lets Klein Samuel fall to the ground. Then walks away without another glance.

A small boy in the crowd cries loudly and his mother shouts out in Sotho, '*What did he do? Modimo – dear God. What did the poor man do?*'

When it is over, Jannie is silent. His skin is grey, as if his internal struggle has used up all the blood meant for his surfaces.

'What kind of world is this, Jannie?' Mokheti says at last.

Jannie does not trust himself to speak.

Mokheti's words come from the Bible stored somewhere in his orator's heart for this moment. 'Because the way I see it, the ones that do not want to die, fall like fine fruit before their time, unprotected by our law and order.'

Jannie feels a bubble of grief make its way up his body. He wants to ask his boss to stop talking before it bursts into his head.

'And those who are ready to die, to spare their families and themselves, are kept alive.'

When Mokheti speaks again, it is with a quiet intensity. 'Jannie, make out a warrant for their arrest.'

Jannie's head snaps up, 'Sure?'

I don want truble plse. Do wat is rite in gods eye.

Mokheti looks at Jannie over his glasses. 'I am.'

Jannie is on his feet already, heading for the door.

Mokheti returns to his computer. He clicks open the email, hits *Forward*, and a stream of addresses begin to fill up the *Send to* column.

The two men, one white, one black – one old, one young – make something of ripple in the crowd as they walk along the road towards Mercy's shebeen.

It is not every day that the stallholders and commuters gathered here see such a twosome sharing such silent intent. There is nothing heroic about their passage, just a banal one-foot-in-front-of-the-other sort of determination to get to where they must go.

Mercy hangs her washing in the yard outside her house when she catches sight of the two men. *I don want truble plse. Do wat is rite in gods eye.*

And so they have.

She doesn't show any alarm, but calmly picks up one child from the ground and takes the other by his hand. She walks out of the low gate and is soon swallowed up by the people milling around the taxi rank.

When Mokheti and Jannie reach the front gate the older man stops and the younger continues to the front door.

For Jannie, the path away from his mentor towards certain confrontation with his foe, is all-his-years-of-living long. He can hear his breath move in and out of his lungs, a wheezy sort of breathing that he associates with *Mr Right Thing To Do* and he is grateful that Mokheti is back. He does not underestimate the storm that will follow this arrest.

He knocks on the door of Mercy's shebeen. Out of the corner of his eye he sees a flicker of movement in the far side of the yard. Before he can turn to look more closely, the door opens and Detective Officer Ntombela smashes his fist into Jannie's fine face. The young detective feels his features shudder and realign but he does not fall.

'*Blerrie moffie,*' Ntombela spits.

Jannie never again wants to hear those two words and certainly not from such a man. *He sees Klein Samuel's body bounce up into the air in a smooth arc, graceful even, until his bound hands bring him back down with a jerk.*

Enough. Jannie brings the barrel of his gun down on the side of Ntombela's head. The policeman falls.

A shout from Mokheti and Jannie turns just in time to see Detective Bezuidenhout bearing down on him. The burly policeman slams Jannie into the wall with the force of his impact. The air leaves Jannie's lungs in a single rush and he slides to the ground. Bezuidenhout seizes his chance and kicks Jannie in the stomach with his heavy boot. And again.

Jannie cries out and curls up foetus-like to protect himself from more. One, two, three, maybe more, bone-snapping kicks rain on the small of his back and he closes his eyes and wonders if this is it for him. A thick, dark feeling begins to separate him from the pain in his body.

Ntombela and Bezuidenhout can see that he is vanquished. They step over Jannie's prone form and move towards the gate.

It is only when they notice Mokheti standing sentry in the road that they begin to doubt their unassailability. His gaze makes it clear that he has busted rank and is here to see that they are held to account.

Behind them, Jannie feels the air rush back into his lungs. He gets to his feet.

When the two detectives see Jannie coming at them they turn and run, seeking cover amongst the people over whom they hold such poisonous power.

They do not see the pharmacist waiting on the pavement ahead. Or Mercy and her clutch of market-stall owners gathering at the end of the road where their police car is parked. They do not see the children putting rocks into their pockets in the alley that runs parallel to their street.

Mokheti sees it all, and as he closes in on Ntombela he knows that these two men have had their day in the sun.

For a moment, Mokheti would like Jannie to be released from being a seeker. He would like it for himself too, but the truth is that it is the fate of decent men in a dark time.

Did they not know that Klein Samuel was a somebody?

Did they not know?

Ntombela sprints for his police car parked just beyond the blue bus. Mokheti's age does not help the pace of his pursuit and the guilty man is almost at his getaway car when a small boy sitting beside his meagre store of apples sticks his foot out in Ntombela's path. The detective trips, his arms flail as he tries to right himself, but gravity wins out and he hits the dirt road hard.

Mercy and her gaggle of people descend on the scrambling policeman. His abuses have left a fearful rage amongst his victims. Some here were witness to Klein Samuel's agony, many have seen smaller acts of cruelty and most have found their meagre incomes pilfered by the rackets run by these two men. *Enough!*

A young man kicks the detective in the head.

Only now does Mokheti catch up to them, breathing hard.

The irony that he will be the one to save the cowering policeman from the fury of the people does not escape him.

Jannie feels rather than sees Bezuidenhout exploit this moment to dodge, still moving fast, behind a makeshift stall and then slip, unseen, into the maze of pathways that spread cobweb-like beyond the taxi rank.

Jannie darts along the narrow paths between the shacks in pursuit. He feels the wound over his eye open anew and the pouring blood makes him blind. He must rely on the world of sound and its messages. It is quieter here, away from the taxi rank and the market stalls. People have taken refuge in their homes in the hope that this time the trouble will pass them by.

Jannie stops, listens for the sound of breath and footfall but there is no sign, no movement, no next move.

An old lady appears in her doorway in a faded petticoat. She puts her finger to her lips and points to the shack next door. Her eyes say *He is in there. Please find him and take him away.*

Jannie steps silently onto the path leading up to the door of the small shack. The trickle of blood from the wound above his eye has found its way to his mouth. He wonders who will suture the cut now that Ouma is gone.

Gone, and *free*; those two facts tumble, twinned, into his mind. She is free. He can hear Gogo say, *Thanks be to God.*

There is no more for him to do.

Jannie's grief flaps up into the air as he approaches the sagging door of the shack where the detective hides.

He knocks. There is no answer. Jannie tries the handle and the door swings open. He steps into it, half blind but ready for a fight. There, on the floor, crouches the one he is looking for.

Epilogue

The coming of evening does not bring relief from the heat in Klein Samuel's distant homestead.

It is thick-aired, and quiet in the dark hut where he lies. Through the small portal that the doorway provides to the outside world he sees his wife and the village *inyanga* hunched together in salutation.

He knows that as his light fades they must alert the *amadhlozi* of his departure from this world. Klein Samuel feels the benign presence of his distant kin. Also, his mother, father and his fallen children too, just beyond the reach of his gaze.

'*Soon, soon,*' he says and he closes his eyes. First, he must take his leave of the others who live in him, the ones who will not know where to find him when they die.

If he could rise up and fly, winged, southward, to the door of Mercy's shebeen he would see it empty out after a busy night.

Above and along the river of lights on the highway from Mercy's to the town of Brits, he would see Jannie bent over his bath, blood streaming.

He would hear the doorbell ring and see the brown man with a poetry book waiting there for Jannie to open it.

And if he left them there and flew along the ridge of mountains towards Ouma's farm he would see Gundwane drinking in the calm shallows on the edge of the dam.

He would see the girl Delilah and the new boy walk down the driveway in their school uniforms.

He would see Gogo on the bench under the Acacia tree just above the slope where Ouma lies. He would notice this time of fleeting quiet when the day creatures are at rest, and the nocturnal ones have yet to start their hunting.

And he would see Groot Samuel, *oh how that would make him smile,* as he kneels down to check the water level before he switches off the tap.

Then he would wait for the one he wants the most. Night would come to the water and make it ink black. Then Cheetah would be there.

And he would whisper, *Swim, Cheetah.*

He would see that the moon has yet to rise when she steps out of her muddy overalls and wades into the shallows.

And he would feel, through her, where the mud at the bottom of the dam gives way to vertiginous space as it deepens. He would see her hesitate for a moment, fearful.

Swim! he would say, for everyone knows water is where the divine can be borne out.

He would know, before she did, that the source of the sliver of light on the water ahead is the emerging tip of the rising moon.

He would see her throw one arm forward and then surge up onto the surface of the water.

Swim, he would beseech her, so the lives they lived can be healed. Never mind that the boy Dumisane lives in the softly moving liquid alongside them. Never mind that.

Swim, he would say, so his own madness can be forgiven when he kneels at the feet of his *amadhlozi*.

And he would see how, one stroke at a time, Cheetah makes her way over the place where Ouma lay, and beyond it to the far end where the acacia tree stands. And he would see her wait there, and he would know that she was listening for him.

Klein Samuel opens his eyes to greet the world into which he will pass. He feels the warm air of the night close in around him, tight. His chest rises up, up, and he is gone.

His dutiful wife murmurs, '*Usephelile*,' and begins her soft lament. *He is finished*.

The jackal, watching Cheetah from the mountaintop, turns on his heels, lopes across the short yellow grass and vanishes over the brim of the hill to hunt, as he likes to do, under cover of the night.

GLOSSARY

A

ag	oh
ag nee, man	oh no, man – exclamation of annoyance, irritation
aikona	no (Zulu)
amadhlozi	ancestors
asseblief	please

B

baas	boss, sir
bakkie	small truck, usually (but not always) open on the back
binnegoed	insides, internal organs
bly	stay, remain
bly stil, julle	keep quiet, you (pl)
bobotie	dish of Indonesian and Cape Malay origin made with spiced minced lamb, with an egg-based topping
boer	farmer (literally), but can be used to refer to a man who is Afrikaans speaking, an Afrikaner (Boer); its use may be either derogatory, affectionate, or descriptive

boerewors	spiced sausage, usually beef or lamb; staple ingredient for a traditional braai or barbecue
bokkie	small buck (literally), most often used as an affectionate term for either male or female
braai	barbecue (n. and vb.)
braaiplek	space outdoors constructed especially for the barbecuing of meat
bredie	stew, usually made with vegetables and meat (lamb or beef), slowly cooked together over several hours, flavoured with a variety of spices that might include ginger, cinnamon, cardamom, cloves
buchu bos	indigenous shrub (*Agathosma betulina*) well known for its medicinal properties

D

dankie	thank you
die	the
dis hy wie die land winsgewende gemaak het	he's the one who made the land profitable
doek	headscarf, worn by a woman, usually tied tightly round the head, concealing the hair
dood	dead
drie	three
duiwel	devil
dumela	hello (Sesotho)

E

een	one
eish!	exclamation denoting annoyance, frustration, sorrow, or regret

ek is nie genoeg nie	I am not enough
ek kannie	I can't, I am not able to

F

fokken	fucking (adj.)

G

gah!	exclamation of disgust (pronounced with a guttural 'g')
gegly	slipped
gemors	mess
genoeg	enough
gevaar	danger
gly	slip
gogo	grandmother
groot	big, large

H

haai	hey (may be used as a greeting; also used as an expression of mild disbelief or disapproval)
hayi	no
heerlik	lovely, delicious
het ek so gemaak?	did I do this?
hoed	hat
hoërskool	high school
hy	he

I

inyanga	diviner, traditional healer (Ndebele)

J

ja	yes
ja-nee	literally, yes-no; a greeting, acknowledgement, with something of a deep sigh implicit in it
jislaaik	expression of annoyance, exasperation
jou	you (s.)
julle	you (pl.)
julle mense	you people
jy het nie	you didn't
jy is die duiwel se kind	you are the devil's child
jy weet	you know
jy weet dit mos	you know it

K

ka mehla	always (Sesotho)
kameeldoring (boom)	camel thorn (tree) (*Vachellia erioloba*)
ke a leboha	thank you (Sesotho)
kind	child
klap	slap, smack
klapwoord	a word that stings, hurts
klein	small
kom	come
kom nou	come now
kom, my liefie	come, my love, my darling
kraal	enclosure for livestock
krag	strength, power
kwaai	angry
kyk net	just look

L

laager	originally used to describe a defensive positioning or circular, enclosing formation of the wagons of

	the Boers when moving or trekking; often used to describe a mindset that is closed or defensive, e.g. a laager mentality
lappie	small cloth or rag
le kae?	how are you?
leef	live, alive
leef hy nog?	is he still alive?
liefie	love, darling (term of endearment)
loop	walk, go
los	leave, or leave alone
luigat	lazy person, lazybones

M

maak gou	hurry, be quick
mbaqanga	a style of South African music, with roots in Zulu music, which evolved out of swing, jazz and kwela and which retains many of those elements
medemenslikheid	humanity, feeling for fellow man
meid	maid, servant; usually used insultingly or in a derogatory way
meneer	mister, sir
mense	people
menslikheid	humanity
met	with
mieliepap	porridge made from ground maize (or 'mielie'), mealie meal
mielies	maize, corn on the cob
miesies	missus
Modimo	God (Sesotho)
mme	mother
moenie	don't
moenie so praat nie	don't talk like that, don't say that

moffie	slang (Afrik.) for a homosexual man; 'queer' would be the equivalent English language term; often used in a derogatory sense, but can also be used in an affectionate tone
mooi	beautiful
muti	medicine
my	my

N

nagapie	bush baby
nê?	not so?
nee	no
nee dankie	no thank you
niemand nie	no one
niks, niks nie	nothing
nog	more, in addition to
nou	now

O

oom	uncle
ons	our
ou, oud	old
ouboet	literally, 'old brother', affectionate term, as one might say 'old thing'
ouma	grandmother, grandma
outjie	little chap, little boy

P

pa	father, dad
pap	porridge
phuma	get out (Zulu)

piep en tjank	whining, making a fuss ('piep', peep, make a small noise; 'tjank', the whimpering sound a dog would make)
poes	cunt
praat	talk

R

rinkhals	ring-necked spitting cobra
rooigras	tufted perennial grass (*Themeda triandra*) that turns a pinkish colour with age

S

saam	together
senuweeagtig	nervous, high-strung, of a nervous disposition
sies	exclamation of disgust (Afrik.)
sisi	sister (Zulu)
skattie	literally, 'little treasure', used as a term of endearment
skyfie	segment, as of an orange
soetdoring	sweet thorn (*Acacia karroo*)
soos	as, just like
spaza shop	small convenience store, selling a variety of goods, mainly foodstuffs
stil	quiet, still
stoep	a raised platform or veranda running along the front and sometimes round the sides of a house of Dutch architecture
stompie	cigarette butt
stywepap	stiff porridge, made from *mielie* meal
sissie	little sister (Afrik.)
swart	black
swart gevaar	black danger
sy het nie gegly nie	she didn't slip

T

tamatie bredie	stew with a thick tomato-based sauce
tannie	auntie
tel	count
tiekiedraai	traditional Afrikaner dance, notable for its spins and turns (literally to 'turn on a tickey coin') danced to *Boeremusiek*
tsamaya hantle	goodbye (Sesotho)
twee	two

U

usephelile	he is finished (dead) (Ndebele)
unontlori	stick insect

V

veld	flat, open countryside
verlange	longing, or feeling of longing
vir ewig en altyd	for ever and always
voetsak	slang for get out or leave; given as a crude instruction or command and very impolite
vrou	woman, wife

W

wa bona	you see (Sesotho)
wag maar	wait, hold on
wag-'n-bietjie bos	buffalo-thorn tree (*Ziziphus mucronata*) literally, wait-a-little bush
wat gaan nou aan?	what's going on now?
wat sê jy?	what did you say, what do you say?
wat sê Ouma nou?	what are you saying now, Ouma?
weet	know

ACKNOWLEDGEMENTS

This book marks something of a homecoming for me; to my country and also to some of the early teachers who were my guides. My father, Professor Neville Proctor, fragile and brilliant, who left us too soon but whose deep humanism I hope is honoured in these pages. Thanks to my brothers Andre and Jonathan – who asked important fraternal questions about my purpose in writing this book. Jonathan, also, for translating the poem 'Ouma' and for helping me to remember. Andre, for updating me on fruit stalls in Lavender Hill and other local knowledge, and for saying, in the end, 'Just do it.' For Lily Ndlovu, our first caretaker who lived through the abuses of the Fifth Brigade in Southern Zimbabwe and told me those tales. For Bucks and Timothy, presences in my childhood, whose precarious lives opened my eyes to how it was. For my first real storytelling teacher and great friend, the director Barney Simon, who I miss deeply. For Gcina Mhlope, with whom I shared transformational years at the Market Theatre and whose writing and friendship I have treasured since. For Robyn Slovo, who I thank for a rich, decades-long conversation about place and purpose. For Gail Gerhart, historian and dear friend, who illuminated our history in her seminal series 'From Protest to Challenge' and who continues to tether me approximately to historical accuracy. For Bill Drayton, whose work, vision and friendship have always quietly guided my thinking. For Shomit Mitter, a most steadfast collaborator on this book and its first supporter. For Jon Riley, editor-in-chief at Quercus, who published my first book and then, miraculously, my second. I am so very grateful for his belief in the work and for his guidance on how to make it better. For Rose Tomaszewska for her kindness and sure-footedness even when the clock was ticking. For Alison Lowry, who worked tirelessly at the end to correct my inaccuracies and test my certainties. For Nicky Stubbs at Jonathan Ball who led me to Alison and launched the book in South Africa. For Truida Heymann who introduced me to Professor Lina Spies, poet and academic, who advised on the Elisabeth Eybers poetry and its translation. Her lifelong study of the poet's oeuvre makes an invaluable contribution to our understanding. And for Elisabeth Eybers herself whose rare visits to my childhood home gave me my first exposure to the idea of *Writer*. For Mercia and Elna for their years of service to the South African Police and for their tireless guidance on questions of investigative practice. I thank them for their generosity and their patience with my ever-expanding research. To my agent Peter Straus and Emma Patterson for their dedication to this book. Evelyn Gunayon for taking care of us with such grace. Thanks to Kerry Ratcliffe and Doug Henderson who shared their retreat on Swan's Island, Maine, for the critical summer when this book took its first steps. For Lisa Montgomery whose friendship helped make my other job, mother of a graduating senior, more than edifying. For Rasha and Hassan Elmasry, Danna, Omar and Yarra for being family. For my friends and fellow trustees at the American School in London, especially Coreen Hester, for being a guiding light to me and to the institution she leads. For lifelong friends Francis and Lindy Wilson, Jessica, Tanya, David, and especially Hannah and Julian, in the company of whom the final words of this book were written at Hogsback, Eastern Cape, New Year 2014. And for Susanne Kapoor and Shefali Malhoutra for being, as always, my sisters.

READING GROUP QUESTIONS

In what way is the landscape of De Wildt a key part of this novel, and in the lives of the characters? Does it affect their decisions, the relationships between people and the law of that region? Is it sympathetic, hostile, or an indifferent backdrop?

'You are paid in full, Ouma.' Do you believe that Ouma is justified in seeking assisted suicide? How do the subsequent events in her family affect your opinion?

Is Jannie a good detective? Does his history with Ouma and feelings for Groot Samuel bias him on the case of her death? How does his investigation shape the plot?

'She could be either angel or devil'. Why was Cheetah the only one who knew how to help Ouma die? How did you respond to this character, her history, her relationships with Klein Samuel and Dumisane and the example portrayed through her of Cape Town and AIDS in South Africa?

In your view, does the novel meet the challenges that face many writers who attempt to explore employer/servant relationships? Is Gogo a credible character and is her story sufficiently revealing of the complexities of her life? If not, what more would you want to know?

Mokheti doesn't believe that there can be close relationships across the races in South Africa. How is he proved right, and proved wrong, by the events of the novel? Are the white people in the novel more optimistic, and if so, why do you think that is?

'The ones that do not want to die, fall like fine fruit before their time, unprotected by our law and order . . . And those who are ready to die, to spare their families and themselves, are kept alive.' Do you agree with Mokheti's ethical reasoning? In a place where the law is always at risk of corruption, can one justify any allowance for straying from the rules?

Gogo claims that parts of her mother's body were stolen during the post-mortem. The trade in stolen body parts is widespread yet rarely reported. Do you think the way this is represented is truthful, and how does it fit in with the way responses to crime and ethical dilemmas are presented in the book?

Suffering follows Ouma like a shadow. Important is rescued from the pound. Groot Samuel kills a snake and tries to save a baby baboon. And the nameless jackal roams the hillside. How much do the animals in the novel reinforce its depiction of savagery, and how much do they mirror the experience of their human counterparts?

'The word thief'. 'Her plea is in Afrikaans to better appease Ilse'. 'They pilfered each other's language'. Words and language play an integral role in the characters' lives. How much do the layers of imagery, and the different languages – English, Afrikaans, Sesotho, Ndebele and Zulu – enrich your experience of the novel? And how much is left unsaid by any words at all?

Ouma lived through apartheid and beyond. What meaning does her memory – and its loss – have in her family and her world? In her dementia and her death, is the author saying something about the future of South Africa?

Join the conversation:

www.elaineproctor.com
Facebook/Elaine-Proctor
Twitter/@ElaineProctor2

www.quercusbooks.co.uk